THORN OF ROSE

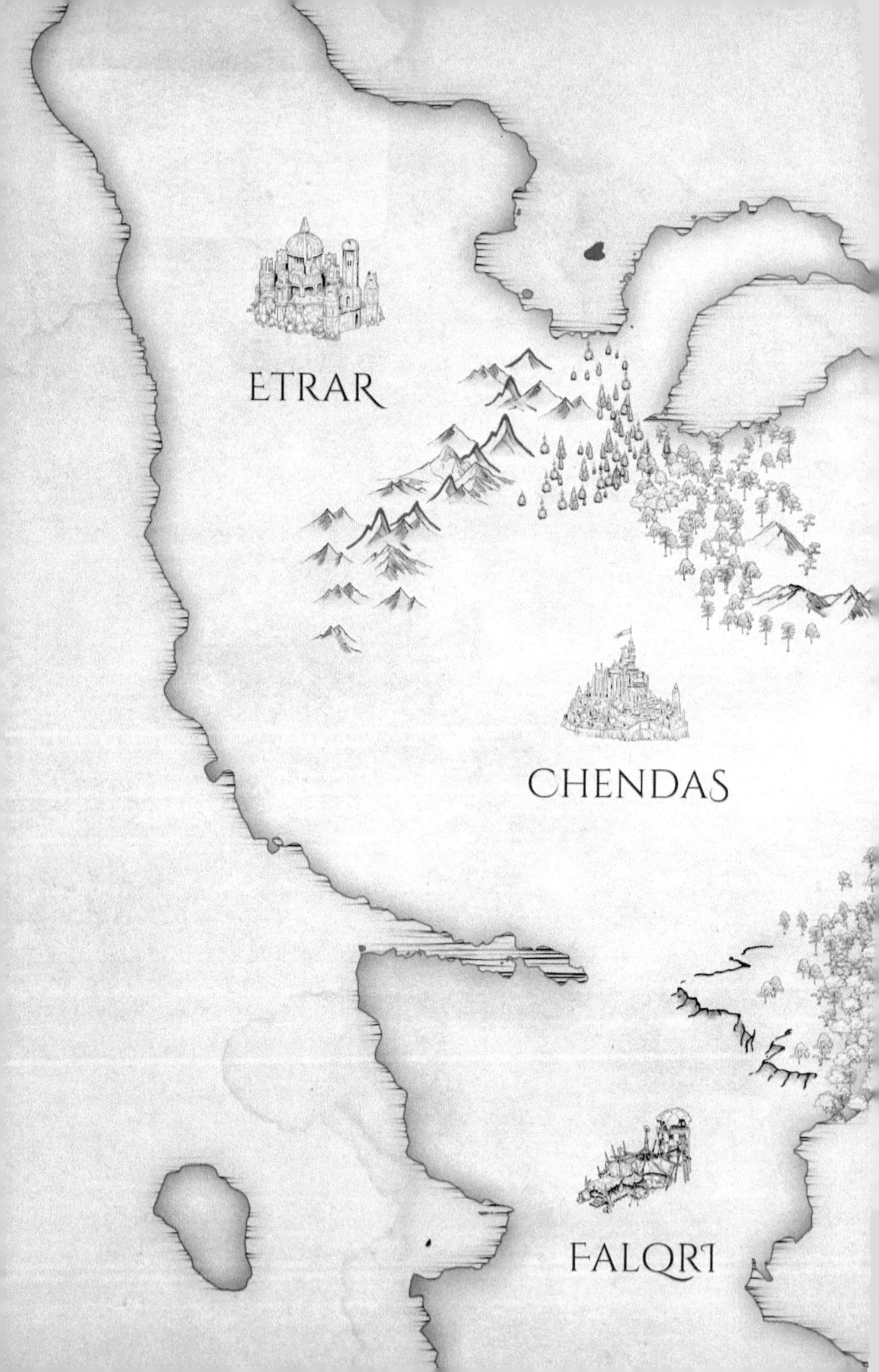

ETRAR
CHENDAS
FALQRT

ALLYS
ISELDIS
Isle of Exile

THORN OF ROSE
A BEAUTY AND THE BEAST ROMANCE

EMILY DEADY

Editor: Allison Erin Wright

Cover Design: Covers by Combs

ISBN: 978-1-7349865-4-9

❀ Created with Vellum

For Grandma Beth,
for sharing with me her love of history and reading.

CHAPTER 1

"I wish I had known that Allysian women were so bewitching." The man leaned over Isa, breathing down her neck as they danced. "I would not have wasted these last seasons in Iseldis."

Isa stiffened as he pressed himself closer. He had stopped trying to hide the fact that his gaze was constantly drifting from her face to the bodice of her elaborate ball gown.

This was her seventh dance partner of the evening, and all but one of them had made her skin crawl. The other had been endearingly tongue-tied, stumbling through the dance as though unable to believe she had consented to dance with him.

Her current partner tightened his arm around her waist, forcing her body closer to his. She instinctively leaned her shoulders back to create as much distance between them as possible.

"Smile for me," he whispered in her ear. "Are you not enjoying this dance?"

"No," she replied without hesitation. "I am not." She pressed her free hand against his chest to remove herself from his embrace.

He fought her resistance for a moment, smiling inanely at her as though she were playing a game or flirting with him. Eventually, he must have realized that she was not only serious but also not above causing a scene in the middle of the crowded ballroom. His eyebrows narrowed and he released his firm hold.

An excuse to leave was on the tip of her tongue, but Isa chose not to condone his overbearing behavior by feeding him a complacent lie. Apparently, the men in Iseldis were no different from those in Allys. Not that she had expected otherwise, but it was disheartening. Ignoring the voice in her head that also told her to smile in farewell, she turned away from the confused look on the man's face and made her way toward the edge of the dance floor.

"Are you unwell?" He was at her heel, following her through the swirling couples. "Do you need something to eat or drink?"

She shook her head, keeping her eyes trained on a spiral staircase that promised a quick escape from the stifling dance floor.

"Surely you will dance with me later this evening?" He grabbed her wrist as she stepped onto the staircase.

Isa's jaw clenched involuntarily at the uninvited contact. "No." She twisted her wrist free from his grasp and hurried up the steps. She did not miss the way his confused expression began to contort into anger.

Thankfully, though, he did not follow her.

She slowed her pace as she reached the second-story balcony. The Iseldis ballroom was a beautiful sight, even if her dancing partners had failed to impress. The magnificent hall was lit by large candelabra overhead that spread a soft warm glow on the elegantly dressed nobles below. It was far more lovely to enjoy the view from above than to be among the confining crowd.

Unfortunately, the balcony she had climbed to was still quite crowded. Considering that Ian, the Crown Prince of Iseldis, was choosing his bride from among the women in attendance tonight, it made sense that even the spacious ballroom was filled far past its capacity.

Isa stepped back onto the spiral staircase and continued spiraling up to the highest balcony in the room. She wondered if it would be rude to leave the ballroom and search for the castle library. Surely they would have something new she had never read before.

Despite climbing so quickly, her breathing eased as she neared the top. Windows and doorways around the back of the highest balcony were open, allowing the fresh evening breeze to clear the air. Exiting the staircase, she slowly wound her way through groups of chatting older gentlemen and tired matronly women. Her shoulders relaxed. She would find no uncomfortable dance partners here.

Reaching inside a hidden pocket on the skirt of her amethyst-colored gown, she pulled out a small hardbound book and opened it to a marked page. Now this was how a proper evening should be spent.

Having taught herself the invaluable skill of walking while reading, she skimmed the open page while keeping a practiced lookout for an empty area to enjoy a moment of peace. It helped that she had already read this particular tome multiple times and could practically quote the entire story from memory. Noticing a quiet corner at the far end of the balcony, she made her way through the light crowd with only two accidental shoulder bumps. Muttering her apologies, she never lifted her eyes from the page, where Andrew was about to declare his undying love for the princess Amelya.

Making it safely to her destination, Isa leaned against the balcony railing, soaking in the words of her favorite story. The princess, tired of her constant stream of selfish suitors, had recognized the true love offered to her by the swineherd Andrew and declared that she loved him in return.

Isa closed the book, keeping her finger between the pages to mark her place. She loved that moment. It was early in the story rather than at the ending. The two young sweethearts had many trials ahead, but at least the reader knew that they would face them together from this moment onward.

As she let the happy feelings inflate in her chest, her eyes dropped to the room below.

On the center dais, Crown Prince Ian was dancing with a woman in a light-blue dress. Everyone else wore the darker jewel tones that were popular in Iseldis. In her own kingdom of Allys, it was too warm to wear dark colors, so Isa felt an instant connection to the girl in blue. The prince was chatting with his blue-gowned partner in an animated way, but the young woman soon stepped off the dais and greeted another young man. Her face lit up when the young man placed his hand at her back.

Interesting. Isa herself had danced with the prince early in the evening, and though polite, he had not been nearly as animated with her as he had with the girl in the sky-blue dress. It seemed the one woman in the room that the prince had any interest in was already interested in someone else. Isa wanted to know more. A romantic story was taking place before her very eyes. Without any additional information, though, the only story she could consume was on the pages in her hands.

The sounds of music and chatter disappeared as she returned to her book, losing herself once again in her favorite story.

"I disagree," a young male voice said from somewhere

nearby in the real world. "Aphronsius was not speaking of art itself, as any cursory glance would tell the reader. He was referring to labor."

Isa drew her mind back to the present, intrigued by the voice. However, it was not the youthfulness or the maleness of the voice that intrigued her; it was the mention of one of her favorite writers.

"Only you would argue against the inherent value of something beautiful," another male voice scoffed.

"On the contrary, I am the greatest proponent of the beauty of art, as you well know," the original voice continued with a sniff. "I merely think that Aphronsius was either wrong in his calculation or veiling his true point."

Isa looked over her shoulder to get a better view of the two men speaking behind her. The first speaker was a young man, likely close to herself in age. He was dressed completely in black. Although his clothing was finely tailored, it held no ornament befitting the occasion of a royal ball other than a small strip of yellow silk tied at his throat. It seemed incredibly rude to attend the event in such simple clothes when he could clearly afford something better. Hopefully, the royal family of Iseldis had not noticed the clothing choice of this particular guest.

The second speaker, slightly taller and considerably older, made no effort to hide his exasperation. "And what point would that be?"

"That destiny is dictated by calculated action, of course," the younger one replied. "Beauty—or art, if you will—has nothing to do with it."

Isa snapped her book closed, whipping fully around. "You clearly have not read Aphronsius's other works then."

The young man showed no surprise at her sudden intrusion into their conversation, though he did raise his eyebrows. "I have read all of his surviving work. Multiple times."

"Then how could you come to such a conclusion? One of his central themes is that destiny is outside our control. His entire thesis on art was just a supporting argument for that. He said that to arrive at the order associated with beauty, one must travel through the chaos in art. And he used that as a proof of his views on destiny."

"Have *you* read his later work?" The young man was beyond rude. He had completely ignored her point and merely responded with a question.

The older man was awkwardly holding his goblet in front of his face, though he was not drinking from it. Isa noticed him hiding a grin behind the large cup. He was clearly enjoying her spar with his friend.

She focused her attention back to the rude one. "Of course I have read his later work, and his early work. I have read all his work. He is a dear friend." She snapped her mouth shut. Aphronsius had been dead for over two hundred years. No need to let these judgmental men know that she liked to imagine herself working alongside the old philosopher and discussing these very topics with him.

The man in black raised his eyebrows again. "He is a friend?" The corners of his lips twisted into a smirk. "Are you a Majis, then, who has discovered longevity of life?"

Isa's lungs froze at the insult, her body instinctively snapping backward. She bumped against the railing behind her, which startled her even more.

The young man reached for her upper arm to steady her.

She quickly stabilized herself and brushed away his help. "How dare you?"

The Majis had been exiled from the five kingdoms one thousand seasons prior, around the time of Aphronsius in fact. Some current scholars did not believe they had truly wielded magic, but everyone agreed they had been exceptionally cruel and oppressive rulers.

"That was too far," the older man admonished the younger one. Turning to Isa, he said, "My friend spoke in jest. Please accept his apology."

Isa stared at the young man in question. She would not be mollified by a secondhand apology.

He bowed lightly to her. "I was amused by your admission of Aphronsius and was merely teasing you. Forgive my hasty words."

She nodded in response, biting the inside of her cheek. His apology would have been better if he had not brought up her embarrassing statement.

"What are you currently reading?" He gestured toward the small book in her hand.

Thankful to change the topic, Isa held out her small book. "*The Queen of Silverreign.*"

He raised an eyebrow. Although he did not utter a word, his expression was clearly judgmental.

"What critique could you possibly have about the most revered story we have in our language?" Her irritation at his poor apology fueled the exasperation in her words.

He shrugged. "It's boring."

"Boring?" Too shocked to form a coherent sentence in response, Isa began to wonder if this man was even human. He had clearly never felt human emotion. No wonder he thought Aphronsius's treatise on the importance of art was actually a veiled statement on the value of labor. She threw her arms up in mock defeat, not willing to discuss her favorite book with someone who already despised it.

"Which volume is this?" The young man reached out, taking the book from her uplifted hand.

"The first." Isa reached out to retrieve her treasure from his scrutiny.

He flipped it over, tracing the spine with his finger. "This is expertly bound." He opened the book, focusing on the cover rather than the contents.

She pulled her hand back to a neutral space between them, curious to see what else he might say.

"I've never seen such a small work with this new hard binding. It is quite intricate." He kept his face down, which gave her the impression that he was talking only to himself. "Incredible craftsmanship."

Isa felt a flutter of pride. She had bound this copy herself.

"The details are perfection for something of this size. This was a job well done." He looked up, as though remembering he had an audience. He smiled and held the book back out to her, running his hand down the cover respectfully.

"Thank you—" Isa started to respond.

"Poor choice of story to receive this level of craftsmanship, though," he said, speaking over her.

She snatched her book from his hand.

"Not to offend you a second time, of course," he hastily added. "Reading any written word is far preferable to dancing."

"We can agree on that point." She turned to the railing, miffed but intrigued. The conversation had been far more entertaining than any of her dances this evening.

The young man stepped to her side and leaned against the railing.

Raising his goblet, the older man gave his friend a slight nod. "I'm going to find some more ale," he said, disappearing into the crowd.

His absence left an awkward pause. Though they had already shared multiple opinions, Isa scrambled for something new to say. She wondered why he thought *The Queen of Silverreign* was boring, but she was not quite ready to give him an opportunity to ruin her favorite story by asking him about it. Her eyes roamed over the moving people below.

They had not introduced themselves yet. That seemed like a good next step.

She turned toward him.

"She came." The young man spoke to himself while staring at the dancers below. He looked back at Isa, his face transformed into a genuine smile. "Enjoy your book." He nodded curtly and left her at the railing.

As he stepped down the far staircase, she puzzled over his assessments, then tried to forget him. She did not want to waste her time dwelling on someone who thought they had the right to outtalk and outthink everyone else.

Yawning, she blinked her eyes rapidly. It was nearly midnight, so the earliest crowd would be leaving soon and she could politely make her escape. She was anxious to return to her ailing father in Allys, despite the days of travel it would entail.

Something familiar in the dancers below caught her attention. The girl in the light-blue dress was at the far end of the hall, almost directly below Isa's spot on the corner of the balcony. She was with her second partner of the evening, the one who had made her face light up. But they had just been joined by the rude man in black she had been conversing with. He was smiling at the girl in blue and chatting with her. They began to walk along the wall, examining the magnificent tapestry that ran across the back of the room.

Isa's heart went out to the poor girl. It seemed that every man in the room was besotted by her tonight, and that was a fate Isa knew better than to wish upon anyone.

As the trio disappeared from view, she looked down to reopen her book. She had just enough time for another chapter before she could politely leave. But her hands were empty.

Alarmed, she quickly reached into her pocket, where her fingers wrapped around the familiar shape of the small tome.

That was odd; she didn't remember putting it back in her pocket.

She pulled it out and skimmed through the pages, looking for the place where she had left off. The room around her dimmed, obscuring her view of the words on the page. Had the candles all gone out? She looked up as a sphere of light exploded in the center of the dais below and the room erupted into chaos.

CHAPTER 2

*A*den wished he could shut his ear holes. Eyelids had such a useful and overlooked functionality. He merely had to close his eyes, and the visual stimulation of color and light faded away. It would be incredibly effective if he could simply activate a muscle and shut out all sound in a similar manner.

"Any change?" his older brother whispered nearby. Well, Ian probably thought it was a whisper, but the breathy tones pierced Aden's skull, reverberating in shock waves through his drowsy mind.

"No, not yet," Aden heard his mother reply. Queen Cara's voice was more rounded, but it still sounded far louder than necessary.

Aden fought the growing wakefulness in his consciousness. He just wanted to sleep.

He heard a shuffling sound accompanied by the clink of armor. The familiar noise of the palace guard did not surprise him, but the close proximity of it confused his still-sleeping mind. The nearest guard was stationed four doorways and two hallways from his bedroom. Aden decided that his mind was playing tricks on him. Of course, he could not hear the guard from this far away. That would be laughable.

Ian's heavy breathing continued to slice through the room.

Exhaling against the inevitable, Aden shifted his body into wakefulness. His breaths felt infinitely slow and his limbs unusually weighty, as though he had overused them in the practice range. They begged him to be left alone, but he ignored their pleas. Only a fool would attempt to sleep amidst the barrage of sound attacking his defenseless ears.

He opened his eyes. The movement felt foreign, as though he had multiple eyelids sliding open from different angles. The sensation sent chills down his spine. All he could see was darkness. He must still be dreaming.

He tried to open his eyes again but found they were indeed already open. He was not dreaming. Everything was dark, though. Alarm pounded in his chest as he sat up in his bed, his arm brushing against something warm and fuzzy. His pup, Warrior, was supposed to sleep on the floor mat. The pesky rascal must have climbed up to the bed during the night.

He reached down to touch the dog in the darkness. The space next to him was empty, but he still felt a warm body covered in fur. It was . . . his *own* body . . . what kind of nightmare was this?

"He is awake." Ian rushed to the side of the bed.

Aden could hear the movement, even if he could not see it. He felt hands on his shoulders.

"Aden, can you hear me?" Ian shouted in his face.

"Of course I can hear you, idiot." Aden's mouth felt dry, his tongue struggling to form the words. "Stop shouting."

Ian sighed in relief, and Aden grit his teeth against the pitchy breath. A catapult shattering through a stone wall could sound more gentle.

"Stop making so much noise." Aden swiped his arm into the darkness, pushing Ian away.

"Ooh!" Ian jumped backward, and Aden felt two small hands encircling his wrists. "Careful with the claws," Ian said.

Claws?

Aden shook his hand free and held it in front of his face, trying to focus through the hazy darkness. He could make out some clouds of light gray in the room, but they seemed to be moving through gloomy shadows. He could not see his own hand. Panic once again seized at his chest, but he refused to let it show.

"What happened?" he asked, his voice coming out calm and disconnected.

"I was attacked by a Majis at the ball," Ian started. "You jumped in front of me—"

"I remember that part." Aden cut him off as the events of the ball came back to him. "What happened afterward? What is happening now?"

Aden could literally hear Ian turn his head toward the other person in the room. His mother's comforting hand ran up the center of his forehead. She was brushing her fingers from the top of his nose upward. It was an odd choice of motion, but it helped to calm him.

"I can understand that it is quite a bit to take in all at once," she said. "How are you feeling?"

Aden shook his head ever so slightly so as not to discourage the gentle movement of her hand on his forehead. So, the attack of the Majis had blinded him. Perhaps it was not permanent, since he could make out vague shadows. "Tired," he responded. "Heavy."

"Try to get some more sleep then." Queen Cara removed her

hand and stepped away from his bed, then dropped her voice to a whisper. "He's taking it surprisingly well."

"I was expecting a bit more of an outburst," Ian replied to her in the same hushed tone.

"I may be blinded," Aden cut in, "but I can still hear you just fine."

The room around him froze.

A cold fear snaked up through Aden's core and slowly squeezed his lungs.

His mother moved back to his side and reached out to his face, touching his cheek with tentative fingertips. "You . . . cannot see?"

Aden shook his head. "No. Well, how dark is it in here?"

His mother's hand resumed its gentle upward motion. Her silence answered his question.

"So, you did not see your . . . hand . . . when you tried to look at it just now?" Ian asked.

Aden shook his head again. Raising his hand, he strained his eyes through the darkness to make it out. His fingers were stiff, and his wrist could painlessly bend in the wrong direction. "What did that Majis do to me?" This time, he could not keep the growing fear from his voice.

"He cursed you . . ." his mother started to say, her voice calm and comforting. But it caught in her throat and she paused. She was not an overly emotional woman, and that small sound frightened Aden more than anything else had in these last strange moments of wakefulness.

"Let me tell him, Mum." Ian took over, his voice weighted with the responsibility of the eldest sibling and the crown prince of Iseldis.

"You did not cause this," Queen Cara said to Ian.

"The attack was directed at me," Ian responded, his voice

miserable. "It is my fault. I should be the one in the body of a beast."

The body of a beast.

Aden flexed his muscles from his feet to his elbows. Suddenly, all the odd sensations fell into place. For the first time since he had woken up, the shrill sounds around him faded away. He felt as though he were observing the entire situation from far up in the hazy clouds around him. The weightiness of his body, the extra muscles in his eyelids, the claws. He flexed his hand again. Curved daggers slid out where his fingers should have been.

"Get. Out." His calm voice was laced with fury.

His mother's hand tensed on his cheek, but she did not pull away.

"Aden." Ian's own voice broke. "This is not over. We have already sent our swiftest courier to the Council. We will find a way . . ."

Aden reached up and pushed his mother's hand away.

"I need to be alone right now. Please leave." His voice was listless.

"He needs some time to think this through," his mother said to Ian. She finally stepped back, and two sets of footsteps moved toward the door.

Aden inhaled into lungs that refused to expand. "Wait," he called after them. "How long have I . . . Is it day or night?"

"The ball ended around midnight," Ian responded. "That was about three hours ago."

Aden nodded.

"Are you sure you want—" Ian asked.

"Go," Aden cut him off.

The door closed behind them, and Aden listened to their footsteps fade down the hall. He truly could hear them from four rooms away.

He flexed his hands again, horrified at the smooth feeling of the long, hard claws gliding in and out of his . . . fingers? Paws? His stomach turned.

The door creaked open and he tensed, waiting for the returning footsteps of an overly concerned family member. He needed time to pity himself before someone else came in to do the pitying for him. He inhaled and his lungs accepted the air. He was ready to spew an angry retort to send whoever it was away. Instead of footsteps, however, he heard tiny, short panting noises and the soft pads of puppy feet.

For the first time since he had awoken, his heart felt a moment of anticipation. "Warrior," he called, "good pup. Come and keep me company."

The mattress rustled as the dog's small body jumped up next to him, and Aden reached out to find his little friend.

"Grrrrrrrwwww." A small growl formed deep in the dog's throat. Under any other circumstances, the pup's attempt to be threatening would have made Aden laugh. In this moment, the aggressive action of his small companion completely broke his heart. Not even his own dog recognized him.

"Come on, boy, it's just me. The same me." Aden pleaded as though his life depended on it. Perhaps it did.

Warrior barked in response and jumped off the bed, growling all the while.

Completely overcome with the desire to hold the comforting bundle of fluff, Aden sat up. "Warrior, I am not going to hurt you, boy. Come up here. I'll find you a treat!" He swung an awkward leg over the side of the bed and reached down toward the menacing pup. Unfortunately, that was entirely the wrong move to make.

Warrior yelped in surprise, probably at the large size of the monster in his master's bed, and flew out of the room, puppy claws desperately scraping against the stone castle floor in an attempt to flee the danger as quickly as possible.

Aden groaned. The sound came out as a beastly growl, eerily similar to the one Warrior had made a few moments ago. Only Aden's was far deeper and actually menacing. The foreign sound of his own despair frightened even him.

Apparently, the sound was louder than he realized. Armored footsteps sounded down the hall, and moments later two guards burst through the door into his room. Alarmed, Aden stood from the bed as he heard the clang of their swords against his doorway.

"Y . . . Your Highness?" They paused immediately inside the door to his room, obviously unsure of whether they should be attacking their former prince.

He was now considered a threat.

"Everything is fine, James and Mattew," Aden said to the two guards standing nervously at his doorway. "I was merely clearing my throat. You can return to your post." He realized too late that he was their post. They had likely been assigned to ensure he did not go on a killing spree throughout the castle.

Another sound of footsteps hurried down the hallway, and a third figure burst into his room. Why was everything still shrouded in darkness?

"Aden?" It was his other older brother, Onric. "You are awake? I thought I heard . . ." Onric awkwardly stopped.

"A beastly growl?" Aden finished the sentence for him.

Onric did not respond, but he must have gestured to the two guards as Aden heard their deafening footsteps retreat out the door.

"So, you have set your guards on me like a common criminal?" Aden's words were full of spite. Somehow, it was easier to show his frustrated emotions to Onric than to Ian and his mother.

"That actually was not me," Onric replied. "I have been too busy ensuring that Lord Munney is safely locked away and helping Father brief the two messengers that just left for Chendas."

"Lord Munney?"

"Yes. You know, the councilor from Chendas?" Onric spoke as though stating the obvious. "Perhaps you really are addled in the head . . ."

Aden let out a low growl.

Onric jumped backward. "Okay, okay, I was merely jesting. So, you don't know what happened?"

Aden smirked. If a light growl held that much power, perhaps he was not as out of control as he thought. "I know I was cursed by a Majis," he replied to Onric's question, "but I could not get much more out of Ian as he was too busy apologizing for causing all this."

"He refused to leave your side. I am surprised he is not here now."

"I growled at him."

"I don't see what everyone is up in arms about. You have obviously not changed a bit."

Aden could have hugged his older brother. He sank back down onto the bed behind him, awkwardly crossing his unfamiliar arms as he sat. "So, Lord Munney?"

"Turns out, he was secretly a Majis this whole time. He tried to curse Ian at the ball, but some lad heroically jumped in front of him and took the hit." Onric's voice grew serious. "I must say, Aden, that was well done. You acted quickly and selflessly, and I am proud to call you a member of my castle guard. You were the only one who got there in time."

For a moment, Aden forgot he was living in a nightmare. He simply let his brother's words wash over him. This entire situation was miserable, but he did have to remember that he had saved his older brother in exchange for . . . whatever this was. It seemed terribly unfair, but regardless of the outcome, he would have done it again in the moment. "Thank you." His new tongue struggled to form the two simple words.

"Hopefully we will hear back from Chendas in the next few days and they can send us a real councilor or examiner, who might know more about this magical curse. More precisely, how to undo it." Onric sighed.

It was a light sigh, probably not intended for Aden's ears, but he heard it nonetheless. "You have doubts?"

"I'm not sure if it is merely that Lord Munney was thwarting any real efforts the Council made to unlock the secrets of the Majis, or if the Council really has discovered nothing. Either way, it is hard to put my hope in them, seeing as they royally betrayed us the first time. Not that . . . not that you should lose hope, of course. This has only just happened. We have plenty of time to figure it out. How are you, by the way?"

Aden was not yet ready to process whether he had hope, or even whether he should have hope, so he gladly let his brother change the conversation. "Other than the fact that I . . . I mean, I feel different. I can't see myself, though. Is it really that . . . am I really that bad?"

"You can't see?"

"Some hazy light and shadow, but mostly nothing."

"Then how did you know that it was James and Mattew?" Onric asked.

"What?" Aden did not follow the logic behind his question.

"The two guards. You called them by name. How did you know which guards they were if you cannot see?"

"I don't know." Aden thought back to the moment the two guards had entered the room. It was obvious his hearing had changed as well as his eyesight. Perhaps his other senses had increased as well? He inhaled through his nose. His older brother smelt of sweat and cloves, with maybe a touch of patchouli? The scent brought back a memory from a few hours before. He was walking up the staircase to the third balcony of the ballroom to avoid the dancing and gliding his hand along the smooth wooden railing. The railing had the rich aroma of clove and patchouli. That moment felt like a lifetime ago. Interesting.

"Let me know if you notice anything else," Onric said. "I, uh, I may have a deeper knowledge of the Majis and their magic than I . . . Just keep me informed on anything you notice that may be magic related, even if it seems unimportant, please?"

"So now I am just another one of your Majis experiments?"

"I have no idea what you are talking about."

Aden growled again, hoping for the same fearful reaction it had produced earlier. He was disappointed.

Onric did not even flinch. "I should get going. It has been quite the night, and I still have a few things to see to."

"Ashlin?" Aden asked, referring to the servant girl who had stolen his older brother's heart. "Is she alright?"

"I hope so." Onric's voice had completely changed. He swallowed. "There were some . . . complications after you were attacked. I need to go find her and make sure she is safe."

"Go."

Onric's footsteps shuffled toward the door. "Aden, we will figure this out. I promise."

Aden nodded in response. He had nothing left to say.

"Oh." Onric opened the door. "Just so you know, I did order the guards to kill you at the ball. That was before I knew it was you, of course." He sprinted away, calling down the hallway as he ran, "Sorry about that!"

Aden growled in response, letting the rumble in his throat explode into a full roar.

He heard the clinking of armor again.

"It's fine. He's fine. Leave him be," Onric yelled to the guards as he ran past them.

Aden eased himself back onto the bed, relaxing his tired head against his generous stack of pillows. Onric's humor had eased his soul a little. They would figure this out.

CHAPTER 3

Isa knocked on the doorless entryway to the small study. Although she could fully see inside, she did not want to enter uninvited.

A head of gray hair bent over the single table in the room. Brother Elias had not heard her knock. Perhaps she had been too quiet. The gentle sound of a sonorous chant filled the air. The other monks were singing their prayers in some other room of the villa-turned-monastery.

Isa rapped on the side of the doorway again. The creamy brick might look warm and inviting, but it was definitely not kind on her knuckles. She cleared her throat.

The old man looked up from his parchments. His eyes found her, then crinkled into a smile. "Come in, child."

Isa smiled in response and entered the room. Stacks of scrolls and parchments covered every available surface. A few hardbound books were stacked in a place of honor at the corner of the desk. She felt right at home in the chaos.

The owner of the study, however, looked a little out of place. His wrinkled skin was covered in a fine sheen of sweat, and his eyes seemed lost, as though he were not fully aware of the physical world around him.

"I see you have not taken up my suggestion for linen robes instead of wool?" she gently chided.

"I cannot conjure up an entirely new set of clothing for nine monks in a few days, my dear."

"What if I conjured them up for you?"

He brushed away her offer with his hand. "You have already given us so much."

"Were they not so generous in Iseldis?" Isa attempted to hide her kindness so the perspiring old monk would accept the much-needed gift. "This is the Allysian way. You will just have to get used to it."

"Perhaps it is just the Bielsa way." He smiled knowingly at her. "Your family has welcomed us here so graciously. How is your father?"

Isa kept the smile on her face, though there was no longer any sincerity behind it. "No change."

For a moment, the uncomfortable weight of reality broke through the comforting walls of parchment around her. She had arrived home from Iseldis the previous evening and had spent the entire morning at her father's bedside. His fever remained constant, and he rambled unconsciously. Her poor father was frequently ill, but he had never suffered this severely for an extended period of time. She shoved those thoughts aside and changed the topic of conversation. "How goes the sorting?"

"I never found the final scroll of *The Queen of Silverreign*," the old man replied. His eyes roamed the room, rescanning each pile as though he might find the missing book from his chair.

"You have checked everything?" She could not hide her disappointment.

"Everything," he confirmed. "It was all so rushed when we left; we had no time to properly transport the entire library. A collection of centuries, filled with countless treasures." He sighed. "I am afraid *The Queen of Silverreign* is not in this house at the moment and probably never made it to Allys at all."

Isa sighed. "I was dearly looking forward to finishing the story."

"If I remembered it, I would recount it. But I was younger than yourself the last time I read it." He absently wiped the perspiration from his face with the corner of his billowing sleeve.

The cold temperatures of silverreign had only just given way to the warmth of spring. If the poor man thought this was hot, Isa did not want to tell him what a true Allysian goldenreign would feel like. At least by then her mother could ensure that the good monks had proper linen robes. Having spent their entire lives on the cold shores of Iseldis, their woolen garb had made sense during every season. But over the last few years, the sea's storms had grown increasingly erratic and dangerous, so the Council of the Five Kingdoms had ordered the monks to leave their monastery and find a safer home. After traveling northeast, most of them had settled in Allys.

"I will find a copy of it someday," Isa promised herself aloud. "Surely someone has preserved the full tale."

The small tome she had brought to Iseldis only contained the first two manuscripts of the beloved story, and she had never been fortunate enough to read the ending. Her father had spent years trying to find the final installment for her, but it seemed that few of the ancient scrolls had survived through the ages.

"How was your trip to Iseldis?" Brother Elias looked up at Isa from beneath his drooping eyelids. She did not miss the small note of wistfulness in his voice.

She smiled, her heart feeling for him. He had been asked to leave his entire life behind. "Quite memorable. The city and palace were beautiful—well, before the attack, that is. I don't think I want to go back anytime soon."

He nodded grimly. "That must have been frightening to witness."

Despite the balmy weather, Isa felt goosebumps run down her arms. She hugged herself. "It was. I couldn't see much, as the room went dark. Fortunately, I was already on an upper balcony and was able to make it out of the hall immediately before they closed the doors to apprehend the attacking Majis. I am not sure what happened after I left. They say a member of the palace guard saved Prince Ian's life. Last I heard, the guard was quite ill but still alive."

"That was a brave man to put himself into unknown danger."

"His magic dimmed the whole room," Isa said, recalling the attacker. She had not shared the full details with her mother or sister, not wanting to burden them with worry or relive the memory too closely herself. But as her mind unraveled the chaotic events of three days prior, a deeper fear began to surface. "I had no idea that one Majis could be that powerful. The Return is only three seasons away. If one Majis could do that, what will it be like when hordes of them return to the Five Kingdoms, eager for revenge after their exile?"

The old monk nodded solemnly, his eyes in that far-off place again.

"I thought we were prepared," Isa continued. "Iseldis will hold them off at the shore. But Iseldis could not even stop an attack on their crown prince! Are we prepared? Is there any hope of victory against that kind of terror?"

Her heart raced, the chills on her arm turning to an uncomfortable flush of warmth. Brother Elias had not turned to her, but his solemn expression told her he had heard her words.

"I do not know if it is victory that we should be hoping for," the old monk finally said. "The future is always far more complicated than that."

Isa exhaled as her mind swirled. It was too much—the extended worry over her father's illness, the shock of witnessing the Majis attack in person, the ever-growing dread of the Return. She wanted to run away, to escape to a world before these problems existed.

As if sensing her change in mood, the old man finally looked toward her, his eyes present. "I did not say that there was no reason to hope at all. No one knows what the next silverreign will bring."

Isa could not keep the confusion from her face. If he had meant to comfort her, he had failed. "Is that not the problem, though—the not knowing?"

"No one knows what the next silverreign will bring." He repeated his own words slowly, to himself, as though he had never heard them before.

Isa waited for him to elaborate.

He did not.

"Do you know something that you are not telling me?" she asked, eager for answers of any sort.

"No one knows." He shrugged. Perhaps the heat had affected him worse than she had thought.

"Isa!" a cheerful voice called as a younger girl stepped into the room. "It's been so much longer than a minute."

Livia, Isa's younger sister, must have grown tired of waiting at the shops across the street.

"Let's go home." Livia slipped her hand in Isa's arm, pulling her toward the door.

Isa hurriedly glanced around the room as she stumbled after her sister. "Wait, Livia, I'm not done." She shook her arm free.

Livia rolled her eyes and crossed her arms impatiently. "We've been gone for hours."

Ignoring her sister, Isa carefully sifted through a nearby pile of scrolls. "Do you have anything else I might borrow?" she asked Brother Elias. "I've been trying to read to my father, and I was hoping that maybe something new would be good for him." Not that he could understand anything that was said to him. Something new would keep her own mind occupied as well.

"Feel free to take anything you like," Brother Elias responded. "I know my dear friends are safe in your hands." He gestured toward the entire wall to his left, which was piled with damaged scrolls. "When your father is better, we can get to work restoring these and establishing a true library here."

"Thank you," Isa responded. "Oh! I did bring you this." She held out a bound book. "You said that you had never read an original Viliamu?"

Her words brought a look of pure joy to the old man's face. He bounced up from his chair and came around the table to take the book from her hands. "An original Detritus? I never thought I would see the day. No one ever thought to bring that old Falqri warrior to the eastern sea, too controversial." Brother Elias had the book open and was instantly lost in skimming through the pages.

Isa left him to his musings and took a quick turn around the room, picking up two tomes she did not recognize from the extensive Bielsa family library at home. She followed her sister out of the study, not bothering to disturb the old man with a goodbye.

"Why the rush to go home?" she asked Livia as they wound around the overgrown plants in the open courtyard. "I thought you could not wait to get out this morning?"

"No reason in particular," Livia responded, keeping her eyes straight ahead.

"You can't fool me." Isa poked her sister's shoulder. "What are you hiding?"

"You're not my tutor anymore." Livia leaned away from her. "I don't have to do what you say."

"I'm still your older sister!" After finishing her own studies, Isa had tutored Livia. It had quickly become clear that not enough learning was happening between all their arguments, and they had ended that experiment as quickly as possible. Isa poked Livia again as they left the open courtyard and stepped onto the busy street.

"Ladies," a smooth voice called out to them, "how excellent to run into you."

Isa kept walking, pretending she had not heard the voice.

Livia had stopped, though, and turned to face the young man quickly approaching them.

Forcing a smile on her face, Isa turned as well. "You are back from your trip so early?"

The young man faltered for a moment. "No, today was . . . were you not expecting me?"

"Of course we were." Livia smiled at the young man, throwing a small glare toward her sister. "Isa has only just returned from Iseldis herself and has not been paying attention to these things."

"How did you find Iseldis?" The young man, Macklin Surrell, turned to Isa. "I am sure none of the uncouth warriors could compare to our more learned society?"

Isa lifted her head to nod, trying to decide if she actually agreed with him or if she was merely too tired to engage in a prolonged discussion.

"She has told me nothing about the prince's ball," Livia said, inserting herself back into the conversation. "So, I'm sure it was nothing worth noting. How did you do on the exams?"

"I passed them," he responded, his smile wide with news of his achievement as he glanced between them, "with highest honors, of course."

Isa tried to ignore the way his shoulders were so close to his chin, as though he were puffing up his chest or trying to appear taller. She reminded herself that he had every right to be proud for passing his exams. They were the mark of a true scholar, like her father, and it was not Macklin's fault that women had never been invited to participate in the exam process.

"So you can continue to be my tutor, Professor Surrell?" Livia asked, also smiling wide.

"Yes," Macklin responded to Livia, but his eyes were on Isa. "If your father will have me."

Isa's stomach twisted uncomfortably. The way Macklin was smiling at her . . . it felt as though he wasn't even seeing her. His smile was entirely for himself. He seemed to be looking forward to an award he deserved. Isa would argue with her dying breath that the reward on his mind had nothing to do with securing his position as Livia's tutor.

She reached for her sister's elbow. "Were you not anxious to be getting home, Livia? We really should go."

"What?" Livia replied innocently. "Why would I need to rush home?"

Isa's jaw clenched. Her sister was no longer a child, but she was indeed acting like one.

"That is precisely where I was headed." Macklin seemed to have missed the non-verbal interaction between the sisters. "I will accompany you."

Livia smiled up at him.

Isa quickly turned and took out her anger by setting the pace as quickly as she could for home. Her home. Her home, which was once again about to be the home of Livia's returning tutor. Not for the first time, Isa bitterly regretted going to the ball in Iseldis. She would have stayed home had her mother not insisted that she accept the invitation. If she had declined it, she could have enjoyed a blissful three weeks of life at home without Macklin Surrell's presence. The same Macklin Surrell who had picked up his pace to catch up with her.

Just as he reached her side, Isa rounded a corner and nearly ran into a young woman coming from the opposite direction. Recognizing her childhood best friend, Isa instinctively smiled at Marlena.

For the smallest fraction of a second, Marlena returned her smile. But then her eyes landed on the young man at Isa's side, and her smile disappeared. With a sharp inhale, Marlena looked away and stepped around them.

"Pardon us," Macklin said, stepping aside to let her pass.

Isa's eyes burned. She tried to inhale, but her lungs constricted tightly instead of expanding as they should have done. She and Marlena had always been best friends. But every time Marlena fell for a boy, he would inevitably overlook her and shower his attention on Isa instead. Isa had done everything in her power to discourage this, but Macklin Surrell's obvious preference had finally been too much for Marlena, and their friendship had not survived.

"How is Lady Marlena doing these days?" Macklin asked. "I have not seen her in some time."

Isa opened the book she had borrowed from Brother Elias. "I wouldn't know," she choked out, hiding her face in the pages.

"Do tell me about Chendas, Professor Surrell. I've always wanted to go." Livia caught up with them, taking her place on the other side of Macklin. "They say the castle is the most glorious masterpiece in all the Five Kingdoms."

Isa silently whispered her sincerest thanks to her sister for drawing the man's attention away in that moment.

CHAPTER 4

*A*den sat with his arms crossed, ignoring the three physicians huddled together on the far side of the room. They whispered about his condition in uncertain tones, unaware that he could hear every word. His vision had partially returned over the last three days, but he still could not properly see the three physicians themselves.

"A lifetime as a surgeon did not prepare me for this," the bald one whispered. "I have never encountered anything so hideous. He is no longer even human."

Aden ran the tip of his tongue around one of the sharp-pointed teeth in his mouth. He, too, thought this body was grotesque. However, the bald one was here to fix the problem, not be disgusted by him. Aden only knew the man was bald because he could make out a bright spot of light bouncing off his reflective head.

"We cannot be expected to treat a magical condition with our scientific remedies," the tallest physician whispered. "I do not know what to tell Their Majesties. It will greatly hurt our credibility."

Aden once again felt as if he were viewing this scene from somewhere outside himself. At least that way he could pretend the feelings of shock and anger coursing through his foreign body were not his own.

"I wish we had information to understand this problem, but all we can observe is the end result. We have no basis for understanding how the change happened, or even if it is permanent. If this were a medicinal issue, we could attempt a process for treatment. But how can we apply a process when we have no information to base any decision upon?" This final voice was female, and while her words were hopeless, they were the most intelligent any physician had offered thus far.

Which was not very impressive, considering that this was the seventeenth physician to have visited Aden in the last three days. Or was it eighteen physicians? He had lost count after twelve. Some had offered herbal remedies, most had promised they would further research the problem, and one had even suggested sacrificing the life of Lord Munney to whatever gods the Majis worshipped in an attempt to break the curse. Fortunately for him, Lord Munney was being safely transported to Chendas, and his fate would be at the mercy of the Council.

It took two days for the fastest courier to travel to Chendas, and it had been three days since the ball. At the very earliest, aid from the Council could arrive on the following day. Hopefully, they would come soon and provide some answers.

In the meantime, Aden knew that summoning more physicians would be useless, but his mother had insisted. She needed to take action, which Aden understood, but he could feel the change in his entire body. He was not wearing some magical mask that gave him the appearance of a monster. He had truly been transformed into a beast. The only thing that could save him was a magical reversal of the curse, and what Majis would willingly—or even unwillingly—perform that change? They were the ones who had cursed him to begin with.

"Thank you for your time with us today, Prince Aden." The tall physician walked back toward him, raising his voice to a normal speaking level. "We have learned much, and we will continue to discuss what treatments we can apply. I am sure we will have a remedy to recommend as soon as possible. In the meantime, do your best to rest."

Aden grunted. The man had literally just whispered that nothing could be done. The physicians bowed, and their scuffling feet told him they were preparing to leave the room.

"My eyes," Aden growled. "Is there nothing that can be done about them immediately?"

Surely treating poor eyesight was a standard procedure whether it was applied to a man or a beast?

"Of course, Your Highness," the bald one said. "You said that your eyesight has improved in the last few hours since you have woken? That is excellent news and bodes very well for this entire predicament."

"I am not sure seeing some shapes and gray shadows or flashes of light counts as much of an improvement." Aden's voice was filled with anger as he made no attempt to hide his frustration with the spineless physicians.

They cowered back, away from him.

"You cannot see any color whatsoever?" The woman physician had remained in her place.

Aden shook his head, letting his open eyes roam throughout the room. "Most everything is gray. Though I can perceive some greens and browns. Nothing brighter than that."

"That is not entirely uncommon among men," she replied. "You could see more colors before this incident?"

"Yes," Aden growled. He felt like an object, being poked and prodded and assessed. It humbled him beyond words to be subject to such basic scrutiny.

"I am afraid there is not a treatment for those who cannot see the full spectrum of color. The best we can suggest is that you rest your eyes. I will come back this evening with an herbal paste that you can apply on top of your eyelids to encourage them to heal in other areas. I do not know whether it will help, but at the very least it should not cause any harm to a regular . . . it should not cause any harm."

Aden nodded and watched the three hazy shapes bow again and leave the room.

He closed his eyes, disgusted by the sensation of the dual eyelids sliding shut across each eye. His head pounded from the extended effort of trying to focus his vision through the cloudiness around him.

Rest? All he had done was rest, and he had never been more exhausted in his life.

He shifted his body back into a reclined position on the bed, every sensation and movement feeling foreign. He hated himself. His foreign limbs trembled with unused energy.

His sensitive ears could pick up every noise in the castle, and he had not found a way to sleep through the constant stimulation.

He longed for quiet. He longed to go outside and leave the prison of this room. Although that would put him at risk and ruin the story they had shared with the populace. Too many people had seen the beast in the ballroom to ignore its existence, but the palace had only informed the people that the Majis had created the beast with its curse. The beast had been intended to ravage the ballroom, but the competent palace guard had quickly overpowered the animal.

And his room was safe. Other than the constantly visiting

physicians and family members, no one could see his unusual body. He was not ready to be seen.

Especially since he had not been able to even see himself yet. Everyone was too polite to say anything to his face, but he could hear what they whispered in the hallways as they walked away from his room.

He was distracted from his self-pity by the sound of a horse's hooves galloping into the front courtyard of the castle. The speed of the gait instantly alerted Aden that this messenger was on an urgent mission.

Was it the messenger from Chendas? It was too early, but perhaps they had made the ride in record time.

Aden jumped from his bed, ran to the door and stepped out into the hallway, more quickly than he had moved in days.

His younger brother Erich peeked out from his own bedroom. "What's going on?" he asked.

"A horseman just arrived in the courtyard. It sounds urgent."

"Stay here," Erich commanded. "I'll go find out what's happening."

"Come back as soon as you find out," Aden growled as his younger brother dashed out of the family wing.

Aden returned to the seclusion of his room, where his tired mind and restless muscles had nothing to do but wait. He strained his ears, but he could not pick out any particular conversation above the level of chatter he heard throughout the large structure.

Of course, Erich never returned.

The noises continued to grow. Guards were moving swiftly down hallways. Horses were galloping out of the front gate.

Whatever news the messenger had brought was not about him, and it was causing a panic.

Aden realized that perhaps he was being foolish, hiding away. He wasn't actually going to hurt anyone, and they could not hide the truth forever. Surely the dozens of physicians who had seen him were already spreading stories of his monstrous body throughout Iseldis and beyond.

As the tension in the castle mounted, he stepped out of his room again. His eyes failed him, and his body froze. He had never navigated the castle blindly before. He looked toward the door at the end of the hall, breathing deeply as his heart raced. Oddly, the distant door itself was more visible than the stone wall beneath his fingertips . . . claw tips?

He started moving toward the door, determined to find out what was happening.

"I should be the one to go," Ian's voice sounded loudly before the door slammed open.

"You are staying here," King Frederich responded, following his son into the hallway. "That's final."

"I am the head of the elite guard! It is my responsibility to lead them into battle," Ian argued, closing the door behind him and speaking to his father in a respectful but passionate tone.

"It is your responsibility to remain here. This is a test, a ruse. The real war is yet to come, and you will not recklessly endanger yourself before then."

"What's going on?" Aden asked, as neither of them seemed to have noticed his presence.

"The Majis have attacked the northern shore, near the old monastery," King Frederich explained.

"Already?" Aden replied. "Their exile does not end until next silverreign."

"It is simply an opening message, an invitation if you will," his father replied. "I think their only goal is to feel out what they are up against."

"Which is why we should be responding with our full force, to scare them off," Ian interjected. "To show them that they cannot return here and bend us to their magical will."

"I am responding with my full force," King Frederich said, his voice calm and low. "Under Erich's leadership."

"Right, because your fourth son is expendable," Ian replied, his voice unusually bitter.

Aden heard his father's deep sigh. Although he could not see it, he could imagine the worry in his father's eyes.

"You are all my sons," King Frederich responded. "None of you are expendable. But you have a different responsibility. One that I expect you to fulfill."

"Yes, Father," Ian replied, his voice returning to his usual respect at the mention of duty. Aden's oldest brother was nothing if not honorable.

"Erich is gone?" Aden asked. That would explain why he'd never returned.

"Yes," his father replied. "Two unidentified ships are still offshore. I need to write messages for the other kingdoms. Ian, come. You can help me with that."

Aden listened to the sound of the footsteps disappear down the length of the hall. He returned to his own room, more restless than before.

He and his brothers had trained for war their entire lives. Iseldis was the kingdom of warriors. Now that a battle was on their doorstep, Aden was useless.

He paced his room until the sun set. At least the rest of the castle was as restless as he was.

As he lay in bed not sleeping, he heard a small scratch at the door. Just as he had been for the past few nights, Warrior was at the door, looking for his old friend.

Aden got up from the bed and stepped gingerly toward the door. For being twice as large and heavy as he had previously been, he could walk more quietly than he ever had. When he reached the door, he undid the latch and opened it a crack.

Warrior wriggled into the room. Aden could hear him

sniffing his way to the bed, then wandering around when he discovered the bed was empty.

It took him a surprisingly long time to discover Aden, who was still standing behind the door. Snarling through puppy teeth, Warrior growled at the massive beast who had replaced his favorite person.

Hopefully, the pup's future fierceness would compensate for his lack of brains. He was not the smartest wolfhound Aden had met.

After the dog had dashed from the room, Aden closed his door again and dragged his broken heart back to bed. He was heartened that Warrior kept trying to find his old friend, but that only made it all the more difficult to bear his barks of rejection.

Just when his tired mind had finally dozed off, another scratch at the door brought him instantly to wakefulness.

"Psst. Aden?" Onric's voice whispered through the door. "Are you awake?"

"I am now," Aden grumbled back. "Your tramping through the halls would wake even a hibernating bear."

As his brother entered the room, Aden quickly recognized the softer footfalls of Ashlin Cabril, the girl who had stolen his brother's heart.

"Who else is with you?" Aden asked, referring to a third set of footsteps.

"Mistress Cedrice, the seamstress from town," Ashlin responded. "She . . ."

When Ashlin paused, Onric finished the sentence. "She may have some insight into your . . . condition."

"I said no more physicians." Aden's voice came out closer to a growl.

"I am here in secrecy, Your Highness," Mistress Cedrice

interjected, "because I have a trifling knowledge of the Majis and their ways."

Aden could not make out any identifying features of the older woman, but her presence was calming. She was nothing like the physicians and surgeons that had bowed and scraped their way into his presence. "Tell me what you know, seamstress."

"Very little, I am afraid," she replied. "These two have given me several accounts of what happened that night, but I should like to hear what you experienced."

He thought back to the events of that horrible night, as he had many times, but the specifics were as hazy as his eyesight. "When the room grew dark," he said, "I saw Ian just standing there, and I knew the ball of light from the attacker was gathering power. So, I jumped forward to protect him. I do not remember anything else. I did not even feel the orb hit me. I just woke up some hours later with a sharp pain in my head and . . . like this."

"You heard the attacker chanting?"

"I suppose I did. I do not recall it as I was focused on getting to Ian in time."

"This self-contained orb is beyond my limited experience." Mistress Cedrice sighed. "I have no idea how powerful this Lord Munney was. I have never experienced a magic that was entirely contained in itself. The only magic I have seen requires an object to interact with."

"Like needing the shard of glass to create my shoes for the ball," Ashlin said, her voice dawning with understanding.

"Precisely."

The mention of glass brought a new memory to Aden's mind. "What happened to the glass rose?"

"Glass rose?" Mistress Cedrice leaned closer.

"I was holding an antique glass rose. It was quite intricate and looked to be a piece from the reign of the Majis queen. I was holding it when . . ." That terrible night flashed through his mind once again, but this time with startling detail. He had been examining the glass rose, taking in the delicate twist of its petals, when the room darkened. Seeing Ian in danger, he had jumped across the dais immediately, reaching out toward him with the rose still in his hand. "I was holding it," he repeated.

"Where is that rose?" Mistress Cedrice said. "It likely saved your life."

Or cursed it. Was it worth it to still have his life if everything was entirely different? "I do not know what happened to the rose," he said aloud, keeping his bitter thoughts to himself.

"We have left the ballroom entirely untouched, waiting for the new councilors to arrive. I'll go look for it now!" Onric dashed out of the room.

Some moments later, he returned. As he stepped through the doorway, Aden's senses were overpowered by the powerful aroma of a freshly cut rose.

"This is most unusual," Mistress Cedrice said.

Aden's heart pounded. "Why?"

The older woman stepped forward and pressed something into his hand. It was long and thin. The floral scent grew stronger.

"It is no longer a glass rose," Mistress Cedrice explained. "It has become real. I think it may have blocked the attack and lessened the power of the dark magic."

"What does that mean?" Aden asked, rolling the stem of the rose through his clumsy claws.

"I do not know, but I want to believe it means there is hope," the older woman replied.

"Could you sing for him?" Ashlin asked. "Could your magic reverse this curse?"

"Your magic?" Aden interjected, the feeling of calm dissipating. Was this woman herself a Majis?

"I can try, my dear," Mistress Cedrice responded, "but the remnants of my ancestors' magic is far too weak to balance out the chaotic evil of this curse." Turning back to Aden, she asked, "Can I sing for you, Your Highness?"

"You are a Majis," Aden stated, uncertain.

"My ancestors were," she replied. "I have found that by singing their songs, I can enhance the harmony of certain objects around me. I do not know that I can do anything to directly help you, but I will cause you no harm."

"You have risked much in coming here." Aden stared at her shadowed form. Majis or no, any interaction with magic was enough to warrant her arrest, exile, or possibly even execution.

"You risked much to save your brother," she said simply.

"You may sing," Aden whispered. His condition was already worse than death. What harm could she do?

The older woman took the rose from his paw and handed it to Ashlin. "I do not understand this curse, and I do not want to tamper with anything that could affect this rose," she explained.

The room quieted, and Aden heard the woman take two long breaths.

Then, she began to sing.

Her voice was low and quiet, soothing the pain and tension in his sensitive ears. He did not recognize her words, but the sounds were soft and rounded, reminding him of the old language still found in some ancient writings.

He closed his eyes. Waves of peace seemed to roll over him.

Her words were entirely different from the harsh sounds Munney had chanted at the ball.

Aden opened his eyes to see if the two experiences were dissimilar in other ways. There was no orb of light. The room did not dim.

In fact, it seemed to be getting slightly brighter, evaporating the shadows that plagued his eyesight. In their stead, he could make out distinct shapes. He saw the woman's hands clasped over her heart as she sang, even if he could not make out the features of her face.

"I . . . I can see a little better," he stammered as her words slowed to a hum. He lifted his hand in front of his face. It was still a fur-covered paw, but he could actually make out the shape of it. "Thank you," he whispered, feeling for the first time that there might be hope.

CHAPTER 5

*I*sa held her hands steady, slowly counting to seventy as she applied gentle pressure on the thin square board in front of her. She stood up on tiptoe, leveraging her body weight over the solid wooden desk.

Wrapping the wooden panel of a book cover in soft seasoned leather was her favorite step in the bookbinding process. She loved the tart smell of the wet glue, the crinkling sounds of the parchment, the soft texture of the leather under her fingers, and the finished look of the pressed cover in perfect alignment. The row of books on her father's shelves looked so modern and elegant compared to the stacks of parchment and scrolls that littered the rest of the library.

"Fifty-three, fifty-four, fifty-five . . ." Isa whispered her slow count into the empty room around her. She was in a small study directly attached to the large library in the Bielsa Villa on the western side of Allys. Unlike the library with its crowded but orderly shelves, her father's study resembled that of the absent-minded Brother Elias. It was a chaotic jumble of loose parchments, treated leather, various colors of inks in bottles or jars, wooden tools, and engraving implements. However messy it might look to an outsider, Isa never had a problem finding any item she might need.

At the moment, she was using a new type of glue her father had developed. It was safer for the delicate parchment of the interior pages, but it dried very quickly and thus required close attention during its application.

The door to the studio opened, distracting her count as Macklin entered the room.

Isa bristled at the interruption, attempting to keep her focus on the task at hand. "Sixty-seven, sixty-eight, sixty-nine . . . seventy." She exhaled, slowly lifting her hands from the board in front of her. It remained in place. Not that it was completely dried yet—that would take two full days if it did not rain again —but the paste had set, which meant she could move on to the next step.

That was, she could have moved on to the next step if she had not been interrupted.

"Miss Isa." The young tutor announced his presence when she finally looked up to acknowledge him. "Is it not a little late to be working?"

"It is not work when one enjoys it." Technically, she was a higher rank than he was, yet he addressed her with the patronizing "miss." There was something about the way he said it, as though he were trying to look more impressive by making her appear less important.

She reached for a pile of blank parchments she had stitched together to form the pages of the book.

Macklin stepped farther into the room, a pleasant smile on his face as he watched her movements. "Practicing your father's craft?"

"No," she replied.

She was not practicing. She was binding.

She was not a novice who needed to practice with blank parchments. She was a skilled artisan. Even her father, who had worked with the most renowned binders in the kingdom, said she was one of the best.

"I am testing a new iteration of the gum paste my father created," she explained, "and I do not want to risk harming a valuable scroll if this experiment turns sour." A vast majority of the works in the family library were written on scrolls. Isa and her father had set themselves the lofty goal of binding every one of them in a sturdy hard cover. However, they wanted to ensure the glue they used would not accelerate the deterioration of the ancient parchment. "This new mix of the paste has a higher degree of resin—"

"I know," Macklin interrupted. "I studied that type of paste under the monks at Chendas." He picked up the clay jar and delicately sniffed its contents.

"That's not—" She started to explain it would have been impossible to study this type of paste because her father had just invented a new variation on the formula, but Macklin was already moving on to a different topic.

"I imagine there are many other occupations a beautiful young woman such as yourself would be interested in on a fine greenreign evening such as this one?"

"What does it matter what season it is? If I prefer to be working, I shall work." Isa kept her focus on her hands in front of her. She carefully lined the stitched parchments against the spine of the drying cover to double-check the width. It was perfect.

"How can you keep yourself cooped up indoors when the nights are growing warmer and the flowers are blooming?" He moved around the table toward her.

Isa had the distinct feeling that this was less about her enjoying the positive aspects of greenreign and more about her enjoying those positive aspects with him. "I happen to already enjoy what I am doing." She could not resist adding a final word. "Alone."

"Of course." The smile remained on his face, though it no longer reached his eyes. He stepped to her side by the desk and picked up the cover she had been working on.

"Don't touch that," she cried. "The glue has only just begun to set."

He dropped it quickly at her reprimand.

Her heart flew into her mouth at the sight of her hours of precious work, falling without a thought. She gently picked it up, checking the edges to see if the pieces had slipped. Fortunately, the glue looked to have set properly.

"But it appears," Macklin said, not noticing her concern, "that you have tucked the corners too tightly to fit over the stack of parchment properly." He pointed to the corner of the cover in her hands. "This angle here needs to be at a precise crossover from that one there in order for the two sides to match perfectly in alignment."

Isa stared at him in disbelief. Was he seriously explaining the most basic principle of the process? The process her very own father had created?

"Don't feel aggrieved. A girl as pretty as you doesn't need to worry about doing things right. Let me show you how it should fit together." Misreading the shocked look on her face, he picked up a finished book from the shelf behind him—a book she herself had bound—and opened it to the first interior page. "See this corner here needs to match with that angle. To get the right margin you simply mark the fold in the leather by lining up the interior fold of the parchment with this side here." His voice was kind and explanatory, as though he were doing her a favor.

How stupid did he think she was? "Unless," she said, as she

moved back to where she had been standing and carefully placed the drying cover on the table, "you are experimenting with a new type of oleoresin that requires a larger margin to properly set and thus reduces the potential contact that might deteriorate the parchment."

Her forward movement forced him to step out of the way. "Of . . . of course," he replied. "Unless you are doing that type of experiment, of course." He turned away to place the covered book he had been using as a demonstration back on the shelf against the wall.

She could not see his face, but he seemed flustered. Good. Maybe he would leave. "Did you come here to look for something specifically? I would like to get back to work."

"Uh. Yes, just seeing if your father kept a copy of *Astridonemus* here for tomorrow's lesson with your sister."

Before Isa could reply, her mother's voice rang out through the main room of the library. "Isabel!"

She never used Isa's full name.

"I hate to distract you from your work, but we have some unexpected guests this evening and I could use your help." Lady Bielsa entered the study. Her bronze skin was uncharacteristically flushed.

"Unexpected guests?" Isa replied. "At this hour?"

Her mother exhaled through her nose. "Two councilors from Chendas. Apparently, our response to their letter was not good enough."

"Letter?" Macklin asked.

"Councilors? Here?" Isa exclaimed. The members of the Council held the highest title and rank other than King. They did not run their own errands.

"What letter?" Macklin repeated.

"The Council requested every copy we have of Floutast's

writing a few weeks ago while you were in Chendas," Lady Bielsa replied.

"Floutast?" Macklin sounded confused. Apparently, he had not studied the obscure writer in his recent education.

"An old Allysian author," Isa explained. "His work is mostly disregarded as myth. We sent them the two volumes we have in the library here, but we keep the rest of his work at the mountain villa."

"The audacity," Lady Bielsa fumed. "To show up unannounced, demanding something they clearly know we cannot provide as things are."

"Can't you tell them that father is too ill?"

"I tried." The anger in her mother's face melted into worry. "The first attack in Iseldis apparently uncovered new information on the Majis. And there's been a second attack. The Council examiners in Chendas need the Floutast immediately. They've run out of time."

"A second attack?" Isa's stomach twisted. It was happening, the Return was beginning early. "Then I'll go," Isa said. "I'll go to the mountains and retrieve the books they need."

"Don't be ridiculous. The villa has been empty since last goldenreign. I'm not sending you out there alone no matter what threats the councilors make."

"More threats?" Isa's voice was higher than she intended.

Lady Bielsa waved away her worry. "They are merely trying to convey their urgency."

"My lady." Macklin bowed slightly. "Allow me to go to the villa."

Isa spoke over him. "What threats did they make?"

"Your family has provided me with the most honorable opportunity to tutor your daughter," Macklin carried on. "It is the least I could do to repay my gratitude."

The worry lines on Lady Bielsa's face smoothed away.

Isa shook her head in panic. The image of the damaged scrolls in Brother Elias's study filled her mind. Macklin may have passed his exams, but he had literally just dropped the book she was working on. "I'm afraid I do not trust anyone but myself to package those scrolls for transport," she said. "I'm going."

Lady Bielsa looked between the two of them. "Professor Surrell, I would be most grateful if you would accompany my daughter to the mountain villa."

Isa's stomach twisted. Nothing about this situation was ideal. "What threats did they make?"

Her mother ignored the question as she stepped out of the study. "Come help me to entertain our guests."

Aden stayed in the safety of the shadows, thankful that his father had not called him to his usual place in the family circle. The private salon, lined with chairs and small sofas, was the preferred meeting place of the royal family. Only immediate family and a few trusted members of the household were allowed to enter it.

But they were currently breaking that sacred tradition, holding the most complicated discussion the family had ever had with two newly arrived outsiders from the Council of Chendas.

"You have handled the situation well these past four days," one of the councilors said, nodding his approval. He was speaking to King Frederich, who had just given him a detailed account of everything they knew concerning Lord Munney's treachery and Aden's current state.

The councilor turned his gaze toward Aden, likely attempting to see him more clearly in the shadows outside the reach of the candles on the wall.

Aden could not clearly make out the man's face. Though his

voice had been matter-of-fact, it also held notes of compassion. But Aden made no move to step closer into the light, no matter how honest the councilor appeared.

"And what of the attack on the coast?" the councilor asked King Frederich. "Were your men able to apprehend the two Majis ships?"

"No," the king replied, "our attacking ship was destroyed this morning by a powerful storm. They have recovered some survivors, but most are still missing."

Erich was still missing. A messenger had arrived from the coast mere hours before the councilors had ridden in from the opposite direction. King Frederich had sent another contingent of soldiers to the coast, to both aid in the recovery and fortify their defenses.

"Your son was on that ship?" the councilor asked. "I am sorry to hear that. With your permission, my brother, King Gareth, will send two hundred men to aid you on the coast."

"His aid would be most appreciated," King Frederich responded.

The tension in the room was palpable. Still shocked by the news of Erich's disappearance, the family had not yet had a chance to mourn. The severity of the storm was so intense that only three men from the ship of nearly one hundred had made it back to the shore. Every hour reduced the odds that any remaining survivors would be found.

"What advice do you bring for us to move forward?" King Frederich asked, moving the conversation away from his missing son.

The councilor turned his attention back to the king and queen, who were seated next to each other on a cushioned sofa. "We were deeply shocked and concerned to discover that Munney was hiding in our midst. My brother, King Gareth, has launched a full-scale investigation in Chendas to discover if any other council members are allied with the Majis. We left as soon as we received word from your messenger, so I do not have results on that front."

"And what of Crown Prince Ian, Your Majesty?" the second councilor asked. "Have you moved forward with the request made at the last session?"

Aden noted the lack of tact exhibited by the man whose power was supposed to be in his words. He had hardly offered a condolence concerning Erich, but was pushing forward his own interests in regard to Ian.

The rest of the room remained silent. Even King Frederich did not respond immediately.

Aden could imagine him raising his eyebrows as he emitted his disapproval of the question. The Council had requested that Ian choose his future wife and queen at the ball.

Ian himself was sitting on a wooden chair next to his parents. Aden wondered if his older brother's expression was slightly more livid. Ian was not yet quite as skilled as their father when it came to masking his emotions.

"Under the circumstances, we did not carry out the full extent of that plan," King Frederich finally said.

"Under the circumstances," the second councilor responded, "it may make the most sense to move forward with that plan as quickly as possible. Now, more than ever, the people need see that your kingdom has a united front, especially as it mourns the loss of Prince Erich."

Onric, who had been pacing across the opposite side of the room, had abruptly stopped. Aden felt himself wishing that his brother would start moving again. The steady drumbeat of his footsteps, however loud they were, at least offered an outlet for the tension in the room. Aden perceived a new set of footsteps from some distance down the hall outside the door. They would have a new visitor momentarily.

"Shall we stay focused on the matter at hand?" King Frederich's tone made it clear he was not asking a question.

"Of course, Your Majesty." The older councilman turned his gaze back toward Aden.

Before he could say anything further, he was interrupted by the door of the salon slamming open. Only family members entered without knocking.

"Why was I not informed of this meeting?" Princess Meena entered, the higher register of her demanding voice making Aden's ears throb. Meena had inherited her mother's commanding presence.

"It was late . . ." King Frederich started, but his daughter's crossed arms stopped him short. The side of Aden's mouth twitched as he imagined her indignant expression. She was her father's only daughter, and she knew it.

"I am no longer a child." As the youngest member of the family, she was sixteen.

Their father nodded toward the remaining empty chair.

She sat.

"Now, can we get back to the presence of a traitorous magic-wielder in the Council infiltrating my kingdom and attacking my sons." King Frederich turned his attention back to the councilor.

"Bring in the prisoner," the councilor said, raising his voice to be heard by the guards stationed outside the door.

"Not in the family room," Queen Cara protested.

"I apologize, Your Majesty. Is there another place we can question him without compromising the privacy of Prince Aden?"

"Is this truly necessary?" Queen Cara asked.

"I could transmit the information he has given us," the councilor responded, "but this is a time in which we cannot trust anyone, and I would never presume that you would blindly trust me. This is a matter which concerns you directly, your whole family even, and it is of the utmost importance that you hear any information directly from the source."

Queen Cara gave a single nod, but Aden could imagine that her lips were pressed into a thin line of displeasure.

"Wait." King Frederich turned to his daughter. "Meena, it really is getting late—"

"I'm staying," she responded, cutting him off. "This is my kingdom and my family." She looked toward Aden, her honest eyes likely filled with sympathy.

He resented her pity, but he would not ask her to leave. He remembered how it had felt when he had been the youngest, to be excluded from the meetings and activities that Ian and Onric were allowed to participate in. Besides, his father could only shelter her from the reality of the situation for so long.

King Frederich did not affirm her, but he sighed deeply as he turned back to the councilor, waiting for him to proceed.

The councilor gave a curt nod to the guard who had entered the room at his earlier command. A few moments later, Lord Munney, the previous councilor to Iseldis, was brought into the room.

Aden expected to feel something when he saw his attacker for the first time since he had been cursed—shock, horror, anger—but he felt nothing. Munney had disguised himself during the attack, so it was not as though Aden had known what was happening in the moment.

He could tell that the man's shoulders were bowed and his face turned down. But his eyes must have been scanning the people in the room, looking for him, as Aden heard a sneering hiss in his direction.

That sinister sound, barely audible as it was, made Aden's hair stand on end and the claws in his hands curl out of their protective padding.

But Munney had reached the center of the room and turned his back to Aden, facing the king and queen with his head bowed. Munney's hands had been bound in front of him, and Aden could make out the rough outline of what appeared to be a wooden bar tied across his mouth. Since the use of magic was directly invoked through the power of song, they had probably gagged him as a defensive measure.

"I have extensively questioned former council member Abadia Munney on our journey here from Chendas," the lead councilor was saying. "He will answer my questions now fully and honestly, and you are free to interrogate him after that."

King Frederich nodded.

As everyone's attention remained fixed on the bound man they had once trusted, Aden felt like a strange outsider. This small room, so used to the intimate laughter of his gathered family, now held all the austerity of a throne room. Even if it could once again be filled with laughter, Aden felt that he was no longer part of the family circle.

The confident voice of the councilor brought him back to the present. "What was your intent with the violent attack you made during the ball four nights ago?" Unhindered by emotion, the councilor asked his first question without rising from his chair.

The guard stepped forward to remove the gag from Munney's face so he could speak. Aden cringed at the small popping sound as the man stretched his facial muscles.

"My intent was to kill the crown prince," Munney said, keeping his face downturned. His answer was practiced and expected, but the spite in his voice decried his humble posture.

Ian, who was fully facing the prisoner, inhaled heavily. Aden could imagine the tension in his face. Ian's hands were gripping the wooden armrests of his chair, as though he was attempting to keep himself from strangling the man who tried to murder him. Aden could not blame him. The claws in his own hands slid easily in and out of their casings.

"With what power did you execute your attack?" the councilor continued.

"With the power of the Majis."

"How have you come into possession of this power? Are you a Majis?"

"Yes." Though Munney's answer was a single word, it was laced with pride.

"How have you come into possession of this power?" the councilor repeated.

"My ancestors went into hiding during the exile and have passed down my heritage, father to son, for generations. We have long awaited the time to take back what is our own."

"How did the murder of Ian Omaris Sirilian fit in with that plan?" The councilor asked these questions with a practiced efficiency. He already knew the answer to each one, and he was ensuring that Munney gave a full account of his actions to the king and queen. Aden had to admit that this method was far more effective than he had anticipated.

"Ian stands to inherit a throne that does not belong to him. I may have failed in my attempt four days ago . . ." Munney lifted his head to stare straight at Ian. "But when my people return from their exile, they will take back what is theirs."

The councilor held out a hand to pacify him. "Watch your tongue, Munney," he said to the prisoner.

Munney dropped his gaze once again to the floor, repositioning his feet as he let out a long sigh.

"It is good to confirm what we have already discovered about this situation, but why did your attack not kill my son Aden when it deflected to him?" King Frederich took over the role of the questioning.

"Aden intercepted the intent of the magic, weakening its effect."

"You will reverse this effect?" The tone of Queen Cara's question held certain consequences for anyone who failed to answer it as she desired.

"I cannot."

"You cannot, or you will not?" Her voice was quiet, which only intensified the weight of her words.

"I cannot." This time, the sincerity in Munney's voice surprisingly matched his humble posture.

Not that he was deserving of their trust, which he had already broken. But for the first time during this uncomfortable interaction, he was not speaking with disdain.

The king turned a questioning gaze to the councilor.

"To the best of our knowledge, this is true." The councilor sighed heavily, his own confident aura slipping away with the gravity of this information. "We have questioned him under threat of death—and worse—to reverse this matter, and it seems that what he says is true."

Aden could feel the tension in the room slowly ebbing toward despair. Hopelessness. His own powerlessness to get out of the nightmare in which he had found himself.

"Remember," the councilor continued, "this is a magic that thrives on chaos. It seems that it cannot exert its power in an action that would restore balance and harmony. This coincides with what the examiners in Chendas have discovered about the magic as well."

Aden's body lost its ability to stand straight, his muscles sagging against his unfamiliar skeleton. To hear that there was absolutely no reason for hope felt as though someone had stabbed him and twisted the knife.

The previous night, when Onric and Ashlin had brought the old seamstress from the village, he had felt a flicker of hope. As though his interference with the magic might mean that his condition could be reversed. The woman had restored some of his sight, but the only thing she had uncovered about the situation was the rose.

The rose.

Aden leaped from the shadows, plowing past the seated Meena to grasp Munney's upper arms. He released his claws just enough to cause a little bite.

"What about the rose?" Aden snarled.

"The . . . the rose?" Munney tried to regain his composure, but Aden could smell his fear.

"I was holding a glass rose when your curse attacked me. It was beautifully sculpted, an exquisite piece really. Probably created by your . . . ancestors." Aden flexed his claws to emphasize the derision in the last word.

Munney's face, inches from his own, was merely a wash of color in Aden's straining eyes. But he could feel the man trembling in his hands. Aden relished the sense of power that brought him.

"That rose," he continued, "apparently became a real rose as a result of your . . . little attack."

Something stiffened in Munney's body, as though he had regained some semblance of control despite the beast towering over him. "It did?" Munney asked, a touch of triumph in his voice.

"What did you do?" Aden increased the growl beneath his voice. Without turning his head, he spoke to his brother. "Onric, get the rose."

The sound of Onric's footsteps dashing out the door told him that his order had been obeyed.

"I did not *do* anything," Munney responded. He tried to use the momentary distraction to step backward, putting space between them.

Aden held him firmly in place.

"My magic should have transformed you totally and completely into a beast," Munney continued. "In fact, even I will admit to being surprised that you retained some of your human functions." Munney sniffed. "Though I see now I may have been mistaken in that."

Aden snarled, shaking the man.

Munney instantly went stiff with fright, though he recovered himself quickly.

"You were saying?" Aden pressed.

"This rose, sculpted with the power of my people, delayed the curse. How fortunate for you."

Aden wanted to believe that he was, indeed, fortunate. "So, you can reverse this curse?"

Munney did not respond immediately, though Aden had the distinct feeling the man was smiling.

"I can—"

He was cut off by the door slamming open. Onric strode into the room, the living rose in his hand. It was in full bloom, and Aden could immediately smell its fragrance floating through the room.

Munney made a motion to reach for the rose, remembering too late that his hands were bound.

"You can?" Aden felt the panic rising in his chest. He did not trust himself to control his claws if the man did not divulge his secrets.

"Unhand me," Munney demanded.

"What are you not telling me?" Aden lifted the man from the floor. He felt someone's hand on his arm, urging him to control himself, but he ignored them.

"I cannot reverse the curse," Munney croaked. "But when the last petal on that rose falls . . ." He gasped for breath.

The outside pressure on Aden's arms increased, and he lowered Munney back to the floor.

"You will lose all remaining human functions."

"I will die?" Aden asked, not sure if that was an unwelcome prospect at the moment.

"You will fully transform into a beast. You will no longer be human," Munney sneered.

Aden felt a true roar tear through his throat. He did not even notice when the puny man in front of him was torn from his grasp.

CHAPTER 7

"I hate to leave him again so soon." Isa felt her father's forehead with the back of her hand.

His eyes remained closed, and his breathing was slow but steady.

"By the time you return, he will be back on his feet and eager to see all the progress you've made in the library." Lady Bielsa had hardly left her husband's side since he had fallen ill.

"Have you noticed any change this morning?"

"None yet." Her mother sighed. "He smiled at me a few times, but his words are still incoherent and his mind wanders."

"It will come back soon. You should get some rest, Mama, or you will be sick beside him."

"I would rather be sick beside him than alive without him." Her mother's words were lifeless. She must be pushing the boundaries of exhaustion, as it was unlike her to have such sad thoughts.

"Do not even think about sharing this illness with him. We need you too much." Isa set her hands on her mother's shoulders, massaging her thumbs into the older woman's stiff muscles. "If love alone could heal him, he would live a thousand lifetimes."

Her mother smiled, relaxing into the comforting touch. "If I were going to get sick, I would have caught it by now. I am far too strong to be overtaken by a mere fever."

Isa smiled as she continued to rub her mother's shoulders. That sounded more like the woman she had always looked up to. "I would much rather be strong than beautiful." She could not keep the bitterness from her voice.

"How fortunate for you, that you have been gifted with both." Her mother's response was formulaic. They'd had this conversation many times before.

Isa did not respond. She stopped her methodical massage and absently tapped her fingers across her mother's back. She did not have to be happy about the fact that her mother was right.

"Are you angry that I am making Macklin accompany you?"

Isa's fingers continued to lightly beat out a chaotic rhythm. "I do not enjoy his company."

"I cannot let you travel alone."

"I'll have Luca, and Blanca, and Cam."

Her mother chuckled lightly. "Our dear servants are the most trustworthy people I have ever had the pleasure to meet, and I know they would literally give their lives to keep you safe, but there is more to this state of affairs and you know it." She twisted her neck to look back at Isa. "Besides, Macklin can help you prepare the volumes as well."

Isa snorted. "I'm sure his help would be most valuable if he could shut his mouth once in a while."

"He does like the sound of his own voice, doesn't he?" Her mother dropped her voice to a conspiratorial whisper.

Isa stopped the motion of her hands. "It is just the way he . . . He seems to think that I am unable to think for myself. Does he not realize I have studied all the same subjects he has, possibly even more? He merely sees a pretty face and assumes I am nothing more than that."

Lady Bielsa reached up to her shoulder to place her hand over her daughter's. "I'm afraid I cannot commiserate with you there, since you take after your grandmother. Her beauty skipped me, and your father was the only man who noticed that my mind was more interesting than his own."

Isa leaned forward, looping her hands around her mother to give her a hug from behind the chair. "I love your story."

Lady Bielsa kissed her daughter's cheek. "Someday, my dearest Isabel, someone will see that you are even more wise than you are beautiful."

Isa sighed. She wanted to believe her mother's words, but her experience told her otherwise. She was of average height and considered herself awkwardly round in all the wrong places. Most Allysian women were short and slim, with naturally tanned skin and sleek, straight hair. Isa was curvy, and her thick, wavy dark hair grew in volume and texture when she combed it. She had always thought that her cheekbones were too high and her eyes too dark.

She had noticed some years ago that men would openly stare at her, lavishing their attention upon her while ignoring the friends standing next to her. She also heard the crude comments they made about her features when they thought she could not hear them.

When her own friends had slowly pulled away, jealous of the attention she received, Isa had begun to resent her own beauty. She threw herself into work with her father, where her looks and physical appearance had no sway in how well she could read, converse, or bind books.

A knock sounded at the door. "Sorry to disturb you, my

lady." The villa stewardess poked her head into the room. "The carriage is nearly ready."

As the stewardess disappeared, Lady Bielsa moved to stand.

Isa held her in place for a moment longer. "Mama, what did the councilors threaten last night when you told them Papa was too ill to get Floutast to them?"

Lady Bielsa exhaled, her shoulders deflating. "It was nothing you need to worry about, my dear. Just get the books back safely."

"Mama."

"They said they would be forced to arrest your father for aiding and abetting the Majis." Her mother's voice was barely a whisper.

Isa stood up straight. "They would do that? When he has not been able to leave his bed in weeks? That's not justified! If they arrest him, he'll surely die in prison! He's done nothing wrong! They cannot attack him for the inability to deliver something as trivial as Floutast!"

Lady Bielsa stood as well, placing a hand on Isa's mouth. "Hush. They might hear you. It is their responsibility to keep the kingdoms safe. We do not know what they need this for. It was probably an idle threat just used to convey the urgency of their need."

Isa pinched her lips. "They've acted on idle threats before. Marlena's father hasn't been seen since they took him to Chendas for questioning."

"They are not titled," Lady Bielsa replied, her face pale. "They won't arrest a noble."

"He isn't titled," Isa responded, "but he is the richest man in the city. They are getting more desperate and aggressive, which makes sense with what is happening in Iseldis. Even though it does feel unjust. Don't worry, though, I'll get the Floutast and return in six days, seven at most."

As they left the bedroom, Isa's heart simmered with outrage. Desperate or not, the Council would achieve nothing by throwing a sick man into jail.

In the courtyard, two servants loaded chests into the waiting carriage.

"Miss Isa." Macklin approached her, a broad smile on his face. "I see you are looking forward to a relaxing holiday with me at this fabled vacation villa?"

Isa could not keep the confusion from her face.

His smile faltered slightly. "Seven trunks," he explained, leaning down as though they were sharing a secret jest between the two of them. "That is a little much, don't you think? Packing seven trunks for a short trip to the mountains. What do you plan on doing there, holding a private ball?" He raised his eyebrows. "Not that I would object, of course."

Isa did not miss the small smirk on her mother's face as Lady Bielsa walked past them to greet the two councilmen on the other side of the courtyard.

Isa had packed seven trunks. One of them contained clothing. She had stayed up late into the night, even after entertaining their guests with her mother, organizing tools and implements from her father's study into the other six trunks. She did not want to be caught unprepared if Floutast's scrolls needed extra care for travel.

"And how many trunks are you bringing?" she asked through gritted teeth. "Since you are such an experienced traveler, I am sure I could learn a thing or two from you."

His grin spread. "I am only bringing a modest five." His shoulders puffed out. "And I would be happy to share my knowledge of traveling with you anytime."

"Is that five trunks of clothing, or did you also see fit to bring softened leather for protecting the scrolls and extra linens for the packaging?"

"Of course not, my silly girl. We are merely fetching the Floutast, not rebinding the spare library."

Isa had the uncomfortable impression that he was about to reach out and pat her on the head as though she were a child to even have suggested such a thing. He had never been that forward, but just to be on the safe side, she crossed the courtyard to join her mother.

She forced a gracious smile on her face as she approached the two councilors who had been guests at the villa for the night.

They bowed slightly at her approach.

"It is most admirable of you to take this responsibility upon your shoulders in place of your father," Lord Sanclim said.

"I speak for the whole of the council when I say that we are most grateful to you for getting this information to us in as timely a manner as possible," Lord Ivin added.

"Of course," Isa replied, "I am honored to undertake this service." Her mind was still ruminating on the not-so-admirable threats they used to ensure their request was heeded.

"We have not been able to locate any other copy of Floutast's works," Lord Sanclim said.

Macklin stepped to her side, having followed her across the courtyard.

Lord Sanclim continued speaking, directing his words at Macklin. "Please ensure that they are not damaged in any way during their travel. The examiners must be able to study every single word."

"But of course, my lord," Macklin responded, his expression grave.

Isa lifted her shoulders to make her presence larger. Apparently, Macklin was not the only one who thought she was only going on this trip for the thrill of it. "*I* will personally ensure that Floutast's work is bound and packaged with utmost care."

Lord Sanclim turned back toward her, his smile indulgent. "Thank you." He turned back to Macklin, and his eyes ran up and down the younger man's body as though sizing him up with new respect. "I almost envy you this little adventure in the mountains," he said.

Isa cut in before Macklin could inhale any more air. His puffed chest was already in danger of exploding. "The sun is up," she said. "We really must get going if we are to reach the inn by nightfall."

She dipped her head to the councilors and strode back to the carriage. Her mother followed her, wrapping her in a warm embrace.

"It takes a true strength to withhold one's anger," she whispered to her daughter. "Be safe, my dear one."

"I will." Isa squeezed her back. "Get Papa well. I'll see you in a few days."

$\mathcal{A}$den slipped deeper into the trees as light spilled over the horizon.

Despite the exhaustion in his limbs and his mind, he felt a glimmer of hope as he watched the sunrise. A newer part of his sight was returning. Since he had not ventured outside his room —and the windows had been kept completely covered for his privacy and safety—he had not discovered until he snuck out of the castle in the dead of night that his sight was almost perfect if he was looking at the horizon. He could make things out quite clearly if they were distant, but the closer objects were, the more blurred they became.

As delightful as it was to feel less blind, that minor victory was completely overshadowed by the anguish brought on by Munney's revelation.

The rage that had overtaken his entire body clouded his mind . . . He would have strangled the Majis if his family had not torn the man from his grasp.

His family. His family had witnessed his momentary loss of sanity.

A petal had fallen from the living rose shortly after the meeting had ended, as though signifying the very humanity that was slipping through his grasp.

He could not stay in Iseldis. He would not let them witness another such outburst. Nor could he imagine the outcome of that unconstrained rage against any of his family members.

He would not die when the rose dropped its last petal, but the rose itself would die, taking his humanity with it.

His family would love him to the end, of course; they had assured him of that. But what would happen after the end? Would he attack Meena, so completely alive but so small and defenseless?

Or would he turn on Ian, whom he had always idolized? Heroic Ian would not even raise a hand in self-defense if Beast-Aden attacked him. And Onric . . . cheerful Onric who had just discovered the light and love of his life. Onric deserved to live.

A strangled laugh twisted in Aden's throat, coming out as a gasping sob. No, Aden would not be the cause of further grief and death in his family.

Erich had deserved to live, too. Erich, who would have been more afraid of a lasting scar on his suave face than of death itself. Aden felt a pang of guilt for all the times he had poked fun at his younger brother. Always ready for a party, Erich had the biggest heart of them all and loved to make sure everyone around him was laughing and enjoying themselves. Aden hadn't even had a chance to say goodbye before Erich was gone.

So, Aden had left. Under the cover of darkness, hours after the secret meeting with the councilors and Munney, Aden had climbed out of his bedroom window.

Of course, he had done the same thing many times throughout the years, but surprisingly, the angles and muscles of his agile new body had made it even easier to clamber over the masonry and ridges of the castle.

He'd requested a late-night meal and then packed it in a leather satchel along with the cursed rose—which he had carefully wrapped in damp linen to prolong its life as long as possible. At least as long as it took to get to the northern mountains. Where he could hide in obscurity and wait for the end.

Aden had covered a considerable distance since leaving the castle. He occasionally thought he could hear the sound of footsteps chasing after him, but no one had overtaken him.

Now, as daylight broke across the horizon, he knew he needed to get off the main road. Travelers and merchants would be up and about soon, making their way toward the capital.

Hunched low, he trekked into the woods. He needed to get far enough off the road so as not to be found.

Perhaps, if the forest floor was dense enough, he could continue pressing forward. However, his aching muscles and drooping eyelids begged him to stop and rest.

Feeling safely secluded from the main road, he finally found a mossy area and sank to the ground.

Attempting to hold his breath, he focused his sensitive hearing on the space around him. No other footsteps crashed through the undergrowth.

His heart hammered and his lungs screamed for air as his overtaxed body readjusted to the lack of movement. He inhaled slowly and quietly.

The forest around him was filled with noises, but none of them were threatening. Leaning back against a tree, he closed his eyes. Eventually, the soft ripple of leaves in the morning breeze lulled him to sleep.

He woke with a start to the sound of a snapping twig.

He froze, tensing his muscles, ready to spring into action if a threat presented itself. He did not hear any additional sounds of a living thing, man or beast.

He slowly leaned back against the tree behind him,

attempting to sleep once again. The surge of energy that had sprung his muscles into action disappeared, leaving them even more exhausted and heavy than before. But his mind was now awake, listening even more carefully than before for the sound of an intruder.

The sun rose in the sky above him, but the shade of the trees kept him cool. Surprisingly, the fur covering his body was not as overbearingly hot as he had expected.

Other than its usual sounds, the forest remained quiet. The twig must have been broken by a passing deer. Aden slowly let his eyelids close once again, drifting into an alert sleep.

Again, the sound of a snapping twig woke him. He had not been sleeping long, as the sun appeared to be in the same place in the sky above him. Was exhaustion merely driving him mad?

Perhaps the effects of the curse were already setting in.

He listened for any additional sound, expecting to hear only emptiness once again. His heart raced, though. He could not control the way in which his body reacted to sound, nor could he control the amount of sound that his ears perceived. Sleep was a useless endeavor.

After the space of two breaths, he heard the distinct sound of a footfall on the forest floor.

He eased himself up, his body going on high alert. Inhaling through his nose, he attempted to get a better understanding of his tracker. Much to his frustration, he could not make out any unfamiliar aroma in the forest.

The footsteps sounded again. They were light. Either it was a very small person, or someone who was fairly well versed in quiet movement.

Another set of footfalls sounded too closely to the first. It must be two people. They were close now. Aden stood, not caring if he alerted them to his presence as they were walking directly toward him and would soon be upon him.

The footsteps picked up their pace, and Aden could hear a panting breath. He finally caught a whiff of the intruder, and his mind put the pieces together all at once just before his attacker broke through the thick undergrowth. It was not a person, nor was it two people.

It was Warrior.

The small pup stopped, half-hidden by the bushy ferns as he stared up at Aden. The dog sniffed and barked. It was not a welcoming bark, nor was it an angry yelp. It was something in between.

"Oh, Warrior," Aden cooed, keeping his voice as high as he could despite its natural baritone and his overwhelming relief. He slowly eased himself down into a sitting position to appear less threatening to the small animal. "Good boy. Were you sad to see me leave?"

Warrior stared at him, baring his teeth slightly as Aden moved. The dog sniffed the air carefully, taking a half step out of the safety of the bush.

Aden did not dare to reach out toward him. This was the friendliest encounter the two had shared since the curse, and he did not want to spook the poor animal.

Leaning back against the tree, his mind finally relaxed along with his muscles.

Sensing that there was no immediate threat, Warrior dropped his back end to the ground and stared at Aden.

Aden returned the gaze, blinking occasionally but keeping the rest of his body as still as possible.

Eventually, Warrior folded his front legs as well, dropping his chin to his paws. He seemed to look up at Aden for a while longer, then closed his eyes. From the sound of his deep breathing, the tired pup had instantly fallen into a deep sleep.

Aden's chest expanded, his eyes and nose tingling with a slight burning sensation. He wanted to reach out and stroke

Warrior on the underside of his ears, just where he liked it. He contented himself with listening to the pup's loud and even breathing. The tiny dog was snoring, louder than a grown man.

Aden closed his eyes to whisk away the moisture that had formed there, and eventually he relaxed once again into an alert sleep.

He managed to sleep until the sun was high in the sky, but his still anxious mind would not let him rest for long. The sounds of animals moving through the forest as they went about their daily activities kept his mind from fully entering a deep sleep. He awoke feeling slightly recovered, though anxious to be on his way.

Warrior stirred as soon as he stood.

"What a good boy you are, Warrior," Aden said. He moved away from the dog and slowly, quietly continued his way through the trees. He kept the road on his left side but stayed deep enough in the trees that no traveler could hear him.

He had hardly disappeared before the dog was at his back, staying a safe distance behind him but never letting him out of sight.

For a brief moment, Aden's blood stilled in his body. What if a hunter happened to see a giant beast walking through the forest? They would not know that it was him, and he could be shot dead.

Wouldn't that be a relief, though? An abrupt end to this miserable curse?

An overwhelming grief flooded through him for the life that had been stolen from him. Aden realized that he desperately wanted to live.

Despite his current solitude, he did not have the luxury of processing that realization. He devoted his frazzled energy into pressing forward, Warrior at his heels.

As night fell, he moved closer to the road. The ground

beneath his feet gradually got steeper, and the undergrowth thinned out. He had made it to the foothills north of Iseldis.

In the complete cover of darkness, he traveled along the road once more, working his way deeper into the mountains. When he noticed a small village in the distance, he gave it a wide berth and then found his way back to the road.

Sometime later, he came to a swing bridge suspended by a rope. The shadowy darkness illuminated nothing of the canyon at his feet, but Aden could hear rushing water far below.

Despite its fragile appearance, the bridge was wide enough for a carriage, so Aden hoped it would be enough to support his increased weight. He carefully stepped onto the wooden panels, followed by Warrior.

As the bridge gently swayed beneath their feet, Warrior yelped, dashing forward in fear.

Aden felt his heart stop as the dog disappeared into the dark. He ran after Warrior as fast as he dared across the unstable bridge.

Warrior had made it safely to the other side and was sitting on the solid ground, growling at the bridge.

"You dumb beast." Aden sighed in relief. "You could have gotten yourself killed."

He reached down to pet Warrior, momentarily forgetting that the dog still didn't trust him.

Warrior slowly backed away, still growling, and Aden withdrew his hand.

The spike of energy that had coursed through his body disappeared, leaving him more exhausted than before. He needed to sleep.

He dragged his feet farther up the path, wanting to put some space between himself and the canyon before finding a secluded spot for sleep.

Some distance later, he came upon a tall stone wall separating the road from a spired mansion hidden in the wilds of the forest.

Intrigued, Aden listened for any sound of life. A wrought-iron gate was slightly overgrown with young vines, and he could not make out the slightest sound. If this place were not abandoned, which it clearly appeared to be, then he would expect to at least hear the sound of a horse whinnying in its sleep or the bark of a watchdog.

He heard only silence.

If his mind were less exhausted, he knew he would make a better decision. But at the moment, he could not believe his luck. Tonight, he would sleep in the relative safety of four abandoned walls.

Not surprisingly, the gate was locked. Gauging the stone fence, he used the strength of his powerful new legs to hoist his body over the wall. He was surprised at his own gracefulness and felt rather proud of himself.

A small whine from the other side of the wall reminded him that Warrior could not make the leap quite as easily. Two breaths later, Aden was back on the outside of the fence.

Dropping to one knee, he reached out a hand for the pup. "Come on, Warrior. I can help you over the wall."

The dog took a cautious step toward him.

"That's a good boy," Aden coaxed, "let me help you."

The dog came all the way forward and tentatively licked Aden's outstretched hand.

"Good boy, Warrior." Aden remained completely still.

Warrior stepped even closer.

Aden heard one more sniff, and then the pup returned to his happy panting. Though he could not see it clearly since the dog was so close, Aden could still make out the swishing movement of a wagging tail.

Suddenly, his own sight grew even hazier as tears filled his eyes.

"Good. Boy."

Keeping his rounded claws hidden, Aden reached out and gave Warrior the best ear scratch he could manage with his beastly paws.

The thumping tail whacking against his leg confirmed that they were best friends once again.

"I'm sorry, boy, I won't betray you like that again if I can help it."

He stood up and Warrior happily barked, running around his ankles.

"Can I help you over this wall, now?" Aden reached down and, with no fuss at all, lifted Warrior onto the top of the wall. Swinging over it himself, he carried the dog down to the other side.

Warrior immediately dashed into the large open courtyard of the mansion, exploring the new space.

Aden, however, kept his attention focused on the large house. As expected, all the windows were dark, and the place looked adequately abandoned. Almost ominously so.

Remembering to compensate for his shifting eyesight, he took in everything from this vantage point while he could still make out some level of detail.

It was a massive house, as big as an entire wing of his family's palace though not nearly as tall. Only two rows of windows lined the main building. Large towers at either end of the rectangular structure pointed far into the sky.

He must have crossed into the northern kingdom of Allys, as the lower profile of the building denoted the sprawling style of most Allysian architecture, but unlike the creamy stone used throughout the rest of the warmer kingdom, this mansion was built in a dark gray rock that matched the wild mountain scenery.

In many places, the dark stone was covered in even darker vines and greenery that wound its way around the structure. It even grew across some windows. Clearly, no one had lived here for some time.

Aden also noted there was no scent of the smoke that would have lingered in the air had someone been living here and using the fireplace.

Satisfied that he was not intruding, he made his way to the front door. Not surprisingly, it too was locked. He wound around the house, where he discovered an open back door and slipped inside.

Finding himself once again inside the safety of four walls, Aden realized how truly exhausted he was. Exploring the house could come later. For now, he had one desire.

Relying on his new senses, he made his way out of the kitchen and into a great room with a double-tall ceiling. This was likely the entrance to the building. Crossing it, he climbed a set of stairs into a long hallway on the other side. He passed a few doorways, peeking inside to find salons and studies.

Finally, he opened a doorway to the wonderful sight of a large four-poster bed, complete with curtains on every side.

After Warrior's paws gently padded into the room, Aden closed the door and inhaled a long, deep breath through his nostrils. The room smelled of dust and musty wood. It also bore the soothing scent of leather, reminding him of the library back in Iseldis.

He stepped toward the bed, pushed aside the curtain, and gratefully sank onto the softest mattress he had ever felt. Deciding then and there that he would never again complain about the luxury of castle conveniences, Aden realized what spending a night alone in the woods could teach a man.

He stretched himself out on the bed as Warrior jumped up beside him and turned three times in the same spot, pawing at the mattress a bit before settling down with a contented sigh.

Aden appreciated the warm weight against his knee and breathed his own contented sigh.

His ears, ever alert, tried to identify the usual noises of this new place.

For the first time since the ball, Aden relished in the fact that the broad space around him was free from any human noise.

Finally, his anxious mind relaxed and he fell into a deep, deep sleep.

CHAPTER 9

"**W**e've reached the bridge, milady," the carriage driver called as he brought the horses to a stop.

"Thank you, Luca." Isa gratefully stepped out onto the open road followed by her lady's maid, Blanca. The night air was refreshingly cool, even this high up in the mountains. They had been traveling for two full days, and the bridge meant they were nearing the end of their journey.

"Have we arrived?" Macklin followed her out of the carriage.

Isa ignored his question as she stepped forward onto the swing bridge.

"Is this the only way across?" Macklin asked, stopping short at the edge of the deep canyon.

Isa turned back to him with an understanding smile. If she had not come here every goldenreign with her family, she would have been frightened by the rural bridge as well. "It is perfectly safe," she explained, "though sometimes it trembles in the wind. Papa worried that it would spook the horses, so we always traverse the bridge on foot."

As if to prove her point, even Luca had not climbed back up

to the driver's seat of the carriage. Instead, he approached the bridge, cooing softly to the horses as he guided them onto the structure.

Isa continued moving forward. It was a gorgeous night to be in the mountains. The stars, brightly visible overhead, offered a surprising amount of light. While crossing the canyon, especially without the canopy of the trees overhead, Isa could appreciate their sparkling beauty all the more. She marveled at the raw strength of the craggy mountains on the horizon and the silence around her. Hopefully, her father would be well enough to make their traditional goldenreign trip this year before the city grew too hot to bear.

At the far side of the bridge, she waited for the rest of their party to cross. Blanca's cheerful conversations had kept the journey pleasant, and Isa also appreciated that her presence had lessened the discomfort of sharing a carriage with Macklin. Cam had preferred to sit outside the carriage with Luca.

When everyone had safely crossed the bridge, Macklin coming in last, they climbed back in the carriage for the final length of their journey. It was just long enough for Isa to start to feel sleepy once again, but not quite long enough for her to completely doze off.

Macklin was surprisingly quiet as he took in as much of the old villa as he could in the darkness. Clouds had rolled in, cutting off the light of the reflective stars.

To a newcomer, the old mansion might have looked intimidating. But to Isa, the darker colors of the clay and brick walls were softened by the thick vines that clung to crevices and corners. It was as though the house itself were saying, "Come here and rest. Rest and laugh and play in my walls." As though the house were a book, waiting to be opened and read and enjoyed.

Even though she was here to work, not relax, Isa was simply

happy to be in one of her favorite places. She would not let Macklin's presence disturb her joy.

Entering the double-wide doors, Blanca and Cam quickly lit a few lanterns, handing one to Isa. The small flames threw tall shadows into the large entrance of the old building. Even though she knew she was safe, Isa glanced quickly throughout the great room to ascertain whether the shadows were a real threat or merely playing on her tired imagination.

The tall entryway was just as she remembered it. The house having been built as an old castle, this room had served as the central hub of activity for the once-thriving community that had lived here. It felt as though Isa had stepped back in time. This was where meals would have been served to the entire community, guests would have been welcomed and entertained, and problems would have been sorted. The lord of this manor would have acted as a small king, overseeing the few dozen families in his care who lived off the land here.

On either side of the tall room, two staircases led up to a long hallway that ran down the entire length of the two wings of the castle. Her family had always used the wing on the left when they stayed here. In addition to the bedrooms, it housed salons, activity rooms, and of course, the library, which was the pride and joy of the Bielsa family.

The lower levels of the right wing housed the servants who stayed at the manor, as well as the kitchen, larders, and butteries.

"I will get some fires prepared in the rooms," Cam offered.

"Thank you, Cam," Isa responded. "Blanca, will you get Macklin settled in one of the guest rooms? I can air out my room myself."

"Of course, milady."

Isa held the lantern in front of her to shed as much light as possible on the worn stone steps and long, dark hallway ahead.

She always stayed in the third room on the right-hand side of the hallway. It was one of the smaller rooms, but it had a larger balcony with the best view of the mountains that towered over the villa.

Creaking open the wooden door, she instinctively held the lantern up a little higher to get a good look at her room. Small animals occasionally made their way inside when the family had been away for a long period of time, so she quickly glanced around to ensure that no squirrels or mice had made it their home. It was surprisingly less dusty than she was expecting. Perhaps all the additional rain during the long silverreign had kept the outdoor air cleaner than usual. Everything else looked as she would have expected it to.

The stone walls had been smeared in a cream-colored clay, so the room itself was light in color, which made it feel like her room back at home. The furniture, however, was made from the dark oak trees that were easily found in the surrounding area. A tall, dark wardrobe took up most of the wall next to the fire-place. A small desk sat near the balcony doorway. The ink pots and feather pen she had left out since her last visit here were barely visible in the light of the lamp, but the tall shadows they cast on the desk still rattled her nerves.

Everything looked as it should, and she took a confident step into the room. She did not mind the local wildlife, but she would rather not be required to shoo a bat or raccoon from the room. Hopefully, there would be no surprise spiders—or worse—in the bed.

The large bed against the side wall was mostly hidden by the sweeping drapes attached to the four tall posts at each corner. She had left the drapes down while they were away to keep the bed as dust free as possible. Still holding the lamp, she stepped closer to the bed and quickly threw aside the drooping curtain to ensure nothing had found a new home in her bed.

Her heart instantly stopped beating as a moment of sheer terror overtook her.

A mouse or spider she could handle. Even a raccoon would not have been too difficult. But, huddled under the covers, its fur-covered head resting on her pillow, was the massive form of a hibernating bear.

Separately, a streak of white fur yelped in surprise and flew past her, dashing out the open door of the bedroom.

Isa tried to inhale, but her lungs refused to perform the basic function.

Time stopped.

Finally, her body unfroze, and she inhaled only to instantly release that precious breath in a bloodcurdling scream. In her mind, she knew she should not make a sound, but she could not have remained silent if her life depended on it. Unfortunately, in this case, it did.

The instant the scream left her body, the massive bear stirred, clawing its way out of the pile of blankets and springing away from the source of the scream. Its motion was surprisingly limber for one so large, but it tore through the drapes as it landed on the other side of the bed.

In the light of the lantern, Isa could clearly make out its hideous form. Time stopped once again as her mind registered every horrifying and dangerous detail of the massive animal towering over her bed.

The beast was standing on its hind legs like a fierce mother bear protecting its cubs, the tatters of the curtain hanging over its shoulders. But, rather than the round body of a mountain bear, its face and limbs were pointed, hard, tactile, agile. The beast was the size of a bear, but its features were more like a wolf or a lion who could overpower its prey with a single powerful leap or snap of the jaw. Its mouth was open as it snarled, clearly displaying two large fangs that hung over its lower set of pointed teeth. Ringed in black fur, its yellow eyes gave off a feral glow.

For the briefest moment, Isa felt as if those big, yellow eyes were fully sentient. The way they tracked her movement, searching for whatever was behind the bright lantern, made it seem almost afraid of her.

But as she noticed the sheer height of the beast and the length of the claws that it held up to protect itself, the sentient look in its eyes disappeared.

It made no move to leap across the bed and devour her, so she took a very slow step backward. Although she had a clear path to the open door, she was not stupid enough to make a mad dash for it. She knew how a predatory animal would respond to the quick movement, snapping her in its jaws like easy prey.

Keeping her focus locked on the immobile animal, she tried to look out the corner of her eye to see if there was any weapon in sight.

Since they had been traveling, she still had a small blade sheathed in the belt around her waist. But against an animal this large, it would be useless. The blade would merely glance off the thick fur coat without inflicting damage.

Not that she would have a chance to get it anywhere near its fur before those two fangs sank into her.

The only two objects within reach were on the small table next to her bed. One was a short candlestick and the other a hardcovered book. The candlestick was made of iron, but it was more of a flat, round dish. Definitely not tall enough to use as a bludgeon. The book, on the other hand, would provide no attack value, but it could be used in defense. If she could protect her body with the book, those powerful fangs would sink into parchment rather than . . . her. Perhaps that moment of confusion would buy her enough time to get through the door.

What book had she been reading when she was here last? She banished that thought from her mind. She could not be worried about ruining a book when her very life was in danger.

The animal had not moved, its eyes fixated on the lantern in her hand.

Perhaps the bright light had blinded it? She reached out with her empty hand and picked up the book from the nightstand. It was the second volume of *The Queen of Silverreign*. Her heart sank. She tried not to imagine those sharp teeth shredding her favorite story. At least it was properly hardbound and not a loose scroll. She pushed those thoughts from her mind. The two thin boards protecting the pages of the book, favorite or not, were the only protection she herself would have from becoming mincemeat.

Hopefully Blanca or Cam had heard her cry and would be arriving soon, although she was not sure what help they would be.

She had to stay focused on getting to the door. The beast's eyes were still glued to the lantern, which she moved slowly. Its eyes followed the light.

She set the lantern down on the small bedside table where the book had been.

Its eyes followed the lantern.

She took a small step away from the table.

The beast instantly sensed the movement, and its eyes returned to her. Its paws were still held out in front of its face, claws poised for attack.

She stopped moving. It had been a good idea, hoping the beast would be distracted by the bright light. Her only chance now was to run for the door and hope she could position the book between herself and those jaws if need be. She took a deep breath, all too aware of the fact that it might be her last.

"I am so sorry to have frightened you," the beast said, slowly moving toward the door.

The beast said?

Again, without her knowledge or consent, Isa's breath left her body in a terrified scream, and she flew toward the open door.

Before she could make her escape, however, Blanca and Macklin filled the doorway.

Isa swerved out of the way just in time to avoid landing on the sword Macklin was pointing into the room.

"What's wrong?" he said, quickly scanning the room.

Isa stood with her back against the wooden wardrobe while the beast commanded the center of the room. Its paws were raised defensively as it eyed the sword and newcomers. "Please, I mean you no harm," it said.

"You heard that, right?" Isa whispered, darting a quick glance at Macklin for support.

Macklin nodded. He was looking quite pale, even in the candlelight, but he kept his eyes locked on the ferocious threat in the middle of the room.

Isa's curiosity was piqued, and she felt the impractical urge to ask the beast how it could talk. But not only would that mean starting a conversation with an animal, now was not the time. She had to figure out a way to survive this.

"I . . . I know this is odd," it said again, "but I promise I mean you no harm. I have merely fallen into unfortunate circumstances. Please, allow me to leave you in peace."

The beast's eyes flicked between Isa and Macklin.

When it was not looking at her, Isa grasped the small dagger in her belt. She looked at Macklin and gave him a slight nod.

He dipped his head in response.

If they both attacked the beast at the same time, they might be able to overpower it.

"Blanca," Isa said quietly. "Run. Now."

The girl disappeared into the darkness of the hallway.

Macklin watched her leave, his face betraying a look of envy at her escape. His hand trembled.

The movement startled the beast, and it stared down at the shaking sword pointed in its direction.

Utilizing the distraction, Isa made eye contact with Macklin and held up a fist. Slowly counting with her fingers, she used her head to emphasize each count.

One. She held up a single finger.

Macklin spared a quick glance at the beast.

Two. She held up a second finger.

Macklin looked back at Isa, his neck bobbing as he gulped.

Three.

On the count of three, Isa sprang forward, hoping to catch the wretched thing off guard.

In the same instant, Macklin backed into the hallway behind him and fled out of sight.

Of all the cowardly, chicken-hearted, spineless things she had ever seen! How did he expect her to get out of the room when the beast was standing between her and the door?

But it was too late for her to change her course of action based on his foolishness. Isa had already slammed against the beast, burying her small blade in its shoulder.

With a roar of pain, the massive animal whipped around to face her. One strong arm wrapped around her waist, imprisoning her body against his. Its other paw wrapped around her wrist, which was still holding the dagger.

Claws bit against her skin and she released the blade. It remained buried in the beast's shoulder.

The beast went still, holding her firmly.

Isa struggled to breathe. Her toes were barely on the ground, and her center of gravity was currently where his firm grip was clamped around her lungs. His rough fur was also digging into the side of her face. She could still feel the pressure of the claws on her wrist, though they did not break through her skin.

On the other hand, she could feel every deep breath the animal made. It sounded winded.

"I apologize for causing you alarm," it rumbled, not without some exasperation, "but I would appreciate not being slaughtered for the offense."

Isa kept her body as still as possible while she tried to calculate her next move.

"Your husband is quite the brave one," it continued, gesturing toward the now-empty doorway with its wolflike head. "He should be commended for his act of courage."

"He's not my . . ." Isa started to protest, but then snapped her mouth shut. She was not going to play mind games with some sort of sentient animal when she still had no idea what it was.

"I wouldn't worry too much about it. I have no intention of harming you, so you will have plenty of time to berate him about it later."

Isa could not agree more. Macklin would surely get a mouthful about this if she lived to see him again. The thought of thoroughly chewing him out in the future gave her a renewed resolve to get out of her current situation.

She eyed her opponent warily.

The beast seemed to be considering a similar objective, as he glanced around the room and cautiously sniffed the air.

Without warning, he lifted her from the ground with the single arm around her waist and leaped for the door, slamming it closed.

Surprised, she pushed away from him as hard as she could.

At the same time, he let go of her waist and wrist, and the momentum of her own propulsion caused her to stumble away from him back into the center of the room.

"I do apologize for that," it rumbled, "but I have no idea when your gutless husband will return and I, too, want to make it out of this situation alive."

Reaching up, he tugged the knife loose from his shoulder without even wincing. He held it out to Isa as though he meant to return it.

Isa tentatively reached out for it, afraid the animal was somehow about to trick her. She did notice that the blade did not even have a single drop of blood on it. She was not sure if she should feel disappointment that her attack had been so weak or if she was relieved that she had not viciously harmed another living being, no matter how scary it was. "It didn't even break through the thick fur," she commented, more to herself than to it.

He yanked his hand back, slipping the knife into a belt at his waistcoat. "No. But it will be a lovely bruise by tomorrow, thanks to you," he said, rubbing his shoulder.

Her mind heard his words, but she did not fully comprehend them. For the first time during this entire bizarre scenario, Isa realized the beast was wearing a waistcoat.

It was almost comical. She was looking at a talking wolf-bear who spoke and dressed like a nobleman.

"What are you?" she asked.

The animal stiffened, straightening back to its full height but keeping its weight against the closed door. "I prefer who," it replied. "*Who* are you? See, it sounds much better that way."

Isa waited for the answer. When none was forthcoming, she realized the animal was waiting for her to ask the question properly. Apparently, she had offended him.

She did not stoop to playing mind games with it. But it was thrice her weight, had pointy claws, and was blocking the exit.

She sighed.

"Who are you?"

"I . . ." it said, dipping its head in a dignified bow and inhaling slowly as though to make a point, "am Aden Sirilian, Prince of Iseldis and third in line for the throne."

She was dealing with a madman. Mad . . . beast? "I saw no beast when I was at the—"

"To skip all the awkward questioning," he continued, cutting her off, "I was cursed by a Majis to have the form of a beast. I intend to leave this house alive, so if you will call off your husband and whatever servants are currently dashing toward us down the hallway, I will leave you in peace."

"Milady," Luca called from the hallway as he threw himself against the closed door, "we are coming in to save you!"

The "Prince of Iseldis" had hunched forward, alert and defensive, as multiple fists pounded on the other side of the door. "Call them off," he said, his voice intensely quiet. "I promise you no harm."

His eyes were wide, wild in the flickering candlelight.

If this cursed animal opened that door, it would tear her servants to shreds.

Isa slowly shook her head. Her mother's recent words rang through her head. *They can be trusted with our very lives.* The servants were under her protection, even if it cost her her life.

She locked eyes with the beast as the pounding on the door grew more frantic.

"Call them off," he repeated.

"No."

With a growl, the animal pushed itself away from the door and threw itself toward her.

Her mind screamed in terror, though no sound passed her lips.

Rather than in pain or unconscious, Isa found herself once again pressed to his side, held in place by a firm arm.

The door slammed open.

He whipped around to position Isa between himself and the two, armed men who stumbled into the room. Cam held a small sword while Luca brandished an ax from the stable.

"Kindly step out of the way," the beast said, as though he were passing a pair of noblemen in a ballroom, "or I shall be forced to harm the lady."

Isa frantically nodded her agreement. Her heart pounded. "Stand back," she ordered, attempting to muster all the courage she had left. But to her own ears, her words sounded frightfully weak.

The two men backed out of the room, their weapons still pointed at the beast.

The "Prince of Iseldis" cautiously took a step toward the door, half-carrying and half-dragging Isa along with him.

He must have known where he was going, for he confidently turned to the left and proceeded down the hallway. He walked backward, keeping Isa between him and the two servants who followed him with weapons at the ready.

"You smell nice," the beast rumbled in her ear. "Like leather and trees."

Isa thought he might have been trying to compliment her, though his choice of scent was far from flattering.

"Thank you," she heard herself saying. "I've been traveling for two days." Her fingers gripped the fur on his powerful arm, which held her like a vice as she stumbled to keep up with his surprisingly graceful backward advance.

"Ah, the stairs might prove a touch tricky," he muttered as they reached the end of the hallway. "Apologies, my lady."

Lifting her completely, he leaped down the staircase in a fluid jump and landed at the bottom in a hunched stance to restore his balance.

For a moment, Isa could not breathe as her lungs shut down from the shock. But she was surprisingly unhurt.

A few moments later, they were standing at the large double doors of the great hall.

After fumbling with the handle, the beast stepped over the threshold so that he was standing outside while Isa was still covered by the doorframe.

"Again," he said, "terribly sorry for the inconvenience."

With that, he released his iron grip from Isa's waist and leaped backward into the night.

Isa whipped around, grabbing the door handle to close the door and put a semblance of safety between her and the beast.

He stepped into the open courtyard, cautiously looking back over his shoulder, likely trying to ensure that the armed servants were not chasing after him.

The clouds had thickened, and a light wind whipped through the courtyard, smattering tiny droplets of rain across every surface.

"On second thought . . ." The beast paused, opening his paw to the falling drizzle. "You wouldn't happen to have a guest bedroom for a passing prince?"

All the stress and fear of the last few minutes coursed through Isa's veins, heating her body with anger. "GET OUT," she yelled into the darkness, slamming the door closed.

CHAPTER 10

*A*den jumped back over the fence to the not-so-abandoned mansion.

While it had been a graceful leap the first time he had accomplished this feat, in his current state he felt he looked more like a wet cat awkwardly flinging itself from a moving carriage.

It was pouring rain.

The sun had not yet risen.

And he was thoroughly soaked to the bone.

His thick coat of fur could hold so much water that his muscles were already complaining from carrying the extra weight.

He shook himself like a dog, humiliation radiating through him as water droplets from his fur collided with the falling rain.

He was not just miserable and uncomfortable; rather, the feeling coursing through his veins would be more aptly described as out-of-control righteous anger.

He had not seen Warrior since that peaceful moment hours before when he had fallen asleep in the "abandoned" house.

Striding heatedly to the front door, he pounded on it loudly enough to wake the whole household. No matter that it was nearly dawn and they had probably just fallen asleep after the shock of finding a beast in their home.

Good riddance.

They—no, *she*—had completely destroyed the first real sleep *he* had experienced in days.

The door opened more quickly than he'd expected, and he found himself staring at the cowardly husband who had abandoned his wife to the arms of an apparently violent beast.

Aden brushed off his disappointment at not being granted the opportunity of taking out his frustration on the door by pounding on it for a second time, and instead he smiled grimly at the now-trembling man.

Aden stretched his lips until he felt his long fangs glide into view.

The coward panic-stumbled back into the great hall.

Before he could slam the door shut, Aden stomped his foot into the doorframe.

"The bridge is out," Aden said, toying with him casually.

"What do you mean?" the man asked, turning his head to glance behind him.

Aden could not see his face clearly, but he assumed the man was waiting for backup so he could disappear to safety again.

"The bridge. The bridge that runs over the canyon? It's out," Aden repeated, adding extra words in an attempt to get the man to understand him.

"You probably just missed it," the coward stuttered. "If you follow the road, you'll find it." He made a move to shut the door again, but it only bounced off Aden's extended foot.

"I did not miss—" Aden's less-than-pleasant retort was cut short by the sound of approaching footsteps.

"Macklin, who is it?" The woman made her voice heard before she was even in sight.

"It's that beast again," the man replied.

"Why?" She looked up as she rounded the corner, coming into view. Her hands were busy fastening a belt around the thick night robe she wore.

At least Aden assumed it was a night robe from what he could make out of it. It was rather straight and flat, without the appealing curves of a day dress. It pleased him, however, to note that she had been at least trying to sleep, and he felt somewhat vindicated in his return.

"I don't know," Macklin replied as he scurried from the doorway so she could take his place.

"What is the meaning of this?" she demanded.

If her face was as furious as her voice, Aden was glad he could not make it out properly.

"The bridge is out," he repeated, as though that explained everything.

"That is not possible," she rebuffed.

Aden flexed the claws in his hand. A trickle of rainwater ran under his fur, dripping down his shoulder onto his back. He shivered uncontrollably at the sensation. "Well, it is out, and the two of you are just going to have to accept that. Also. What have you done with my dog?" He followed the last part with a deep growl that he hoped would express his frustration and displeasure.

"I have no idea. Goodnight." She pressed the door against his foot.

He didn't budge.

"Warrior is my companion and friend," he growled. "I will not leave him behind."

"I don't have him." The woman's spine was straight, and she looked him square in the face.

"If I leave here now, he won't know where I've gone." Aden leaned slightly forward, unwilling to back down.

"That is not my problem." Her words were drawn out and sharp, punctuated by short jerks of her head.

He gestured toward the drowning courtyard, a more primal anger rising from his core. "The water will wash away my scent, and Warrior won't be able to follow me."

Grasping the handle, she whacked the full weight of the solid wooden door against his foot.

"As a prince from the royal line of Iseldis," he roared with all the breath he could muster, "I demand entry into this house and a bed for the night, or your king will be hearing from my father." He pointed a bared claw at her chest.

"You would start a war, on the brink of the Return, just for a bed?"

He placed a hand possessively on either side of the doorway and leaned over the woman standing between him and shelter. "A bed. And a dog."

Her lack of response gave him hope that she was at least considering his request.

Releasing a long breath, he decided to try a different tactic. "May I remind you that, had I harbored any ill intention toward you or your household, I could have acted upon it at any other time this night?"

"At any other time this night? Oh, you mean after I found you intruding in my family's villa, in my very bed?"

"For that, I do apologize. I truly thought the place was abandoned, and I needed a place to rest my head." He made his voice as pitiful as he could muster. "You would deny this basic human need when you clearly have rooms to spare?"

"You are probably a Majis in disguise." She threw the words at him half-heartedly, almost as a last attempt to insult him into leaving.

"If I were a Majis, and I had the power to disguise my body into whatever I wanted it to be, why would I be demanding a bed in the form of an ugly, vicious beast?" Aden could not keep the true despair and frustration from his voice.

She pinched her lips, and her head moved up and down.

He could only guess that her eyes were scanning the length of his body. The scrutiny of that action was almost enough to make him turn and run back into the forest.

"One night," she finally stated. "In the morning, Luca will show you the proper road to take to the bridge that is very much still there, as you obviously could not find it for yourself."

"Thank you." He ignored her cutting remark and sincerely offered his gratitude.

She opened the door a touch wider, then stopped herself. "You will cause no harm to anyone in this household?" she asked.

"I will cause no harm to anyone in this household." Aden meant those words with complete honesty, but he realized too late that he did not have the power to completely make that promise.

The rose in his pack had only lost a single petal, so he hoped that he was safe—that others were safe from him—for at least the near future.

CHAPTER 11

The rushing water swirling far below her made Isa's head spin. She stepped away from the ledge of the canyon. Her heart was pounding, causing an uncomfortable throbbing sensation at the back of her neck. Not wanting to show fear, she casually reached up behind her head and gently put pressure on the top of her spine where the pulsing was most insistent.

"I've never seen the water this high before," she said to Macklin and Luca, ignoring the giant beast who was leaning against a tree behind her, well away from the edge of the canyon. She couldn't tell if he was afraid of heights as well or merely gloating in the fact that he had been right.

"It would appear that the bridge is, indeed, gone," Macklin confirmed.

"The changing weather must have caused a freak flood higher up the mountains," Luca speculated. "Washed the bridge clean away."

The only remaining element of the wooden structure they

had recently walked across was some dangling rope and a few twisted posts on either side of the canyon.

Despite the panic signals from her body, which were telling her to run in the opposite direction, Isa peered over the edge once more.

The water was definitely higher than she had ever seen it, but the canyon was so deep that it was still a long drop down. Her mind conjured the image of the rushing river swelling up the polished rock walls, spilling over the edge where she was currently standing, and devouring everything in its path. It was not a pleasant thought.

Her neck pulsed again, pounding against the base of her skull.

She rubbed at the spot, keeping her eyes on the canyon wall to find a safe path down.

The smooth walls plunged to the depths below, with hardly a plant clinging to the rocky surface. Even if someone could safely make it down the risky embankment, not even the strongest swimmer could navigate the swollen torrents and get to the other side. And if he could, he would then be faced with climbing the completely vertical surface.

Panic swelled in her chest, and she backed away from the dizzying overlook. The nearest village was on the other side of the canyon. How would they contact the villagers to alert them of their plight? Who would rebuild the bridge? How would they get home? Who would protect her from . . .

"You did this." She whipped around, pointing at the uncon-cerned figure with his arms crossed in front of him.

Isa had not gotten a good look at the beast in the darkness of the previous night, and she had been terrified to discover that he was even scarier in daylight. He stood on his two hind feet like a man, but he was several hands taller than average and his massive shoulders made him twice as wide.

"You tore out the bridge last night so you could trap us here without aid while you . . ." She wanted to back away from him as she accused him of his future plans to devour them all, but if she stepped backward, she would tumble to a certain death. Even though she fully wanted to believe he planned on eating them all, his coherent conversation and high-handed masculine attitude made him feel at least partially human.

"If I wanted to devour you all," the beast said, pushing himself away from the tree and standing to his full height, "I would have done it long ago."

"I know. I didn't say that," Isa snapped back.

"You were clearly thinking it," he responded, apparently unoffended.

"Milady," Luca cut in. "As much as I do not trust this supposed prince, the damage that has clearly been done all along the canyon is what I would expect from a flood."

Isa's shoulders fell. She knew he was right. It just felt good to have someone to blame. She felt a touch of remorse that her angry words were driven by a fear of their situation and not the beast itself. "What do we do now, then?"

Luca kept his gaze fixed on the canyon wall, and Isa had the uncomfortable feeling that he wanted to tell her the next course of action would be to apologize. It was on the tip of her tongue to do so, but he—it—was a beast. One did not apologize to beasts.

Not that she really knew what one did when with or around a beast.

Nor did she know what to do when her access to the rest of the world was cut off, but at least that one problem could be overcome . . . somehow. "It could be weeks before anyone from the village realizes that the bridge is out. It's not as though they have reason to come to the villa when they do not even know we are here."

Luca rubbed his chin.

Isa saw concern in his eyes that he was not expressing aloud, and it frightened her.

"How far is the nearest way over the canyon?" Macklin asked, looking up and down the river.

Isa turned to Luca. She had never come by any other road.

"Two days' ride to the south, and that is if the canyon is even passable when the water levels out. Could be longer."

"I'll go get help," the beast sighed.

"Or you'll wander off, never telling anyone about our existence and leaving us out here to die," Macklin muttered.

The beast growled. It was deep in his chest, as though he were more frustrated than angry. "What would it take for you to trust I am who I say?"

"Prove to me that you are Prince Aden of Iseldis and I'll believe it," Isa challenged him, grateful that Macklin had given her an opportunity to press the beast for information.

"Well, what do you know of my family?" He ran his hand over his forehead. It got caught in the thick fur there, and he yanked it back down to his side. "Or Iseldis, for that matter?"

"You are the one who is supposed to be giving the information here, not me." Isa crossed her arms. "I am not about to share what I know so that you can use it against me."

"Then how am I supposed to know what will prove my identity to you? Nothing is holding me here. I can just leave."

"Then leave."

The beast started walking down the riverbank. "I'll alert the villagers on the other side when I find a way across," he threw back over his shoulder. "Though it will likely be a sennight or more before someone can make their way back to you."

Isa's heart thumped uncomfortably as she watched the hulking beast stride away.

She turned to Luca, whose expression mirrored the discomfort she was feeling. Neither of them would sit here and wait for the beast to follow through with what he claimed.

"How long will it take to build the bridge back?" she asked.

"By the end of this greenreign, if we are lucky."

That was two months away. "I guess we should pack some supplies and start walking south ourselves if that is our only option to get out of here," she said.

Luca looked at her fully for the first time since they had arrived at the canyon's edge. "You can't make that trip."

Isa instantly felt a flare of anger rise in her chest at his rude remark. But it dissipated a moment later as she realized he was right. She had never spent a night under the stars, much less walked farther than the distance between her home and the library at the Allysian palace—and that was all on a smooth road.

Her shoulders dropped as she exhaled. "I can't very well stay here."

"Macklin, Cam, and Blanca will remain here as well. Just do not leave the house as there are clearly strange things lurking in these forests. I should be back in a week."

The thought of doing nothing while waiting for aid to arrive terrified Isa more than the thought of the beast. "He single-handedly defeated all of us last night. If we split up, we will be even easier to attack. No one can travel south while he—*it*— while it is loose in the woods."

Luca gave her a shrewd glance. "Are you implying what I think you are implying?"

Isa nodded, gulping at her own audacity.

"Interesting. It might be the best option." Luca stroked his chin and turned his eyes toward the retreating figure of the beast.

Macklin looked back and forth between the two of them. "What do you mean? What are you saying?"

"It is not safe for Luca to travel south while we do not know where the beast is. If he attacked Luca, we would never even know it. We would just be sitting at a secluded villa, waiting for help that never comes." Saying the thought aloud sent cold shivers down her arms. "Then it could return to the villa and attack us at its leisure."

"The safest course of action would be to invite the beast to the villa while I go for help," Luca finished, outlining Isa's plan. "The enemy you can see is better than the enemy you can't."

Macklin shook his head.

"This is our best option," Isa said in response to his unspoken protest. The beast was almost out of sight, and they had to make this decision before he disappeared.

"No," Macklin interjected vehemently. "No. If we are going to leave you here, Miss Isa, then you should be protected by the best. I failed you last night. I will not fail you again. I will go get help. Luca is stronger and will be a better guard here. Keep her safe."

Isa found herself touched at his genuine outburst. Perhaps she had been a little too harsh in chewing him out that morning. She turned to Luca.

His face was grim, but he nodded at Macklin.

Isa glanced down the canyon. The farther away the beast got, the more difficult it became to breathe. Being stuck on this side of the canyon, knowing that he was out there and that he knew where they were and how many of them were there . . .

"This is the plan?" she asked.

"This is the plan," Macklin confirmed, though his pale face said otherwise.

The beast was nearly out of sight now.

"Maybe we should send Cam with him," Luca said.

Macklin nodded vigorously.

"Then who would do the cooking?" Isa knew this was not the proper time to discuss the details.

"Blanca and I," Luca responded, his eyes still on Macklin.

"Alright," Isa responded. "If you think that is best." She started moving down the river.

"But that would leave one less person to stand guard over the violent beast we are about to invite into our company," Luca muttered, his face growing red. He clearly did not fully trust Macklin.

Isa did *not* trust him, but she definitely felt no qualm sending him away for help. "I think we will be fine. Send Cam with Macklin. You said it yourself—the beast could have killed us multiple times already and hasn't yet."

The beast disappeared behind a copse of trees.

"Do you have a better option?" Her voice betrayed her lack of patience.

Luca shook his head.

Isa shared a final glance with Macklin to ensure they were on the same page.

He nodded. "I'll get help with Cam."

Channeling her exasperation into a quick sprint, she chased after the beast, careful to remain as far away from the dangerous edge of the canyon as she could.

"Beast!" she called as soon as she could see him again.

He continued walking. He was still some ways away, so perhaps he had not heard her.

"Beast!" she called again as she drew closer.

He did not turn around, though there was no way he had not heard her this time.

She slowed to a stop to catch her breath. "Aden of Iseldis." She made no effort to hide the derision in her voice.

The tall beast finally stopped and turned around. "Yes?"

"Wait here. Macklin will go for help."

He looked suspicious. Not that the animal had a clear facial expression—but somehow Isa knew he looked suspicious. He started walking back toward her.

She refused to show fear, even as he stepped closer and his large fangs were clearly visible.

"Wait here? What a tempting offer. You have been such a pleasant host thus far."

Isa ignored the sarcasm that coated his words. "Macklin will go with Cam, and he knows the area better so they will get to the village more quickly," she explained.

The beast raised his eyebrows, or at least the fur above his eyes, which somewhat resembled the eyebrows a human person would have.

"Regardless, it is not likely the villagers would even listen to you." Isa was desperate to persuade him. "They don't like outsiders much in these parts, and well, they are more likely to hunt you."

The beast remained silent; his eyes narrowed. She did not get the saucy retort to that comment she had expected.

"So, this is about concern for my safety?" he asked. "Or yours?"

Isa shuffled uncomfortably. "I trust Macklin more than I trust you." She could not think of anything else to say, but it was the honest answer.

His shoulders seemed to sag, but she must have been imagining that, for he bared his fangs and licked them absently before answering her. "Let us return and get this Macklin safely on his journey then."

CHAPTER 12

*A*den kept a comfortable distance from the rest of the group as they walked back to the mansion.

The manservant, Luca, had placed himself between Aden and Isa. The cowardly one from the previous night, Macklin, was on the far side of her. Aden did not fail to notice that Macklin was staying as far away from him as possible.

Aden walked in front of them. He could not blame them for not trusting him. He would not want to leave his back undefended against himself.

There was something familiar about this Isa, but he could not quite place it.

He glanced back over his shoulder. He was far enough away that he could barely make out some details of her face. But he was so far away that he also could not see her properly at all.

He adjusted the muscles in his eyes, willing them to bring her face into focus. The action pained him, and he squeezed his eyes shut, blinking rapidly.

He could not recall ever having met someone named Isa. He would have to inquire about her family name; perhaps he knew her father or a brother. Or perhaps his mind was playing tricks on him and the sense of familiarity was derived from their unfortunate encounter the previous night.

The small reminder of the terrifying events of the previous night made his heart race. He had never been more frightened in his life. He could still hear that bloodcurdling scream vibrating in his ears.

These people had just tried to kill him only hours prior, yet he was willingly walking back to their mansion with them.

He could have kept walking south along the canyon when he'd had the chance, but he still had not found Warrior.

Regardless, he could not in good conscience have left these people stranded in the mountains without at least contacting someone from the village to alert them that the bridge was down.

And this Isa had been right. If he had tried to approach anyone in the village, he would have been . . . hunted.

Apparently, the cowardly husband Macklin would be the hero of the day.

"The next bridge is about a two days' walk from here," Luca instructed Macklin behind him.

"After you make it across, come back north to alert the villagers, then travel back to Allys," Isa added. "My mother will send up the proper resources to get the bridge rebuilt as quickly as possible."

"And you are sure you will be fine here?" Macklin asked. His voice was low, obviously not meant for Aden's ears.

"We have plenty of food," Luca responded. "And the weather should be clear and warm. It will be like every other golden-reign holiday, just a touch early."

"That's not what I was referring to, and you know it." Macklin's voice had dropped to an even deeper register.

Aden shot another glance over his shoulder. Macklin had moved closer to Isa and was practically hovering over her.

"Do you have a better idea?" Isa replied, also whispering.

"We could all go together."

That actually was a good point—If they clearly did not trust Aden, why would they not all make the long journey to the next bridge? When Isa did not respond right away, Aden looked back again. They were grouped closer together, as though she had moved toward Luca to include him in this quiet conversation.

"But the Floutast?"

Floutast? Surely they were not referring to the ancient writer. Aden could not imagine why he would be a part of the current conversation.

"Curse the Floutast," Macklin replied. "I don't want to leave you here."

"You were the one who volunteered to go!" Isa sounded flustered.

But then, she had also sounded flustered during all the interactions she'd had with Aden.

"Well, true . . ." Macklin seemed to be fishing for words. "But . . ."

"This is the best option. Focus on your part. We will be . . . safe."

Aden felt the fur on the back of his neck tense, and he shivered. He did not need to look over his shoulder to know they were all looking at him. In an instant, he forgot that he was larger, faster, stronger, and more menacing than any of them. He felt small and guilty. He was the problem.

As they neared the mansion, a streak of white fur dashed through the open gate and launched itself at Aden's leg.

"Warrior!" Aden forgot his momentary despondency as he reunited yet again with his small friend. "Where have you been?"

The poor thing must have been hiding all this time, trying to figure out where Aden had gone.

Aden dropped to his knees, attempting to pet the overexcited pup. It was a useless endeavor as the dog was bounding weightless around Aden, yelping and licking him.

"So, you weren't lying about the dog."

Aden looked up.

The other two men had continued through the open gate into the courtyard, but Isa had stopped next to him.

"Isn't he a little too small and adorable for a name like Warrior?" she asked.

Aden did not immediately deign to offer a reply. Warrior looked like a small energetic pile of fluff, but he also looked like a puppy, which was fairly obvious. "He is a descendant of wolves," Aden eventually responded, not without some pride.

"Oh?" Isa actually sounded interested.

"Well, to be honest, I'm not entirely positive," Aden said. "I mean I found him in the forest outside the palace."

"In Iseldis?"

Aden nodded. If she was trying to trip him up by catching him in a lie, it was not going to work. He was Prince Aden of Iseldis. "Aren't all dogs descendants of wolves?" he said, defending himself. "He'll grow."

Warrior had finally noticed that they were not alone and had turned around, placing himself between Isa and Aden. He hunched forward and growled the tiniest growl at her, as though sensing she was a threat.

Isa took a step back, holding up her hand in a mock defense. "Never mind. A warrior at heart, I see."

"That would have been a little more helpful last night before you abandoned me," Aden muttered under his breath to Warrior.

"What was that?" Isa asked.

Aden forced a cough. "Just agreeing with you about the 'warrior at heart' part."

She stood there silently for several long moments, making no move toward the mansion.

Unsure what she was waiting for, Aden gestured toward the gate. "After you."

She shook her head.

Ah, right. He was the enemy here.

He moved through the gate first. "Come on, Warrior."

The dog had already started to follow him, so Aden's words were unnecessary. But it felt better to say something to fill the awkward silence between them.

The awkwardness returned, however, moments later when he opened the door into the great hall and stepped inside. What was he supposed to do now?

"You can stay in the same room you had last night, in the west wing," Isa said, following him through the door.

The west wing. All the other inhabitants of the sprawling mansion had slept in the east wing the previous night. He nodded.

"If you value your hide, you'll stay in that wing." Without another word, she turned and climbed the stairs, disappearing into the east wing.

Aden felt both chastised and angered at her heartless words. "Come on, Warrior," he muttered again as he crossed the room to the western side, ducking his head as he stepped into a long hallway.

Entering the small room that was currently his, Aden felt a heavy weight settle over his shoulders and chest. The close proximity of every wall in the space immediately meant that he could no longer see anything clearly. Its ceiling was low overhead, weighing down upon him and making it difficult for him to breathe. The room itself was likely intended to house the family's servants; being on the ground level of the mansion.

He could make out the hazy shapes of a bed, a wardrobe, and a table. He knew his traveling bag was on the table. But the clarity of sight he'd experienced outdoors had disappeared. He felt trapped.

He could not remain here.

He could leave. Nothing was stopping him from picking up his bag and walking back into the mountains. Back to loneliness, exhaustion, and waiting for . . .

Perhaps it would be better to remain here one more night. He could sleep in the comfortable bed in this mostly silent house, endure the glares of its inhabitants, and get rested and renewed before leaving in the morning.

That plan wouldn't hurt anyone. Unless the rose died before tomorrow morning, of course.

He quickly crossed the room to his bag on the table. Carefully removing the rose, he unwrapped it from the large piece of linen he had used to protect it. The cloth, which he had dampened to keep the flower alive, was now dry.

He squinted his eyes. The head of the rose was a murky brown. He could not see the detail of the petals, but it had clearly lost its vibrant color.

It was dead.

Suddenly, Aden's limbs felt funny, as though they had lost all sensation. It was happening. He was going to lose his humanity and become less than nothing. Become uncontrolled chaos.

As rage and despair welled up inside his chest, he felt the overwhelming desire to grasp the head of the rose and tear it off, to be in control of the final moment of his destiny.

Warrior barked, nipping at Aden's leg as though he sensed something was wrong.

Momentarily distracted, Aden looked down fondly at his little friend. "You're a good boy, Warrior."

Warrior stood on his hind legs, his front paws resting against Aden's knee. The dog opened his mouth in what seemed like a grin at Aden's encouraging words. His tongue lolled out as he panted up happily.

Aden stared at Warrior's tongue. Something nagged at his mind.

Then, Aden felt a giggle in the pit of his stomach. It grew, bursting out of his lungs in a strange mix of laughter and sobbing.

Aden's knees gave out and he sank to the ground, scooping his dog into a big hug. "You're a good boy, Warrior. Such a good boy."

The dog's normally bright pink tongue, hanging out the side of his mouth, had appeared to Aden to be a dull, hazy brown.

"I can't see color," Aden said out loud, still sobbing with laughter. "I've gotten so used to a colorless world, I forgot that I can't see color."

The rose wasn't dead. At least not yet. It just looked brown to him.

Regaining his composure while feeling lighter than he had in a long time, Aden once again picked up the rose.

He squinted. Other than the blob of brown that indicated the petals, he could not make out any details on the rose. He wanted to see if the edges of the petals were becoming dry and brittle, or if the stem was streaked with decay.

His strained eyes revealed nothing.

Holding it gently under his nose, Aden inhaled deeply. The aroma was overpowering. It was fresh, floral, and complex.

He could not smell any hint of dryness or decay. Not that he had ever spent much time comparing the scent of a living rose to that of a dying one. Would he even know when the rose was near its end? Would he be able to perceive the petals as they fell? Or would he one day wake up to find that the red blob had disappeared into nothingness?

He needed a better method to discern what was happening.

He had noticed the scent of flowers in the courtyard. Perhaps he could pluck a normal, un-cursed rose to use as a comparison.

Carefully rewrapping the rose, he headed back outside.

Sure enough, the courtyard was full of rose bushes. Aden slowly walked around them, smelling the different scents and attempting to find one that smelled like his.

Every breath he inhaled buoyed his spirits. He had never noticed that the color of the flower affected the way it smelled, nor the way the sunlight played over the mountaintops.

Forgetting his strange new existence, he simply marveled at the beauty around him.

CHAPTER 13

"What have I done?" Isa asked herself as she watched Cam and Macklin walk down the road toward the canyon. They each carried a large rucksack on their back, and Macklin had insisted they divide the weight evenly. Somehow, though, Cam's pack looked significantly larger. Maybe it just seemed that way since Macklin was so much taller.

Isa was glad Macklin had volunteered to go for help. She realized—with a pang of guilt brought on by his selflessness—that she would not miss his presence.

She turned back to the villa. Sleep or no sleep, it was time to look for the Floutast.

A movement from the rose garden caught her eye.

Bending over the bushes, inhaling the scent of each rose with all the delicacy of an artist, was the beast.

After smelling a particularly large red bloom, he snapped the stem to pluck it from the bush. The stem did not break completely, though, and he struggled for a few moments to twist it free.

Confused and intrigued, Isa took a step toward him.

He must have heard her, as he looked up instantly. He was some ways away, but his eyes squinted as he stared at her.

She had caught him staring at her earlier today while they'd been walking back from the canyon. Annoyed, she left him to his roses and made her way to the library.

The library room felt older than the mountain villa itself. The windows were positioned high up the stone wall to allow for every possible fingerbreadth of shelving space. And every possible space was, in fact, used for shelving.

The tall stacks of books and scrolls were delicately lit by the slabs of morning light coming through the tall slit windows. Even though no one had been in this room for nearly a year, dust constantly swirled in the pools of light.

Isa coughed, waving her hand in front of her to clear the air.

Here, she could focus and forget the difficulties of their situation. Slipping a large apron over her dress, she surveyed the task at hand. While she knew the location of every book in the library at home, she was not as well acquainted with the one here.

Floutast was over two hundred years old, so he was likely in the far-left corner.

She went to the farthest shelf along the back wall and started gently sifting through its contents.

When she came across something interesting that she had not read herself, she placed it in a separate stack for perusing later. Depending on how long it would take to rebuild the bridge, she might have some time for extra reading.

She was soon too focused on her task to notice the pattern of light changing across the shelves as the morning sun rose in the sky.

A loud sneeze broke through her heavy concentration.

Stifling a gasp of surprise, she turned around to find the

beast standing in the center of the room, gazing up at the shelves that were even taller than his own abnormal height.

"I wasn't expecting so much . . . *Achoo!*" he sneezed again.

"I believe the last words I said to you were 'Don't set foot in the east wing.'" Isa did not appreciate being interrupted. Nor did she appreciate the visual reminder of the danger she had placed them all in by asking the beast to remain.

The beast's shoulders dropped. "Ah. Right. I thought you were referring to the bedrooms in the east wing." He turned to leave.

"I was referring to the east wing, and I meant the east wing." Her heart was still pounding from the surprise of finding him right behind her.

"I'm going," he said, walking toward the door.

It irked Isa that he had not apologized for disregarding her rule or for startling her.

Before he could walk through the door, however, his dog bounded into the room and started dashing through the shelves.

Isa's already-pounding heart flew into her mouth. "Stop him!" she yelled, worried for the delicate scrolls. "We don't allow animals in the library!" Realizing what she had just said, she snapped her mouth shut.

The beast's behavior had definitely been very manlike, from the elegant speech to the way he openly stared at her when he thought she wasn't looking. Her conscience had been pricked when she'd unintentionally grouped him with the animal species instead of the humans. But if he wasn't going to offer apologies, neither would she.

"Warrior. Here," the beast commanded his dog, appearing not to have noticed Isa's harsh words.

The dog also appeared not to have noticed the beast's loud command.

He dashed back in the room to chase the pup.

Isa ran to the other wall, hoping to corner the dog.

But Warrior scampered in the other direction, weaving through the bookcases as though he knew where he was going.

Sliding around a corner, he bumped against one of the lower shelves, knocking a scroll off it.

"Stop him!" Isa yelled again.

"Grrrr-rough!" The beast let out a short but intense growl.

Warrior instantly stopped, his ears shooting straight up in high alert. Afraid of the growl, he turned and ran directly back toward Isa. But seeing her, the dog skidded to a stop and barked in disapproval.

Isa crossed her arms. She did not care whether or not the dog liked her; she just wanted it out of her library.

"Warrior. Here. Now." The beast had stepped to the other end of the aisle, blocking Warrior between them.

Warrior's ears dropped, and he plopped down on the floor. He let out a little puppy whine, as though he knew he had done wrong and was asking for sympathy.

"Bad dog," the beast said, stepping forward and scooping him up off the ground. "I'm so terribly sorry," he said to Isa.

Not caring about the belated apology, Isa pointed toward the door. "Get him out of my library."

CHAPTER 14

$\mathcal{A}$den set Warrior down outside the library. "Bad dog," he muttered, trying to keep his tone neutral despite wanting to take out his frustration on the poor animal. "Not that it's your fault, of course, since I haven't given you any proper training. You're just a pup." He pointed his finger toward the library door, raising his voice in case she was listening. "But some fully grown humans don't have that excuse for their rudeness."

She was the one who had invited him back to her home, if one could even call this partially abandoned mansion a home. She was the one making cutting remarks and enforcing useless rules. Aden hadn't asked to be in this situation. She had invited him.

Warrior plopped down on the floor at Aden's feet, a blur of white against the dark stone background. He could hear the dog's tail thumping rhythmically.

This body—this curse—was an injustice he could do nothing about. However, he could fight back against some of the other injustices in his life while he still had the chance.

"Stay," he told Warrior.

Taking a deep breath to steel his resolve, he reopened the door to the library and confidently stepped back inside.

"Alright, Miss Isa," he started.

"That's Lady Bielsa to you." She was crouched on the floor near the shelf where Warrior had knocked something down.

"Bielsa?" Aden momentarily forgot his fight for justice. "As in Carlo Bielsa, the renowned scholar and innovator?"

"My father." Her reply was terse.

Aden smiled at the unexpected connection. Much to his own disappointment, Lord Bielsa had always been too busy reading, writing, or developing scholarly preservation methods to take on pupils. But he had been kind enough to speak with Aden a handful of times and answer questions about his work. "I met him while studying in Chendas."

"So did everyone else who got to study in Chendas," Isa replied, her biting tone instantly destroying his pleasant memories. "And since he's not here to verify your statement, that means nothing to me."

"I wasn't trying to prove anything to you!" Aden roared back at her callous response. "This has nothing to do with you. *He* meant something to me. I was particularly impressed by his lofty goals of binding scrolls for their preservation. He is an incredibly wise and resourceful man, and he has my deepest respect."

"So, this has nothing to do with me? Oh wait, except for the fact that he is *my* father."

"You are deliberately missing the point!" Aden recalled the reason he had returned to the room.

"Then why don't you spell it out for me, since I am so stupid?" She stood to her full height as she challenged him.

Aden took a few deep breaths, blinking through the hazy

light to try and make out her facial expression. Something in her reckless words hinted at a deeper hurt.

"I said you are deliberately missing the point." His voice was still full of frustration, but he tried to keep the volume to an acceptable level. "I think you are smart enough to know what the point is, but you refuse to see it. So no, I will not spell it out for you, since you are more than capable of discerning it."

She did not immediately respond. Rather, she turned away and seemed to be placing something back on the shelf next to her.

"Did Warrior damage a book?" Aden asked.

"No." She moved away from him, working her way to a corner on the back wall.

"Good. I will be sure to keep him out of here in the future." He remained where he was.

"But . . . ?" she asked, as if sensing that he was not done speaking.

"But, I am actually quite fond of books. And I intend to utilize this library."

She said nothing, which irked him.

"I did not ask to be here," he continued, his voice less calm than he wanted. "You invited me here. I did not have to accept." He stepped further into the room as he gained confidence in his argument. "In fact, you could say that I am here for your comfort. An enemy you can see is better than an enemy you cannot, right?"

He could not see her face, but he heard her sharp intake of breath when he repeated the exact words she and her manservant had used at the side of the canyon that very morning. He had heard the entire conversation, of course.

"I may have agreed to your *plan*," he continued, "but I will not tolerate being treated like an *animal*." He paused, waiting for her reaction.

"You are quite fond of books?" she finally responded.

He nodded. Not the response he was expecting.

"Then read to me while I work, Prince Aden of Iseldis."

"Gladly." That seemed simple enough, although this was definitely meant to be some sort of test. "What would you like me to read from? Astridonemus? Mirza?"

"Oh, no. They would put me quite to sleep. I prefer something with a little more drama." Walking back to him, she held out a small hardbound book. "*The Queen of Silverreign*."

As Aden took the book from her hand, two things became immediately clear.

He had met this woman before.

And he could not read a single word in his current condition.

Curses be damned.

Glancing around the room to stall for time, he saw a large armchair and made his way to it. Sinking down into it—thankful that it held his weight—he carefully opened the tiny book.

She was the woman he had spoken with on the balcony at the ball right before the curse. That was why she'd seemed so familiar. And she clearly knew who he was; she was proving it by handing him the book they had discussed that night.

The Queen of Silverreign.

Aden could barely make out the shape of the book in his hand, much less the words on the page. He knew many works from memory, sections from his favorite philosophers and lyricists, but he had only read this myth once and that had been too many years ago. He could not pretend to read by reciting it.

"Shall I start at the beginning?" he asked.

Did she actually want him to read it? Or was she simply too proud to say that she knew who he was, and this was her way of showing it?

"I'm currently on chapter six. Although you can start from the beginning if you need a refresher on the story? I'm assuming you've read it?" Her voice was light, innocent. Too innocent.

Aden focused the muscles of eyes, exerting every bit of power he had to force the words on the page to come into focus. His hand tapped anxiously on the wooden arm of the chair. The room felt warm and suddenly much smaller than before.

He could not remember a time in his life when he could not read. His mother often bragged about the fact that he had learned to read like his older brothers almost before he could talk. He had read all the great works and could discuss them with ease and clarity.

In the chaos of the past few days, he had not even looked at a book or letter or parchment.

He could not make out the simple words of an ancient myth.

Aden closed the little book, slamming it a little louder than necessary. "I do not play games, Lady Bielsa. I say what I mean and prefer for others to do the same."

Standing, he placed the book on the chair behind him and left the room.

CHAPTER 15

"Quiet," Isa whispered as a stair creaked behind her. She froze, listening for any other sounds.

"My knees are too old for this," Luca muttered back to her. But he paused nonetheless, looking over his shoulder.

"He heard our entire conversation this morning," Isa replied after a few moments of silence. Lifting her foot, she continued her climb. "His hearing ability is uncanny. I don't know how far it extends."

"Do you suppose he heard us leaving our rooms?" Blanca asked. She was carrying a lantern and leading the group of three up the staircase into the watchtower on the eastern side of the villa.

"I hope not. The one thing we do know is that he sleeps deeply." Isa hoped her own words were true. At the very least, the large beast would not be able to creep up on them at the top of the tower without making considerable noise on these same stairs. "But quiet now, save your whispers for the top room."

Luca breathed heavily behind her. "I'm not sure which is worse—early mornings, late nights, or cursed creatures."

"Shhh." Isa smiled at his grumpy humor, but she kept her own opinion to herself. One of these things was far worse than the other two, and they were about to officially decide what to do about it.

Upon arriving at their destination, Luca carefully closed the door, easing it silently shut behind them. Blanca placed the lantern she was carrying in the center of the room.

The top of the tower was less a room than it was a slightly enclosed space in the open air. It had round walls and a roof, but seven tall openings led to an outer rampart that circled it. The rampart was an excellent place to watch for visitors coming up the road, and an even better place for uninterrupted time with a book.

Isa gathered three wooden stools around the lantern, and they all sat down. The chill evening air danced through the tall openings around them.

"This is the worst possible scenario we could have imagined," Isa began, stating the obvious. "And I appreciate your staying here with me more than I can say." She paused, looking at their familiar faces in the flickering candlelight. They deserved to know the whole of the truth. "If we do not deliver the Floutast, the Council threatened—"

"We know, dear," Blanca said, cutting her off.

"Oh." Isa nodded, smiling to cover her embarrassment. "Of course you do."

"It's part of our job to know such things," Blanca confirmed.

"Though it ain't part of our job to eavesdrop," Luca muttered.

"Right. Well, regardless, thank you all the same," Isa reiterated.

"So, what is the plan of attack?" Luca asked. "Or should I say plan of defense?"

Isa smiled. She truly was thankful not to be in this alone.

"Well, until the bridge gets replaced and help arrives, I'll stay focused on finding the Floutast so it is ready as soon as possible."

"I'll take care of you," Blanca said, "and take on some cooking and cleaning duties since Cam is gone. Though I can't say my meals will be as tasty, I can surely keep us all fed."

"Thank you," Isa responded. "That is more than enough."

"That leaves me to find food and fuel," Luca said.

Isa nodded. "Excellent. That covers Cam's absence. Hopefully we can keep it up until help arrives."

"Speaking of which," Luca said, "we should also plan on keeping a watch down at the canyon once it is likely the villagers have been alerted. Probably don't need to worry about that for a week or so, though."

"Right." Isa nodded. "I can help with that as well when the time comes."

"That will be difficult, as our packed food stores will be running low by then." Blanca clicked her tongue as though thinking of other solutions.

"This would be quite the adventure," Luca said, "except that we have not addressed the real reason we are huddled at the top of a tower and whispering like naughty children."

Isa sighed. She had hoped the easy part of the conversation would last longer. But Luca was right; they had to decide what to do about the beast. "First, I think we must know where it is at all times."

"He," Blanca said. "Prince Aden."

"He?" Isa bristled at the correction.

"Do you not believe he is who he says he is?" Blanca asked. "You were at the Iseldis ball and saw the Majis attack."

"Right." Isa shifted uncomfortably. "And I did not see a beast."

"I agree," Luca cut in. "I think we must know where this beast is at all times."

"As in, play nursemaid to a monster?" Blanca asked, chuckling at her own jest.

Isa rolled her eyes with a small chuckle of her own. "That's one way to put it. But how will we accomplish that? I already tried restricting him to the west wing, and that failed. He defied me immediately. We can't exactly punish him like a naughty child."

"Maybe a less restrictive approach," Blanca offered. "We can ask him to help us with our various tasks. That would give us an excuse to have him close by."

"But how much trust are we willing to extend here?" Luca pushed back on her suggestion. "We have no idea what he's doing here, in such a remote place, by himself. I don't know that we should be spending time alone with him until we know more about him."

"I agree," Isa said. "If he is who he says he is, what is he doing all the way out here and why did he leave Iseldis?"

"Exactly," Luca responded. "One of us needs to find out."

Isa nodded, then realized that both Luca and Blanca were staring at her. "What, me? Why me?"

"He's more likely to answer your questions than ours," Blanca said.

"And your task leaves the most time for chitchat," Luca added.

In other words, she was the only one with the courage and patience to face him. "Fine," Isa conceded. "I'll try to find out why he's here, but that means the two of you are responsible for keeping an eye on him."

Luca nodded.

"Wait," Blanca said. "If this Prince Aden has such powerful hearing, can't he just stay outside and listen for any sound coming from the canyon?"

Isa gaped at her over the lantern, unable to ascertain whether she was jesting or serious. "We can't trust him with that kind of responsibility!" she hissed.

Blanca shrugged, seemingly undeterred by the incredulous looks that both Isa and Luca were giving her. "It could save us loads of trouble. We'll be running ourselves ragged just trying to keep us all fed and safe. He might as well make himself useful. Besides, it allows us to keep him within our own watch. He watches the river. We watch him watching the river. None of us have to watch the river." She nodded her head emphatically.

"That sounds good to me," a new voice rumbled from the doorway. "I am more than happy to help."

Isa, Luca, and Blanca scrambled to their feet as the hulking beast squeezed himself through the small door. He looked even larger in the confines of the small room.

"You are quite right," he continued. "I can hear the river running, even from up here, and we can test that tomorrow by sending someone down there to yell things back up at me." He joined their circle, sitting himself comfortably on the floor next to the lantern.

Isa stared down at him. How much of their conversation had he heard?

"Sit, sit." He pointed to the stools around him. "Now that we have confirmed who I am, we can get to the matter of why I am here. Although, I would also like to know why you are here."

Blanca was the first to return to her seat.

Isa was last. "So why are you here?" she asked tentatively.

"Because I heard three sets of stealthy footsteps in the middle of the night and did not want to be left out. Ian and

Onric used to have secret meetings without me all the time. I hated it."

Isa crossed her arms. "No jesting. This is a serious secret meeting. Why are you here in the northern mountains? Running away from your kingdom, perhaps? Are you a lawbreaker and this curse is a punishment?"

The beast's eyes flickered, and Isa shrank back.

She was not sure if the candlelight was playing tricks with her or she had truly inspired his anger.

"That was too far, Lady Bielsa," he said, carrying an ominous rumble in his voice. "The power of the Majis is nothing to jest about."

"Of course," Isa responded, his words sparking something in her memory she could not fully recall. "No kingdom would utilize that magic even if they could."

He said nothing, his eyes still glowing yellow at her over the lantern. Perhaps he was waiting for her to apologize.

She said nothing further.

"I was cursed while defending my brother Ian at the ball six days ago."

"That was a palace guard who defended him," Isa said.

"I am the third in line for the throne of Iseldis. I am a palace guard." His tone was dismissive, as though everyone knew this information.

Isa had never been incredibly interested in the succession traditions of other kingdoms, so she had no rebuttal.

"When it became clear that this curse was unable to be reversed, I left my family before they could smother me with their sympathy. And now I am here, at your gracious mercy." He accompanied these words with a casual inspection of the lengthy, protracted claws on his right paw. "Thankfully, you have not been as forthcoming with the sympathy. For that, I am grateful. Any questions?"

Isa looked to Luca.

He shook his head.

She turned to Blanca, raising her eyebrows.

Blanca nodded. She seemed satisfied with that explanation.

Isa, however, was not. She turned back to the beast.

He had been staring at her over the lantern, his eyes frequently flicking closed.

She was beginning to believe that he truly was Prince Aden of Iseldis, but she was growing increasingly more annoyed by his blatant staring. "You left your family because they were being too nice to you?"

His eyes dropped to the lantern. "That was a polite way to say that I left my family because I was ashamed of my new circumstances. I am not exactly in a position to be proud of what I am. Their kind gestures only reminded me . . ." He shook his head and looked back up at Isa. "For my first round of 'nursemaid' tomorrow, I choose Lady Bielsa. I'm sure she will find me a great help in the library."

"I think we've learned everything we need to here," Isa replied, glaring at the beast. "This secret meeting session is over."

CHAPTER 16

Aden held a rose in each hand. Why was he still here?

The rose in his right hand was the one he had plucked from the garden two days prior. Without water, the base of the blossom had become wobbly on the stem. It still smelled quite fresh, though he could detect hints of warmth in the scent that had not been there before.

The cursed rose, in his left hand, seemed unchanged. He had filled a jar with water to keep it in, but other than that, he had no idea how to care for it or extend its life. It had lost no other petal and smelled as fresh as the roses in the garden.

Should he leave this mansion and its inhabitants?

He placed the cursed rose back in its jar and left the garden rose to decompose on the table next to it.

He felt no different this morning than he had previously. The movements of his body were less foreign, and he could not deny that the comforts of the mansion were far preferable to living in the wilds. Unlike Ian and Erich, Aden's role as a castle guard had required very little training in the wilds of Iseldis.

Perhaps he had a little more time than he'd expected. He

could stay a few more days without endangering the good people here.

At ease with his decision, he left his room.

"Is it my turn?" Blanca asked as Aden poked his head into the kitchen.

Aden nodded. He had spent the previous day lounging on a comfortable chair in the library while Isa meticulously sorted through the shelves in the back corner. He had considered offering to help, then decided against it when he'd realized he wouldn't really be able to help at all since he couldn't read the book titles. So, he'd grabbed a random tome and pretended to read by the fireplace all day. Isa had shut down any attempt he made at conversation. Contenting himself with the fact that his presence annoyed her, he merely sat there and pretended to read.

Isa would get to work in peace this morning, though, as Aden had decided to enforce the plan the servants had come up with for keeping him in their view at all times. It would be simple enough for him to ease their worries by remaining in their presence while they went about their daily duties.

"Anything I can help you with?" he asked Blanca.

"Oh, no. Not at all, Your Highness . . . ?" She stepped away from him, tittering uncomfortably.

"Well, I shall do my best not to bother you," Aden said, attempting to put her at ease. He truly had no intention of scaring the poor woman out of her wits. Stepping into the large kitchen, he followed his nose to the larder. It appeared fairly empty, but it held an interesting myriad of scents mixed in with the perpetual dust that seemed to be in every room of the mansion.

He scrunched his nose, sniffing away a sneeze before it hit him.

Carefully picking up an item at random, he gave it a whiff.

Dried garlic? He flexed his paw, gently squeezing it. The satisfying crinkle of the dried paper shell greeted his ears. Dried garlic, it was! He placed it back on the shelf and picked up another item.

"Are . . . are you hungry?" Blanca asked from behind him. "Some porridge will be ready shortly."

"Oh, no." He turned around. "Just amusing myself." He held out the object in his hand, which he had not yet identified. "Close your eyes."

Blanca said nothing, seemingly frozen in place. The woman was so still, Aden was afraid she had stopped breathing.

"Oh!" He must have frightened her. "Here, I'll do it." He placed the unknown object back on the shelf and left the larder to sit on a bench in the kitchen.

Blanca was still silent, but Aden assumed that, if he could see her face, she would be looking at him as though he were crazy.

He should have just said nothing. Maybe being ignored all day yesterday in the library had bothered him more than he'd realized. "Pick any object in the larder, and I'll try to guess what it is using only my nose."

Again, she said nothing, but Aden heard her muffled footsteps as she walked away from him and into the larder. She returned a few moments later, and an overpowering scent surrounded Aden.

Keeping his hands over his eyes to prove he was playing fair, Aden breathed in deeply through his nose. A little too deeply, as the bitter aroma struck the back of his throat. "Oof," he said, leaning away. "Fermented cabbages."

"That was too easy!" Blanca laughed.

Aden opened his eyes. The older woman was standing a full arm's length away from him—but she was laughing. Aden smiled. He knew his face would not look any less frightening, but he hoped it would appear as non-aggressive as possible.

"Another," she said. "Wait here!"

Aden's tentative smile melted into a real one as he placed his hands over his eyes once again.

"What is this?" she asked when she finally returned from the larder.

Aden inhaled. He definitely smelled fish and salt, so he assumed it was some sort of dried fish. But there was something strange mixed in with it as well, something sweet. He inhaled again. It smelled terrible.

She was laughing under her breath.

"Honey salted fish?" he finally guessed just before opening his eyes. "Who would eat such a thing?"

Blanca laughed louder, holding up two separate hands. One contained dried fish; the other held a jar of honey.

"You cheated!" He laughed along with her.

"What's going on here?" a grumpy voice spoke over their mirth. "Are we getting breakfast, or do we have to wait for dinner?"

"Sorry, Luca." Blanca wiped tears from her eyes. "Go see to the horses and I'll have some porridge ready before you can turn around." She moved across the kitchen, lifting a wooden pail.

"I've already seen to the horses," Luca muttered from the doorway. His head kept pivoting between Blanca and Aden.

"Then quit complaining and get me some water." Blanca forced her pail into Luca's empty hands.

He left, continuing to mutter under his breath. Aden only caught the words "bad knees" and "chop the wood."

Blanca dipped a wooden spoon into the pot hanging above the fire.

"Shall I grab you some fish for that porridge?" Aden asked. "It would add a nice flavor, especially with a drizzle of honey."

"Absolutely not." She laughed at him. "But you can make yourself useful by fetching me some salt."

Aden happily obliged.

Later that night, when he collapsed into bed, Aden felt light and . . . normal. Following the older woman around the kitchen and villa as she made the place more livable had turned out to be surprisingly enjoyable. And if her constant stream of light-hearted chatter was anything to go on, she seemed to have enjoyed his company as well.

CHAPTER 17

*A*den knocked on the library door.

He heard a sigh of frustration from the other side that was probably not meant for his ears. His mouth twitched into a smile. He enjoyed the fact that his presence bothered her as much as it did.

"Yes?" Isa said, opening the door.

"It's your turn."

"My turn?"

"To play nursemaid to the crazy beast inhabiting your castle," Aden responded.

"It's hardly a castle, and I thought you didn't play games," she said, using his own words against him. She kept the door only partially open, not fully inviting him into the room.

"Oh, it's not a game, Lady Bielsa." He kept his expression sincere. "Of course, if you'd prefer, I can wander the grounds unattended, causing damage and tearing through draperies." He lifted his paw, giving her a glimpse of the knife-like points of his claws.

She stepped back and opened the door all the way.

He stepped inside, having accomplished his goal, but was startled by the force with which she slammed the door closed behind him.

"Do not toy with me." Her words were quiet but angry. "And do not bother me." She returned to the shelf at the far corner of the room.

Aden watched her. The sounds of her firm footfalls emphasized her anger. He did not know why that pleased him.

Being a prince, he was quite familiar with people trying to flatter him. This was often a source of frustration, and it was delightful that she did not even bother trying to impress him.

He moved over to the empty chair by the fireplace and made himself comfortable.

He was not sure which was more enjoyable, spending his day in a library or continuing to bother the fiery woman behind the tall shelves. Growing up, he had watched Ian and Onric constantly fight to best each other, and since he could never keep up, he had found his own solace in the library at home. He preferred the more even playing field of an intellectual debate. This woman did not mince her words.

Unable to read, he sat, listening to the sounds of her shuffling through the contents of the shelves. Whatever she was looking for, she was entirely focused on her task.

Aden, however, was growing steadily more bored. As much as he admired this woman's confidence and focus, he did not appreciate being bored.

He stood from his chair and wandered toward her, pretending to stop and browse different shelves on the way.

"What are you looking for?" he asked as he drew closer.

"Nothing that concerns you," she replied.

"Would you like some help?" Aden offered, remembering too late that he would not be able to read the titles in order to properly aid her.

"No. I would like to not be bothered."

Thinking of nothing further to say, Aden returned to his chair.

As the day wore on, the wood beneath him seemed to grow more and more uncomfortable—as did the icy silence from the other side of the room.

But what could he get her to engage in? The only thing he knew about her was that she enjoyed reading.

He stood again. "Lady Bielsa," he said, "what is your favorite book in this library?"

The shuffling behind the shelf stopped. "Why do you ask?" she responded suspiciously.

"To determine the quality of this library, of course."

She stepped around the shelf, bringing him into view. "How does knowing my favorite book have anything to do with the quality of the library?"

"I asked for your favorite book in *this* library."

"That still seems like an unfair assessment," she replied.

"Why don't you answer my question and then we will find out." Aden had no idea where he was going with this, but he was delighted that she was finally engaged.

She disappeared behind the shelf again. "I don't know this library very well, so I don't feel comfortable answering that question."

"Oh." Aden turned back toward the chair, hoping his voice sounded uninterested. "I take it you are not as well-read as I had assumed."

"Excuse me?" She reappeared. "This is merely a holiday villa. We don't spend much time here, and we use it as extra space to store the books that don't fit into the library at home. If you are going to judge the quality of a library, it should be that one. Not this one. Also," she continued ranting, hardly pausing to draw breath, "I don't think you should be judging a collection of books to begin with. Who are you to make an unequivocal decision based on a personal opinion? You keep claiming to be so in love with reading, but I haven't seen you even open a book."

Aden was speechless. He had wanted to poke her out of her high-and-mighty attitude, and he had absolutely succeeded. "I . . . uh . . . you are right."

"Of course I'm right. You can't just stare at my face and instantly assume that I am stupid."

"I wasn't—" Aden was confused as to what she meant, but she did not give him a chance to explain.

"Stories are not meant to be critiqued like some student's first attempt at calligraphy. They are meant to be enjoyed, studied, learned from . . . savored." She slowed down at the last word, emphasizing her point. "What's your favorite book, anyway? The *Manual of Weights and Measures?*"

Aden couldn't stop the smile that spread to his face. "Why, because I like judging things so much?"

"Obviously." She sounded pleased at her own cleverness.

"I have read the *Manual of Weights and Measures*, I'll have you know," he said. "My father made me study it in preparation for being a just leader."

"And?" she asked.

"And what?"

"Is it your favorite book?" A giggle accompanied her words.

"Absolutely not. It was dull and boring. I had to jump around the room every few pages just to keep myself from falling asleep."

She laughed outright at that.

Aden smiled as his heart beat a funny rhythm in his chest. He could not even recall what this woman looked like, but he was beginning to like her in an entirely new way.

CHAPTER 18

"Ah-ha!" Isa could not contain her cry of delight when she finally found a scroll with Floutast's unmistakable signature near the clasp.

"Did you finally find it?" a deep voice rumbled from across the room.

Isa kicked herself internally. She had forgotten he was there, as he had been completely quiet all day. So quiet, in fact, that she hadn't even heard a page turn.

She decided not to reply. Ignoring the beast had worked thus far on the days he spent with her in the library.

She carefully set the scroll on a side table behind her and returned to the same spot on the shelf. Her father kept his books meticulously organized, so it was likely that any other Floutast would be on the same shelf.

She was in luck! The next three scrolls were exactly what the councilors had requested.

A weight she had not realized she'd been carrying slipped from her shoulders as she surveyed her finds.

They were in poor condition, but they had been found. She could handle everything from here on out. Her father's life was safe.

She carefully opened the latch on the first scroll she had found and gently nudged it open. A section of the outer parchment broke away from the rest of the scroll. "Curses," she swore.

"Present," the deep rumbling voice of the beast sounded behind her.

"Go away." She did not have time for this.

"What happened?" he asked.

"What are you? Blind?" she snapped.

"Well, actually—"

"These are in worse shape than I thought," she muttered to herself, remaining focused on the problem at hand. She wanted to unroll the scroll further, but she knew better than to aggravate it.

It was time to get to work.

Wanting all the surface area she had available, she started clearing off the largest table in the library.

"Where do you want these?" the beast asked.

She looked up to see him holding a stack of books. "There." She pointed across the library to a shelf that still had some space on it.

With his help, the table was cleared in a few short moments.

"Grab those chests and stack them on this side," she said, pointing to the chests by the library door. Macklin might have laughed at her for bringing every possible tool for every possible eventuality, but she was glad she had done so. This was a full-on emergency makeover.

As the beast brought over the chests, Isa opened them, unpacking their contents into a pile of organized chaos on the newly cleared table.

Her heart still felt fluttery. Seeing the all-important Floutast disintegrate in her fingers had been unnerving. What would the Council do if she found the information they needed and then proceeded to ruin it? She reminded herself that the worst thing she could do was allow the scrolls to travel in their current state. She had seen firsthand what that had done to Brother Elias's library.

Looking up, she realized the beast was standing on the other side of the table, staring down at her. "Thank you for your help," she said dismissively. She truly was thankful, but she also hoped that he would leave. His staring made her uncomfortable.

"This seems like a stressfully fixated effort for an ancient writer who is largely disregarded as myth or fancy."

Surprised, Isa looked back up at him. He had not moved from his side of the table. "You know Floutast?"

"Of course. He's a primary source of ancient battle tactics. Although, to be honest, the only real reason I read him was because everyone said he was so useless. I had to read it for myself just to prove my professor wrong."

Isa walked across the room to where she had left the three Floutast scrolls. She picked one up and carried it to her newly prepared workspace. "Did you?" she asked.

"What, read it? Yes." His eyes followed her careful progress across the room.

"No, prove your professor wrong." She set the first scroll on the table and returned for the next.

"Oh. Sadly, no. I found the writing rather dull and uninspired. Just boring accounts of daily details and such. In the few battles Floutast actually wrote about, he spent most of the time cataloging the number of barrels of wheat each army had and how many wagons of fuel were brought in each day. If you are going to tell the story of a battle, the least you could do is actually talk about the battle." He stopped speaking as she approached the table with the second scroll. "Have you read him?"

"No," she replied. She positioned the cylindrical parchment against a jar so it would not roll off the table. "He sounded boring. And I rather liked my professors. I don't think I ever felt the need to prove them wrong. I spent more time trying to prove them right."

"Prove them right?"

"For taking a post as a girl's tutor," she said over her shoulder as she picked up the last scroll on the other side of the room.

When the beast said nothing in response, she looked up at him as she walked back. His eyes were scrunched as though in confusion. "What did you have to prove to them? Weren't they just paid to take the post?"

"That I could be as smart and interesting to teach as a male pupil even if I would never be able to take the exams and earn the real scholarly title." Her jaw tightened as she arranged the scroll on the large table. She had put as much energy into being a good student as she had put into the actual studying itself. One would think those were the same thing, but somehow, they were different. She wished she had spent more time enjoying the material than trying to learn her professors' differing perspectives. She felt like she had not been able to draw her own conclusions about the books she had read. It was complicated to explain.

"Did you want to take the exams?" Aden asked.

Isa nodded, though she felt embarrassed for having admitted it.

"Is that why you are looking for Floutast, then?" Aden asked.

"What? So that I can take the exams and prove how smart I am?" Her mind was still ruminating on her old tutors.

"No. Why would you have to prove how smart you are? It

sounds like you already did, exams or no. Are you looking for Floutast because you haven't read him yet?"

"Oh. No. I . . ." Isa stopped, finally realizing that she was having a conversation with the beast. The councilors had not stressed any sort of secrecy, just urgency, but she had already shared more than she had intended. "I need to deliver it to the Council."

The beast raised his eyebrows. "What are they looking for in Floutast?" His voice was deeper somehow, slipping into a growl.

Isa shrugged. What the Council was planning was none of her business. Having no desire to speak of it further, she returned her focus to the table in front of her. Everything was set and ready to begin binding the scrolls, but she had lost her focus.

"Come eat supper with me tonight," the beast said.

Isa looked up, confused. "What?"

"You haven't left this room in four days, and you've hardly eaten a thing. You found the scrolls. Take the rest of the night to refresh yourself, and come sit down and eat a proper meal with me."

She shook her head. "I can't. Binding these will take days, if not weeks."

"When is the soonest the bridge will be replaced?" he asked.

She shrugged. Maybe if she avoided looking at him again, he would leave the room and go eat the supper he was so excited about.

"By Luca's calculations, it will be four weeks at the soonest, but that is relying on the speedy success of your valiant husband and his fearless manservant."

Isa snapped her head up when he called Macklin her husband. She glared a warning at the beast, but he did not seem to notice.

"I don't want to say that I have any doubts about those two," he carried on, "but let me just say, I have some doubts."

What was it with this beast and his complete inability to read social cues? Maybe he was a human man after all. "Stop saying that!" Isa yelled.

"What? Oh. That was rude of me. Of course you should not harbor any doubts about the capability of your husband."

"He's not my husband!" she yelled.

That seemed to have gotten his attention. He blinked at her. Then his inhuman mouth spread into a very humanlike grin. "It would seem, Lady Bielsa, that we finally have something in common."

"What is that supposed to mean?" she asked, completely at a loss for where he was going with this.

"It seems that neither of us can stomach Macklin the Cowardly."

Isa felt the giggle in her throat before it burst out in a wave of laughter, but she was too humored to try and stop it. "Macklin the Cowardly?" She snorted as she inhaled. "He doesn't deserve that."

"He did abandon you in a moment of danger," the beast said, defending his position.

Isa sobered at the reminder of that night.

"Perhaps he will redeem himself by saving us all," the beast continued, offering another viewpoint.

Isa looked up at him, searching for the humanity in his beastly features. "I did get the distinct impression," she said, her voice slow and thoughtful, "that he volunteered to go as an excuse to put more distance between himself . . . and you."

The beast sighed. "You are likely right. Although I cannot say that I blame him."

Isa nodded. Somehow Macklin's second betrayal felt worse than the first. That first night, his actions had been despicable, but his intentionally leaving her stuck in the mountains with a dangerous unknown beast felt more calculated and truly cowardly. The last thing she wanted to think about was Macklin's actions toward her. On that account, she could not care less. "Let us go see what Blanca has managed to conjure for dinner," she said. "A break will do me good."

CHAPTER 19

"*B*lanca." Aden poked his head into the kitchen, nearly running into the older woman as she headed out the door with a tray of food in hand. "Lady Bielsa and I will be dining together in the great hall," he continued. "I hope it is not too late to make arrangements for that?"

"Just in time," she replied. "I was about to bring this up." She set the tray down and started removing items from it. "It's a bit sudden to change plans, but more difficult things have been done, such as convincing that girl to come out of the library. However did you do it?"

Aden shrugged. "Must be my striking good looks."

He left the lady's maid-turned-cook laughing over a stack of plates and went to see if the great hall needed any other preparation.

He had known, of course, that Macklin was not Isa's husband; it had just been fun to annoy her repeatedly by saying it. She had done her own share of throwing verbal barbs at him, and he'd felt it was only fair to return the favor.

What he had not counted on was how fun it would be to make her angry.

He was not sure why he enjoyed teasing her like he did his mother and sister, or why he was even excited to have dinner with her. Perhaps it was just an excuse to feel more human.

Tonight, he would switch tactics and actually try to not make her angry. He just wanted something normal. A normal supper. A normal conversation.

Blanca followed him into the room a short time later and arranged some plates and tableware.

The great hall felt like the palace at home, just a more rural version of it. The walls were darker and the textures more rustic. Even the smell of the stew Blanca brought to the table felt like the homely version of what the palace cooks would have served.

Aden suddenly found himself nervous.

It was just dinner. Yet, it was dinner with just the two of them.

He was the middle child of five siblings; he had never had a quiet meal in his life. What were they supposed to talk about? Their conversations up till now had not been promising. Except for the first time they'd met, at the ball. What had they talked about on the balcony?

He couldn't remember. The normalcy of that moment had been drowned in the chaos that followed it.

"Where is milady?" Blanca asked, coming back into the room with a bottle of wine and two glass cups.

"I don't know," Aden responded truthfully. "She said she wanted to freshen up but that she would meet me here."

"I'll go see if I can find her," Blanca said. "Everything else is ready."

Aden pulled out a chair at the end of the long table and sat down. Perhaps she had been so exhausted from her search that she had fallen directly asleep, unable to resist the soft comfort of her bed.

The stew smelled delicious.

He partially extended his claws and drummed them absently on the side of the table.

Feeling a little rude but also impatient, Aden closed his eyes and focused his hearing on the castle around him. All was quiet. He could hear neither footsteps nor voices.

Maybe she *had* fallen asleep.

Aden sighed.

It was no use letting a good stew go to waste.

He opened the lid of the serving dish and flailed his hand around the rim, searching for the ladle. Locating it successfully, he gave the pot a good stir and lifted out a generous spoonful.

The ladle was halfway to his bowl when the door slammed open, startling him.

Caught in the middle of something he should not be doing, he instantly plopped the ladle back into the pot and slammed the lid back onto it. "This stew smells delicious, Blanca," he said, covering his embarrassment.

"Thank you," she responded. "No fish in it, or honey for that matter."

Aden grinned up at her, then slowly brought his eyes over to Isa.

She had changed her dress, or perhaps she had just removed the large apron she always wore in the library. He couldn't quite tell since he had not been paying attention. She did smell faintly of roses, as though she had freshened up with a scented soap or something equally nice. However, his sensitive nostrils could still smell the faint whiff of leather and wood he had noticed that first night when he'd held her in his arms.

That thought brought a blush to his face, which he hoped was not visible through his thick fur.

What was his mind doing? He had not "held her in his arms" that night—he had fended off her armed attack! He shook the thoughts away, then realized he was still sitting and jumped up from his chair.

"Lady Bielsa!" He bowed. The extra formality made him feel utterly ridiculous in his beastly form. "Welcome to the feast!"

"It does smell delicious," Isa said, speaking to Blanca.

"Thank you, milady. It's just a stew." Blanca left the room.

Aden would have guessed she was grinning from ear to ear, but he couldn't quite tell.

Looking back at Isa, Aden gestured to a chair at the table, then pulled it out for her as she approached.

"Thank you," she said, opening the lid of the pot and serving herself.

Aden reached for the bottle of wine, realizing too late that he would not be able to get a proper grip on the slippery surface. He pulled his hand back, hoping she had not noticed.

He picked up the ladle next, balancing its long handle between his claws.

"Tomorrow is Luca's turn for cooking, so I would eat well tonight if I were you," Isa said.

"Should I be worried?" Aden asked, helping himself to another spoonful just in case.

"I don't know. I've never had his cooking."

She reached for the wine and thankfully poured for them both.

That ancient legend . . . they had discussed it on the balcony, but what was it called? "Tell me about *The Queen of Silverreign*?" he asked, hoping she would enjoy speaking of it again.

"*The Queen of Silverreign*?" She sounded surprised.

"It's your favorite book, isn't it? Why do you like it?"

"I do love it," she said. "It's the opposite of how you described

Floutast. Unlike other ancient works, it focuses on the story instead of getting mired in boring details."

Aden nodded. He could appreciate that perspective, even if he did not care for the work in question. "I always struggled with it," he said. "It felt so romanticized."

"Not enough battles?" Her voice carried both a jest and a warning. This was a topic she cared about.

Aden leaned forward. This was a conversation he was interested in having. "Too unbelievable. Except for the ending, which was the only part I did like."

Isa jumped out of her chair, leaning forward over the table. "You've read the ending?! How does it end? Is it perfect? Where did you find the final volume? I've been searching for it for ages!"

Aden leaned back, startled at her sudden outburst. "So many questions. Slow down! Start from the beginning. Wait . . ." He stared at her face, wishing he could see her expression. She was so excited, so eager. "It's your favorite book and you haven't read the ending?"

She shook her head, sinking back into her chair. "It's so old, I've never been able to locate a copy of the final volume."

"Oh, we have the full collection in Iseldis."

"No!" she cried, disappointed. "I was so close! I was *just* in Iseldis. I knew I should have skipped the ball and gone in search of the library instead of wasting my time dancing."

"You don't like dancing?" Aden was intrigued. He hated dancing, a trait his siblings had always teased him about.

She shook her head again. "I like dancing, just not the crowded rooms and constant noise and obnoxious men."

Aden nodded, squeezing his eyes shut. The strain of continually trying to make out the features of her face was making his head ache and his eyes sore. He looked back at her so it would appear as though he was listening intently, but he let his eyes relax until she was merely a blur.

"You are distracting me," she said. "Tell me how it ends! No, wait. I'd rather read it for myself. Let's go to Iseldis, right now. We can jump over the canyon and be there in two days!"

He laughed at her eagerness. "Do you want me to tell you or not?"

"Tell me. You said it was your favorite part, so it can't be disappointing."

"Favorite might mean something different for me." Aden did not know this young woman well, but he realized that what he was about to say would probably ruin her excitement. "Wouldn't you rather read it yourself someday?"

"Yes! And I will. But tell me. Do Amelya and Andrew defeat the evil invaders and finally come back to each other to spend the rest of their days together?"

"They do defeat the invaders," Aden confirmed, speaking slowly.

"And?" She was leaning over the table again.

Aden realized that his eyes had refocused so he could better read her body language. He picked up his wine glass. He needed to relax his eyes and ease the growing pain in his head. Having deftly practiced how to get liquid from a cup into his oddly shaped mouth, he expertly poured the wine onto his scooped tongue.

"Rude," she said dismissively.

Embarrassed at his clumsy workaround, Aden brought the glass back to the table with more force than was necessary.

"I am sitting here waiting for the most exciting moment of my life," she continued, "and you are rude enough to pause for a drink. What do they do after they achieve the victory?"

Aden exhaled in relief. She had not been reacting in disgust to his body—just impatience for the story. "Well," he said, "Andrew is deeply wounded during the final attack, but he goes back to the battlefield to search for Amelya while their army is celebrating victory. He finds her . . . but she is dead. She died a hero's death defeating the enemy general. In his grief, Andrew collapses on top of her and dies from his wounds while their people are shouting in victory." Aden had forgotten the melodramatic tone of the great saga, and recalling the heroic actions of the final chapters had stirred his own appreciation for the work. "It really was poignantly beautiful, the way they had sacrificed their time together in order to bring about peace for their people. It seems fitting that they died in the end. They had committed their lives to this war already. It really would have cheapened the whole story if they'd gotten to live in happiness after all they went through."

"Fitting?" Isa said, incredulous.

Aden snapped his mouth shut.

"Sacrificed?" Her voice was dangerously high pitched.

Aden resisted the urge to cover his poor ears.

"Cheapened?!?" She was standing once again. "They died?! After all they went through to achieve a state of peace, they died?!" She threw something down at her plate. It must have been a piece of bread, as it bounced up lightly and fell off the table.

Aden brought his eyes back to her fuming face.

"They died." She sank into her seat. She had seemingly forgotten he was there. "He should never have left her to seek out the magician. She wouldn't have been forced to lead the army, and then they could have lived—happily and in love. That would have made such a better story."

"More satisfying in the moment, perhaps," Aden said, attempting to offer some consolation. "But then you would never have heard the story at all."

Her head didn't move, but he thought he saw her eyelids flick toward him.

Hoping that he had her attention, he kept talking. "It's a legend, a saga. A story that is told for the purpose of passing on wisdom from one generation to the next."

"I know what a legend is!" she said. "Enough with the literature lecture."

Aden clumsily continued making his point. "It was only because of the bittersweet ending that the story became a legend at all."

Isa pushed her bowl of stew toward the center of the table. "Thank you for ruining my absolute favorite thing in the entire kingdom and beyond. I find that I have quite lost my appetite. Goodnight." She stood.

"But real life doesn't end happily for everyone!" Aden said, his voice coming out louder than he intended. "Just because you're disappointed doesn't mean you should disregard the entire story."

"I'm not disregarding the entire story, but I am disappointed. I don't want real life to look like that. If I loved someone that immensely, I would never walk away from them on the eve of battle." She clutched the back of her chair with one hand, gesturing wildly with the other.

"That's admirable," Aden said, "and having seen your courage firsthand, I have no doubt that you would remain on the front line. But don't you realize that if Andrew had not gone back, they would have lost the entire war? Everyone in the army would have died that day, and their families would have been enslaved."

"Oh, yes, now I see what you mean," she said, her voice thick with sarcasm. "You would have no problem abandoning someone you loved, just like you ran away from your family!"

Aden stood. The force of his abrupt movement sent the chair

behind him toppling. "Enough!" he roared. "You have no idea what you are talking about." The thunder of his rage exploded out from him, shaking every item in the room and reverberating off the tall stone walls.

Blood filled his vision and the room around him turned black.

Reining in his anger, he took a few stabilizing breaths. As his sight returned, he thought Isa had left the room.

A movement behind her chair drew his attention. She had been cowering behind it. She slowly stood, backing away from him. "Neither do you."

"Isa!" He lifted his hands to cover his face in shame. "I'm so sorry. I . . . I don't know what came over me. I'm so sorry."

She did not respond.

When he withdrew his hands, she had left the room.

Having lost his own appetite, Aden walked back to his own room. Somehow, before he even opened the door, he knew that the rose had lost another petal. He was right.

He was right.

INTERIM

Salt.

His first conscious thought was salt. Everywhere. It was in his nose, his throat, his eyes—even his stomach felt upset, like it had been dried from the inside out with salt.

He was alive. And it felt terrible.

He coughed, trying to expel the bitter flavor from the back of his throat. But lying on one's back was not ideal for coughing, and his attempt devolved into a choking gag.

He tried to roll over to his side. His limbs refused to move.

His skin itched, everywhere. Probably from all the salt.

His eyes burned as he tried to crack them open. Even that tiny movement was painful, with his eyelids as dry as they were.

The sun beat down on him, warming him from above while the sand baked him from below.

He remembered getting on the ship with his squadron of the elite guard. The storm had hit when they were a few hours away from the shore. It had appeared instantaneously. The clear blue sky had been blocked from view by waves that could have eclipsed a mansion.

It was no ordinary storm.

The Majis were demonstrating that they were the ones who controlled the sea.

He felt as though he were about to fall over, even though he was already lying down. His tongue, stuck to the top of his mouth, begged for water.

Every breath smelled and tasted of salt. His stomach turned.

The massive wave had crashed over their ship, smashing it into pieces with its crushing force. His last conscious memory was one of complete terror.

The discomfort in his stomach grew as he realized how helpless they were against such unrestrained power.

He forced himself to breathe deeply, turning the discomfort to anger.

He would not be cowed by their power. He loved his life too much to sacrifice it to their tyrannical whims. They could try to destroy him, destroy his brother, destroy his family, destroy his kingdom.

He would be the one to destroy. Their exile should have been permanent, or worse.

He would show them.

As soon as he'd had a moment to rest.

He closed his eyes again.

The sun would burn his skin if he did not find some shade, but his body was not ready to move.

His last breath, as his mind drifted back into ignorant sleep, did not smell of salt. It was a far more pleasant floral aroma, like a fragrant lotus.

Which was ridiculous. The lotus flower did not grow in the salty sea.

CHAPTER 20

Having not seen the beast for two days, Isa called another secret meeting.

She had kept herself secluded in the library while starting the delicate process of separating the parchment of the scroll into uniform pages.

Neither Luca nor Blanca had complained about the beast in the meantime, but Isa wanted to make sure their original plan was still secure enough for everyone's safety.

After witnessing the ferocity of the beast's anger, she was not sure that it was.

"It is likely he can hear our every word," she whispered over the lantern in the tower room, "but it is more important that we meet regardless. I think it might be time to find a way to trap the beast in his room and not let him out until help arrives. It might be difficult to plan, since he could overpower us all if he finds out, but I think I've come up with a way to make it work."

"That seems a little bit unnecessary to me," Blanca said, her eyes narrowed in the dim light.

Isa was a little surprised that Blanca was quick to be against the idea, but the woman was so kindhearted she likely did not want to hurt anyone's feelings. Isa had noticed that Blanca laughed more frequently when the beast was near.

"Luca?" Isa asked, knowing she could expect more support from him.

"Well," he said, dragging his words out, "that does seem just a tad extreme."

Isa furrowed her eyebrows in confusion. He had been the most distrustful of the beast during their first meeting.

Luca glanced toward the door, as though expecting the beast to appear at any moment.

"Oh," Isa whispered, understanding his reticence. "If you are afraid he will hear you and retaliate, just nod your head yes to my idea."

Blanca immediately shook her head, mouthing a silent, "No."

Luca, too, shook his head.

"I knew you'd come around," Blanca whispered to Luca, jabbing him with her elbow.

"Hmph," he responded, rubbing his arm and inching away from Blanca. "Someone's been keeping the woodpile chopped, and it's not me."

"He's ferocious and volatile," Isa hissed, scrambling for something they could all agree on.

Blanca shook her head. "You've been too locked up in that library to notice anything."

"He *roared* at me," Isa responded. "Surely you heard that? The villagers on the other side of the canyon likely heard it. He lost control."

"After you rudely insulted his family." Blanca clucked her tongue in disapproval.

"You heard that, too?" Isa asked, surprised for a moment. Of course they had heard it; they were surely listening in through the door. She crossed her arms. "He may have you all fooled that he is part human. But I think it's clear to see he is all beast, and we need to do something about it before he loses control again."

"He did not exactly lose control. He got angry but quickly calmed back down. He's under a curse," Blanca replied, as though that simple fact explained everything.

"Right. Cursed to be a beast. Which makes him not human."

"And you think that curses can't be broken?" Blanca was deadly serious.

"He himself said it can't be," Isa responded.

Blanca lifted her hands in the air. "What does he know of curses?"

"What do you know of curses?" Isa retorted.

"You've read me that story a hundred times while I've combed your hair."

"*The Queen of Silverreign?*" Isa asked, not particularly interested in being reminded of that story at the moment. "That's just a myth."

"A myth in which that Andrew boy manages to break a curse." Blanca said it as though she were explaining things to a ten-year-old.

"A myth that isn't true," Isa said, responding in the same condescending tone.

"How do you know that? It was written hundreds of years ago. Who are you to say whether it is based on truth or not?"

"It's clearly a scholarly work, based on its use of metaphor and linguistics. It's a story that is only told for the purpose of passing on wisdom from one generation to the next." Isa clenched her jaw shut as she realized she was using the same explanation of the story that the beast had used on her.

"You are just like your father." Blanca shook her head.

"Generally, I would take that as a compliment, but why do I have the feeling your statement does not have a positive intent?"

"Sometimes, milady, you are so focused on what's inside of a book that you completely miss what is right in front of your nose."

Isa touched her nose dramatically. "Air. Air is in front of my nose."

"Quiet," Luca whispered. "He might be outside the door this very moment listening to all your nonsense. Get to the point and let us all get back to bed."

Isa let out a long breath. "Sorry. I'm confused and thought we were all in agreement. Apparently, I'm missing something. What am I missing?"

"You burrow yourself into the library all day. Maybe try poking your head out once in a while and see what else is happening," Blanca replied.

"But the Floutast—"

"Can wait. The bridge won't be ready for days yet, likely still weeks. You have time. You always said you wanted space to read and think. Now's your time. Just read somewhere outside the library for a change. Feel the sun. Enjoy the mountain air. Sit in the rose garden."

Isa narrowed her eyes. Blanca was right; she did spend all her time in the library. But she was not quite so blind as her maid was making out. She had noticed that Aden spent a considerable amount of time each morning in the rose garden.

What was Blanca implying?

Once again, Isa was reminded of her mother's words about the trustworthiness of their servants. She inhaled, studying their faces in the soft glow of the lantern's light. They were completely serious, and she knew they would never lie to her.

"So, no drastic measures yet in terms of our guest?" Isa asked.

Blanca and Luca shook their heads.

"And the two of you feel safe with the way things are right now?"

Blanca and Luca nodded.

"I trust the two of you," Isa whispered. "I do not trust this beast, but I trust you. I'll keep my eyes open and pay attention to the air in front of my nose. I guess this meeting is concluded. Let's get back to bed."

Luca picked up the lantern and led the way back down the tower staircase.

That meeting had not gone according to her plan, but apparently Isa was missing something about this beast. She was determined to find out what it was.

Hopefully she did not get her head torn off in the meantime.

The following morning, she did not go straight to the library. Instead, she went to sit by a window overlooking the rose garden.

It was a beautiful morning. The sun peeked over the mountains, spreading long shadows in its wake. Rather than dry out everything in its path, as happened in the city, the light fell on lush green plants that had plenty of access to cool air and water in the mountain climate. Just the sight of the beautiful morning made Isa feel like running out to the garden herself and singing at the top of her lungs.

But on this particular morning, she contented herself with enjoying the view, for she had other plans.

As was his habit, the beast soon appeared below her, walking through the rose bushes and carefully smelling the individual blooms.

Isa smiled, backing away from the window. Tiptoeing on stockinged feet, she wound her way to the west wing and silently opened the door of the beast's room. The servants usually slept in this half of the villa, but she had invited them to sleep on the family's side in the east wing to keep them further from their guest.

The modest room was comfortably furnished and clearly inhabited. The blankets on the bed had been clumsily straightened, the wardrobe door was slightly ajar, and a leather pack lay open on the side table.

A small feeling of guilt gnawed at her, but she pushed it away. This was her villa, and she had a right to know who—or what—was occupying it.

She started with the wardrobe. A loose shirt, larger than any she had ever seen, was tossed over the center rod. She had not realized until this moment that the beast had been wearing the same waistcoat and breeches every day. At least he had a second undershirt.

She turned to the table, pausing to ensure no lumbering footsteps were coming down the hall.

All was silent.

The rucksack held nothing unusual. A few slices of dried meat, an empty water skin, and a few coins. No letters, parchments, or special trinkets.

The only remotely unique item in the room was a single rose, standing tall in a jar of water.

It was stunning.

She examined it more closely. It was the most perfectly delicate bloom she had ever seen.

And it was absolutely not from the bushes in the courtyard.

The mountain roses were small, fluttery blossoms on twisted, thorny branches. This beautiful specimen was large and full, its petals perfectly nestled within each other, rippling out to a bold open blossom. Even the stem was tall and straight, adorned with only a few pointed thorns.

Lifting the rose from the jar, Isa cupped her hand beneath the blossom and brought it to her face. The velvety petals brushed her skin as she inhaled its scent. It was glorious. She closed her eyes. The soft aroma reminded her of sunny days and flowing streams and picnics in a grassy field. Nothing about the scent was too bright or overpowering, as it was on some roses. This aroma was soft and delicate and completely full. She inhaled again, perfectly happy to smell this scent for the rest of her life.

"PUT. THAT. DOWN."

Isa clenched the rose, guilt and anger flushing her cheeks as she turned to face the beast.

His hulking frame filled the doorway, so much so that he had to duck his head to fit under it. His shoulders were hunched as he reached toward her, claws extended. One paw gripped a bouquet of freshly picked roses. His animalistic eyes flashed bright yellow in anger.

Though the power of his voice was yet again strong enough to shake every piece of furniture in the room, Isa was better prepared to face it this time. She refused to be intimidated.

"How dare you speak to me like that in my own home." She shook the rose at the beast to emphasize her words.

"Put that down," he repeated. His eyes tracked every movement of her hand, as though he were a dog waiting for her to toss him a scrap of food. A deep rumble growled from his throat.

It was a sound Isa had not heard from him before. It held menace and a threat. Rather than scare her, it fueled her desire for control. "What are you hiding from me?" she asked, holding the rose out of his reach. "So what if you've been cursed? You're a prince. Your family has access to every physician and even direct access to the Council!"

He slowly inched toward her, his feral eyes still glued to the rose.

The mention of the Council had triggered an anger deep

within her, and she squeezed the stem of the rose, shaking it again. "They wouldn't threaten your father with imprisonment for something he could not deliver! He's a king! They would bend over backward to have their examiners heal you. Why did you run? What are you hiding from me?!"

The beast had stopped moving just out of reach. The quiet rumble in his throat turned into a roaring growl as he launched himself forward without warning.

Isa shrieked, uselessly holding the rose as high as she could reach.

The beast's body slammed into hers as he wrapped one arm around her, keeping them both on their feet. His other hand easily plucked the rose from her grasp.

Once again, Isa struggled to breathe. It was not because he was holding her too tightly; rather it felt like her heart had leapt into her mouth, blocking off her throat.

As soon as the rose was safely in his grasp, he released her.

She stumbled away from him, attempting to inhale. Her tiny breaths seemed unable to move past the lump in her throat.

"Never touch this rose again," the beast said as he placed it back in the jar of water. His voice was calm, and he was standing tall. All that remained of the ferocious beast from moments before was the fur on his body. He turned back toward her, holding the jar and rose protectively against his chest.

"Never touch me again," she spat, backing away from him as her lungs finally received air.

"Gladly," he responded.

Isa slowly worked her way toward the door. She was not ready to admit defeat, but she did want an easy escape route. "What are you hiding?" she asked again.

"Nothing that concerns you," he responded. "Thank you for

your gracious hospitality, but it is no longer safe for me to remain here. I will be taking my leave in the morning."

"No longer safe for you?" Her voice was incredulous.

He waved a paw at the floor. It was littered with a few broken roses. "I picked those this morning to offer as an apology for yelling at you the other night. I'm afraid that apology is rather useless at the moment, but I would like to extend it to you regardless. I lost my temper, and I should not have roared at you."

"Does this apology also extend to the yelling that just happened?" Isa could hear the recklessness in her own voice. Part of her mind screamed at her in warning. If she was not careful, she would end up on the floor like the broken roses. But she was still not ready to cower in fear. The fact that he had twice attacked her without so much as scratching her fueled her defiance.

"I haven't decided yet." The beast had scrunched the fur above his eyes. "I feel rather justified about that, and I'm not going to ask forgiveness about something I do not feel sorry for."

Isa nodded, accepting that explanation. She felt strangely calm inside, as though she were somehow disconnected from what was happening around her. "Where will you go?" she asked.

He shrugged. "Deeper into the mountains."

"There is nothing deeper in the mountains."

"I know."

"Well," Isa said. She was confused by his course of action, but she had no reason to deter him from it. "Goodbye, then."

The wild yellow of his eyes had calmed to a regular brown. He blinked at her for a moment, then squeezed his eyes shut.

This motion annoyed her. It was as though he were trying to

commit her image to memory. A movement at his chest caught her attention, and she dropped her eyes to the rose in his hands.

A single petal gently detached from the base of the blossom. Slowly, seemingly lighter than air, it danced its way to the ground.

The beast released a slow sigh, as though pained in some long-suffering battle of patience. "Goodbye," he whispered.

CHAPTER 21

*I*sa narrowed her focus on the leather square in front of her. She confidently scraped across certain areas of the leather's softer side with a piece of dyed wax. It left clean lines and markings to denote where the various stitches and pieces of the cover should be placed.

He was leaving.

She should be glad. She was glad.

But she could not get him out of her head. Why would he go deeper into the mountains? If he made it through the mountain range, he would eventually find Chendas to the southeast. But no one traveled through the mountains to get to Chendas; they went around them.

Was it right to let him set out into dangerous unknown territory? Her personal wants struggled against her conscience. If she continued working—and said nothing—then Blanca would fill his sack with whatever food they had to spare. And she would never have to see him again. They had already bid each other farewell.

However, would she be able to sleep that night knowing that

somewhere, cold and alone, Aden the beast was attempting to sleep on the hard ground?

He was a *beast*. He didn't need her help or her opinions. No one ever wanted her opinions, except for her father. And he was the one who should be her sole concern at the moment.

She looked down at the leather in front of her, trying to remember how she had added the measurements to arrive at the distance between the markings.

She needed to focus, but her ears kept listening for the clapping sound of the doors in the great hall. Had he left yet? Should she go down to the kitchen just to see?

A knock sounded on the door.

Grateful for the distraction, she hurried to open it. The beast stood before her, holding three roses.

Isa was genuinely relieved to see him. She was not sure she should invite him to stay, but at least her conscience could stop bugging her.

"Lady Bielsa," he said, "I have never been particularly good at making apologies." His brown eyes looked down at her as he stumbled over his words. "To be honest, I have not had many opportunities in my life to do so. I am sorry for, uh, pouncing on you this morning and yelling at you. Again."

She tentatively accepted the proffered flowers. "Are you actually sorry about what happened this morning?" she asked, recalling his earlier words.

He raised his eyebrows.

Isa noticed how, despite the fur that covered his entire face, he had two distinct streaks of darker, longer fur above his eyes.

Blinking his eyes shut, he shook his head.

"At least you're honest about it." She stepped back so that he could enter the room. If he had come back up to talk to her, she was at least open to one final conversation.

He followed her in. The leather pack from his room was

slung over one shoulder. It looked full.

"I should apologize as well," she said. Approaching her work table, she set the roses on the side of it, out of the way. She turned back to face him. "I should not have made that rude comment about your family the other night," she said.

He nodded.

Isa could think of nothing further to say. "So, you are leaving?"

He nodded again.

"Be safe . . ." she started to say, but then stopped. Now was her chance. He might scoff at her opinion, but if she did not speak up now then she would regret it later. She hated the feeling of regret. "Actually, I can't say that truthfully. The deep mountains are not safe, especially for one man traveling alone. If you are trying to reach Chendas, then you should go on the route around the northern peaks. It's longer in terms of distance, but it will save you time in the end. Just travel south down the canyon until you can find a way to safely cross the river and get back to the main road."

He nodded. Again. "Thank you."

Her shoulders relaxed. He had not contradicted her or used his own opinion to refute hers. "Blanca gave you food?"

His wolf-like jaw spread into a small smile. "More than enough."

Again, at a loss for what to say, Isa merely stood there awkwardly.

He did the same. His eyes roamed around the room, then came back to land on her. He bowed a small bow. "Thank you again for your generous hospitality."

She nodded. "Of course. Thank you for . . ." She closed her mouth.

"For not eating you?" he finished for her.

"No! I mean, yes." She looked down in embarrassment.

Despite his terrifying appearance, he had proven multiple times that he had no intent of hurting them.

"Goodbye." He turned and walked away from her.

She watched the back of his head, glad that she had offered him advice but oddly sorry to see him go.

At the doorway, he stopped, placing a paw against the door-frame. After the space of a few breaths, he turned back to face her. "This morning," he said, "when you said the Council wouldn't threaten my family . . . what did you . . . Did they threaten your family? Is that why the Foutast is so important?"

Isa narrowed her eyes.

He seemed completely serious, concerned even.

"I don't know that I can, or should, respond to that," she said. She turned back to her work table. She didn't *not* trust him, but she couldn't afford to speak ill of the Council.

"Can I sit here for a moment before I head out?" he asked.

Isa nodded. "Yes." She opened a jar of her father's new gum paste and laid out the tools she would need to start building the first cover.

Behind her, the beast pulled out a chair and sat down, setting his pack aside. "Shouldn't you put those in some water?" he asked, pointing to the roses lying on the table beside her.

"Is it important that I keep them alive?" she asked, confused.

"Well, no, you can do whatever you like with them," he responded. "But supposing you did want to keep them alive for as long as possible, what would you do?"

"Put them in water," she responded. It seemed as though he just wanted to delay his departure.

"That's it?"

"That's all I know of caring for cut flowers. If you don't want them to die, then you shouldn't pick them in the first place."

He nodded.

She turned back to her work table and once again stared at

the leather in front of her. Flustered, she twisted the square around to view the markings from a different angle.

She picked up the jar of paste again, but her mind refused to focus. She could not apply the quick-drying glue unless she was clearly focused. No matter how hard she tried to ignore them, she kept noticing the roses on the side of the table. Perhaps if she put them in some water, she could focus.

She made a quick dash to the kitchen for an empty jar. As she reentered the library, the beast looked up from his book. His squinted eyes tracked her movement in a feral way, making her feel like his prey.

"Stop that," she said, angrily giving him a wide berth as she made her way back to her work table.

"Stop what?" he asked.

"Staring at me!"

"I was just trying to make out your face," he responded, his eyes still glued to her.

"Why does everyone stop to stare at my face?"

"Is something wrong with it?" he asked innocently.

"I wish there was!" she said, hoping he had rested enough to get up and leave.

The beast stood from his chair, lifting it easily from the back and rotating it. When he sat back down, his back was facing her work table.

Isa stared at him for a few moments. That was not exactly what she'd had in mind, but it was surprisingly effective. The simple fact that he was not staring at her instantly calmed her racing heart.

With the roses sitting happily in water and the glaring gaze of the beast removed, she could focus on her work.

Lifting the jar of paste again, she vigorously stirred its contents to recombine the liquid with the heavier resins.

"That smells odd," the beast said. Getting up from his chair, he sniffed loudly as he crossed the room to her worktable.

"It's the binding agent for the hardcover," she said.

"I watched your father at work in Chendas," the beast said. "His craftsmanship was incomparable. If I recall correctly, though, the paste he was using had a, uh, softer smell to it."

"That would have been the old wheatpaste glue," Isa responded. She handed him a different jar.

He sniffed it, the whiskers on his nose fluttering with the slightest movement. "Ah, yes, that is more familiar. So, what are you using now?" He handed the jar back to her.

Isa turned away from him, spending longer than necessary arranging the jar amid the items on the other end of the table. She was suddenly reticent to share her knowledge. Why should she explain a concept if he was just going to talk over her with some fact he learned while studying in Chendas?

As if noting her discomfort, the beast turned his back to the table and promptly sat down on the floor. He leaned back, resting the back of his head against the edge of the table.

"What are you doing?" Isa asked.

"Not staring at you."

"Thank you?" Isa said, unable to stop herself from staring at the back of his head. The thick brown fur looked unruly and soft. He was definitely less menacing from this angle. And once again, his gesture had a similar effect. Her breathing calmed.

"Do you mind telling me about the new paste you are using? Is it better?" he asked. "I am genuinely interested."

"Previous attempts in binding proved unstable because the wheat paste can subject parchment to decay," she said, continuing to stir the glue in her hand. "This made my father's work rather useless, if the process he developed to protect these works only accelerated the chance of destroying them from the inside out." She paused.

Aden sat quietly, listening.

She breathed. "He has been experimenting with a new type of resin made from the sap of an Etrarian tree," she continued. "This new resin is supposed to help the paste dry completely but produce a less brittle texture."

"And it has been working better?" Aden asked.

"It seems to be safer for the parchment. However, it dries more quickly, sometimes too quickly, making it more difficult to fix mistakes later on in the process. One should only apply it on a book if they can give the project their full concentration."

"Are you applying it now?" he asked.

"I'm about to start," she responded.

"Then I shall stop distracting you." He stood, turning to face the table. "Thank you for explaining that. You have your father's skill in more than one respect."

Isa looked down, her cheeks unexpectedly warm.

"How is your father?" the beast asked. "I hope he is well?"

"Actually . . ." Isa looked back up at him. "He is not. I am here to fetch the Floutast in his stead."

"I'm sorry to hear that," the beast replied. "I should have asked about him much earlier. It must be difficult to be away from your family, then, with no way to get back quickly."

Isa nodded. A lump was forming in her throat, and she did not trust herself to speak.

The beast turned again and sat with his back to the table. "The Majis who cursed me was a councilor from Chendas," he said. "The rose that you were holding this morning was . . . is part of the curse."

Isa set the jar of paste on the table in front of her. "I take it I should not apply the glue right now?"

He chuckled, the warming rumble a comforting contrast to the gravity of his words. "You are right not to trust me."

She stared at the back of his head, visible above the tabletop.

"My father has more recently been doubting the Council's

ability to provide any safety for our kingdom when the Majis do return. It was quite a shock to realize that a Councilor was secretly a magic-wielder. It would be just as shocking to learn that the Council has stooped so low as to threaten the quotidian without the knowledge of noble families."

Isa listened intently, trying to understand all the information he was offering her. "How does the rose fit into all this?"

He dropped his head, looking at the floor. "When the last petal falls . . . when the rose dies . . . I go with it."

Horrified, Isa ran around the table, dropping to her knees in front of him to see his face. "You are not planning on going to Chendas?"

He shook his head, refusing to look at her.

"Oh, Aden, I am so sorry." She wanted to reach out to him, to comfort him. But what could she say in the face of such a hopeless destiny? "And I was standing there, shaking the rose like an idiot! I'm so sorry."

Aden's claws slid in and out of his paws as he clenched his hands.

She reached out to place her hand on his, but the image of a single rose petal floating to the ground came into her head, and she pulled her hand back in humiliation. "The petal that fell, I caused that." Heat flooded her face, and she dropped her own head.

A soft paw nudged her chin, encouraging her to look up.

"Don't blame yourself for that," he said, his eyes blinking away tears. "I am fairly sure it was my own anger that caused the petal to fall."

"But your anger was entirely justified," Isa responded. "How would that have caused a petal to fall?"

Aden shrugged. "It's a Majis curse. It thrives on chaos." He pulled himself to his feet and went to retrieve his leather sack. "It is time for me to go. I have tarried too long."

den swung his pack over his shoulder. As the weight settled onto his back, he felt oddly lighter.

He was glad he had told Isa the truth about what had happened concerning the rose that morning. While he had grown more accustomed to his beastly body, he resented even more the idea that someone might view him as nothing more than an animal.

He turned to her to say his final goodbye, but they were both distracted by footsteps running down the hall.

"They made it!" Luca yelled before he was even in view. "Macklin and Cam made it to the village! They're on the other side of the canyon."

"Come on!" Isa said, her voice filled with joy and relief. "Let's go!"

Aden followed them down the hill outside the mansion, slowing his pace to match theirs.

Sure enough, on the other side of the canyon, a group of people waved at them.

"Hello! Hello!" Isa called over to them.

He flinched as her sudden yell pierced his ears.

"Hello!" one of them called back. Aden thought it might be the cook, Cam, who had left with Macklin. "How are you holding up over there?"

"What?" Isa yelled back, cupping her hands around her mouth. "We can't hear you!" She turned to Luca and Blanca, who had followed them from the house. "Could you hear that?"

"He asked how you are holding up," Aden said.

"Good!" Isa yelled back over the canyon, waving her hands above her head in excitement. "Can you hear us?"

"Yes!" came the faint response from across the canyon.

Isa turned to Aden to see what the answer had been.

Aden nodded. "They can hear us."

"It must be the wind," Luca observed. "It's carrying our voices over to them, but dispersing their voices before they can reach us."

"Except for Aden," Isa corrected him. "The sound can reach Aden's ears." She turned to Aden. "Ask them when they will start building."

Aden shook his head. His voice might be loud, but it was deep. The rumbling of the river below would completely wash over it. "You do the asking; your voice will carry better in the wind." He did not mention that the thought of communicating with other humans terrified him.

"When will you start building the bridge?" Isa yelled.

"Soon!" the man responded. "Mr. Surrell continued back to Allys to alert your parents. We'll start with the supplies we have available, but he will be back with better resources!"

Aden relayed the information back to the group.

"Do you need us to send someone back the long way with food?" the man yelled across at them. Aden felt further justified in his guess that the man was Cam. Trust a cook to think of food.

Aden forwarded Cam's question to Luca, who looked at Blanca. They shook their heads simultaneously.

"I think we are doing just fine," Blanca said.

"They should focus their manpower on construction," Luca confirmed.

Isa shouted this information back across the river.

"Are you safe?" came the final question from the other side.

Even though Aden knew the question was justified, he deflated. He dropped his face to the ground, closing his eyes as he repeated the question to Isa, Luca, and Blanca. He did not want to see their reactions.

"Yes!" Isa shouted instantly.

Aden felt a small touch on his arm, and he opened his eyes to see Isa's hand resting just below his elbow. For the second time that morning, tears stung at his eyelids.

"Don't go," she said. Her whisper was so quiet, he wondered if he had imagined it. He tried to focus on her face, but she had turned back to the canyon. "Thank you!" she yelled.

Aden lagged behind the small group as they made their way back up the hill to the house.

Blanca practically danced up the road. "I thought they would never make it," she said. "But that Mr. Surrell, he pulled through for us. I'm so glad our Cam went with him. He likely never would have made it without Cam. I was so worried, but they did just fine. And now everything will be alright."

Even Luca seemed to walk with a new spring in his step. At least, he had not yet grumbled about the pain in his old knees.

Isa turned to face Aden, dropping back a step or two to walk alongside him. "Stay here," she whispered. She placed her hand on his arm once again, and Aden instantly knew he would do whatever she asked him. "You don't need to face this alone," she continued. "Blanca and Luca will be on your side, I'm sure of it."

"And you?" he asked, staring down at her upturned face, wishing against all odds that he could see the color of her eyes or the shape of her lips.

"I'm on your side, too," she whispered.

He smiled down at her, but the relief in his heart was short-lived. She still didn't understand what she was inviting into her home.

She had started pulling forward, pressing to join Luca and Blanca.

He reached out, gently brushing her upper arm.

She stopped and looked back up at him.

He stopped moving altogether, waiting until the two chatting servants were out of earshot. "I still have to go," he said. The admission of that fact tore through his beastly heart. "When this ends . . . when the last petal falls . . . I will likely become dangerous to those around me. That's why I left my family and why I cannot stay here."

"How many petals have fallen?" she asked.

"Three."

"In how many days? Fourteen?"

"Fifteen," he confirmed.

"Prince Aden of Iseldis," she replied, "I saw that rose with my own eyes. It easily has twenty petals or more remaining. Three petals fell in two weeks. You do the math." She shook her head. "You do not have to leave today. I'm willing to bet that you can safely stay until the bridge is finished. Besides, we'll need someone to help us communicate with the villagers in the meantime. Stay."

Aden let himself be led back to the house. She was right. If the rose continued to decay at its current rate, he would still have plenty of time.

But he was too afraid to admit to himself that some things were still in danger of being hurt if he stayed.

He sighed.

If he could not protect his own heart, he could at least attempt to protect hers.

CHAPTER 23

When Isa woke the next morning, she knew the garden was calling her. The Floutast needed to be worked on, but her relief that the villagers were finally starting to build the bridge had given her a new hope. She had made too many small mistakes yesterday. If she did not stop for a breather, her work would only get clumsier.

Although her southern-facing window did not get direct sunlight in the morning, she could still see its golden glow sparkling down on the green deciduous trees outside her window.

Yes, the garden was calling her this morning.

Quickly putting on one of the simple dresses she had brought from home, she grabbed a book from the stack on her table. It was a collection of stories from a whimsical Iseldis writer. The author's name was male, but her father had told her the stories were actually written by a woman, which made Isa appreciate them all the more. She could find precious few books written by women.

The courtyard was dazzling in its morning glory. The crisp

air promised another warm day, but the heat had not yet arrived. Birds sang to each other across the treetops while little squirrels dashed across the pathways, jumping between the safety of the bushes.

A puppy yelp sounded from the rose garden, and she followed the sound to investigate.

Warrior was huddled on his front paws in front of a bush, no doubt waiting for a squirrel to make a reappearance. "Be nice," she scolded. "They just want to get their breakfast, same as you."

She looked past the pup to glance through the empty rose garden.

Aden was nowhere to be seen.

Isa tried not to feel disappointed. She had come to the garden for her own benefit, not to see him.

Walking past a wooden bench, she chose instead to sink into the small patch of grass beside it. The grass was lightly warmed, cushioned with moss, and without a single droplet of dew. It truly was the perfect morning.

Isa opened her book and let herself get lost.

When she eventually pushed open the library door, her heart and mind felt aligned and more peaceful than they had in some days. Reading really was magical.

However, what she saw when she entered the library was not what she'd been expecting.

The circle of chairs near the fireplace had all been pushed aside except for one, which sat in front of a small table. A single leaf of parchment rested on the side of the table along with a quill and ink.

"Ah, there you are." Aden stepped into view from behind a shelf of books. "I was about to start the exam without you. Tardiness will not be tolerated."

"Exam?"

"Sit!" Aden raised his voice, pointing at the chair and table. "I will be the one asking the questions here! The Circle of Scholars sent me, their most highly respected member, to conduct your final exams." He paced back and forth, elaborating on his words with dramatic hand gestures. "They value the important work you are already undertaking and have thus decided to allow your exams to take place outside of their normal process."

Isa grinned and took her place at the table. "I am afraid I was not informed of this generous offer from the Circle," she said, playing along, "so I have had no time to study in preparation."

"Silence!" Aden spun to face her. "A true scholar is always ready to discuss their opinion, studied or not."

"My apologies," Isa replied, folding her hands on the table in front of her. "I am more than ready to take this exam, Professor . . . ?"

"Professor Aden the Wise." Aden scratched the back of his neck as though pretending to be flattered. "That's how I'm known in the scholarly circles, you see."

Isa snorted as she attempted to hold in her laughter.

"Let us begin!" Aden announced. "Start with your full name in the upper corner of the parchment you will find on your desk."

Isa positioned the sheet of parchment in front of her and dipped the waiting feather in the pot of ink. She carefully wrote her name in the upper corner of the parchment as instructed, looking up when she had finished.

Aden stepped forward, lifting the parchment from her desk.

"Are you already checking my work, Professor?" she asked, surprised. "It's just my name."

"It is imperative to ensure you have no opportunity to swindle the scholars. I must check your every answer." He squinted at the paper. "Hmmm. The margin for error is too large." He crumpled the parchment and tossed it into the empty fireplace.

"I messed up my name?" Isa asked incredulously.

"No, but we will continue this exam in spoken word rather than written word." He sniffed, brushing a mop of fur away from his eyes.

"Of course, Professor Aden the Wise, I would never want to be caught cheating my exams. The horror!" She gasped dramatically.

"Excellent. Now, your name."

"My name again? In the upper corner of the air?"

Aden peered down at her over his long, whiskered nose. "Are you mocking me?"

"No, no. I would never dare. It is an honor to have you seated over my exam. My name is Isabel Bielsa."

"Isabel? Isa is short for Isabel?" His face spread into a true smile. "I-S-A-B-E-L?"

"Yes, did you not realize that?"

"No." He shook his head. "Isabel Bielsa." He said her full name to himself, rolling it over his tongue. "That's fascinating."

Isa smiled in confusion. She was quite tired of men complimenting her appearance, but no one had ever called her name fascinating before. "Fascinating?"

"I-S-A-B-E-L and B-I-E-L-S-A. Those are the same letters in both of your names, just scrambled in different ways. That's so clever."

Isa laughed. It was a quiet laugh, a genuine laugh that started in her stomach and melted her face into a smile. "Yes, yes, it is. I've always thought it was quite unique, but no one else has ever noticed it before."

"That's probably because you've never met anyone quite as wise as myself." Aden sniffed again, returning to his professor persona.

"Is that one of the exam questions?" she asked. "If so, my answer is no, I have never met someone quite as wise as you."

"Excellent, I'll give you full marks on that question." He puffed out his chest, lifting his shoulders high. "Now, for the real questions. Can you name the three most influential writers from each of the five kingdoms?"

Isa answered his question quickly and easily.

"Which of these is your favorite and why?"

The questions continued, some of them frivolous but most of them serious. Isa laughed as Aden slipped in and out of his character, joining her in conversation when they hit a particularly interesting topic.

It had been some time since her mind had been challenged in such a way, and she enjoyed the process of remembering her studies and parsing what she thought of them.

When Luca knocked on the door to deliver the noonday meal, they finally stopped to eat together.

"Is that really what the exams were like?" she asked.

"Yes," Aden responded, "except with much less laughing. You would have passed them easily." He set down the carrot he had been munching. "I am sorry you were never invited to take your final exams in Chendas. If I ever make it into the Circle of Scholars, I will ensure that you get the chance to do so, even if it has never been done before."

"Thank you," she said. The smile on her face, however, disappeared as she realized what he had said. He must have momentarily forgotten that he would never have the chance to vie for one of the enviable chairs in the Circle of Scholars.

His downcast eyes told her that he had just remembered his unfortunate circumstance as well.

"This helped, though," she said, hoping to distract him. "Even if it was a fake exam, it lessened the sting of having missed out on the real one. Thank you."

That brought his eyes back up to hers. He blinked

frequently, as he often did when looking at her. Somehow, it did not bother her as much in that moment.

"I wonder if someone will write a legend about us, someday," he said.

"What do you mean?"

"Here we are, striving for the impossible. Me, against an absurd curse. You, against a necessary power that is unjustly threatening your father."

"I'd rather not have a legend written about us," she replied. "Not if it is going to end in sadness, though I can't see how it won't."

"Yours is not a hopeless goal," Aden replied. "You are continuing to make progress on the Floutast, and the villagers are starting construction on the new bridge. We can ensure that you, at least, have a happy ending."

Isa looked at the man sitting across from her. His bushy dark brows were furrowed in concern, and his yellow-brown eyes were focused on her. Instead of wallowing in his own despair, he was thinking of her.

Even if she did get the Floutast back in time, she wondered if she would feel like she had accomplished a happy ending. "I am beginning to understand the choice that Andrew had to make," she said, referring to *The Queen of Silverreign*.

"What do you mean?" Aden asked.

"I still don't think I could choose to leave the one I loved on the eve of battle."

"Hopefully you never have to make that decision."

Isa nodded, hoping he was right but fairly sure he would be wrong.

"Mum is going to murder you!"

Aden squinted across the canyon in surprise. A tall figure dressed in a loud mix of bright blue and orange was on the opposite cliff. The more moderately dressed villagers around him nearly blended in with the surrounding landscape. A reliable group of workers had been at the edge of the canyon each day, constructing the foundation for their side of the bridge. This new figure, with the familiar voice and flamboyant clothing, could only belong to one person: his brother Erich.

Squinting across the canyon at his younger brother, Aden felt a warm glow in his chest. "You're alive?" he called back. He had not expected to see any member of his family again, much less his supposedly dead younger brother.

"Of course I am," Erich yelled. "Did you expect a measly rainstorm to do me in? I'm not as weak as you are, you ridiculous oaf! Do you have any idea how big of a fool you are?" He waved his arms wildly as he moved back and forth along the edge of the canyon.

The warm glow in Aden's chest started to disappear. It was

typical of Erich to insult him as loudly as possible in front of multiple people.

It had been seven days since construction had begun. Aden, along with Isa, Luca, and Blanca, had frequently walked down the hill to check on the progress. Today, however, it was only Isa at his side.

"Who is that new person?" Isa asked him. "What's he saying?"

"My brother," Aden responded. "I'll fill you in soon, he's still talking."

"What were you even thinking?" Erich continued, his dramatic voice easily carrying over the wide expanse between them.

Aden noticed a tall appendage sticking out of his brother's head. It swayed in the breeze, responding to Erich's movements. He couldn't quite make it out, but it appeared to be a long feather affixed to a wide-brimmed hat. Aden had never seen a feather that large before and had no idea how his brother had managed to source it. If they were going to talk about which one was the more ridiculous oaf, Erich should take a look in the mirror.

"Do you have any idea how devastated Mum was to find out you'd left?" He clearly did not expect an answer to his question as he carried on. "Not to mention the rest of us. I didn't sleep for nights, tossing and turning and worrying about you roughing it out in the woods. I, of course, would have been fine. I've recently had to endure far worse than a few nights out of doors and look at me now! But I could only imagine how wretched you felt, all alone . . . the *agony!*"

Aden glanced down at Isa, hoping she still could not hear any of this. Her face was turned toward his. She was probably burning with questions, but she remained quiet. Aden realized that she would enjoy hearing about Erich, and he found himself looking forward to discussing his younger brother with her.

But first, he had to get that brother to stop yelling embarrassing insults. "How did you find me?" Aden yelled.

"What was that?" Erich replied. "You'll have to speak up."

"How did you find me?"

"Oh, right. Rumors started spreading a few days ago about a ferocious talking monster in the mountains east of Iseldis. We could only assume they referred to you, so I changed course on my way to Chendas to give you a proper chewing out. I'm impressed that you managed to lie low for so long; we've had every web of people on the lookout in all five kingdoms. Dead silence for days. Although this bridge situation explains that." Erich stopped speaking. He stopped pacing as well. He appeared to be staring across the canyon. "Is that someone over there with you?"

"Yes!" Aden rubbed his throat. Yelling a handful of words across the river was already making his throat feel sore. He had no idea how Erich could continually monologue at such a volume.

"A woman? And you haven't scared her away with those vicious fangs? Hah. Impressive. You'll have to tell me your ways."

Aden squeezed his lungs, a low growl hovering in his throat. His brother was lucky they were separated by a wide chasm. "Shut your lip if you know what's good for you," Aden yelled, allowing some of the growl in his throat to accompany the words.

Isa placed a calming hand on his arm. He patted it comfortingly. He was not truly angry, just annoyed.

Erich stopped moving again, likely drawing out his face in mock hurt. "Hold your anger, dear brother. It looks as though this pulley system will be able to ferry men across in a day or two. I'll find some suitable lodging on this side and come over as soon as I can. I have news. And it's not great. I wouldn't want to shout it across here for all the village to hear."

Aden raised a hand above his head in acknowledgment. It was not as though his brother had been shouting his personal business for the past ten minutes for the entire village to hear.

"Your brother?" Isa asked. "He seems like quite the interesting fellow. What did he say?"

"Do you have any siblings, Isabel?" Aden had taken up the habit of saying her full name whenever he had the chance. He loved the way it danced across his tongue, and she had not asked him to stop.

"I do, a younger sister."

"Do you love her dearly but sometimes feel like boxing her across the ears?"

Isa laughed.

Despite the fact that she was standing so close to him, her laugh soothed him rather than bothered him. He loved the sound of it.

"That is an apt description," she responded.

"So then, you understand," he replied. "That was Erich. My younger brother."

"He looked excited to have found you," Isa said, staring back over the canyon at the building crew. "I take it your family is a little miffed at you right now?"

"That about sums it up." Aden sighed. "The foundation on that side is nearly ready. They'll have a rope pulley connected to this side in a few days that will be strong enough to ferry him across. You'll get the pleasure of meeting him yourself."

"Should I be looking forward to this meeting?"

"It won't be dull, that's for sure," Aden responded. "It will be good to see another human, won't it? Oh, he said he has news and it's not good. I don't know what that means, but I suppose we will find out soon enough."

"Mhhh." Isa stared across the canyon. "He gave no indication what it was about?"

Aden shook his head. "Shall we head back?"

"I brought a book," Isa responded, holding up a hardcover tome. "I'm going to stay down here and read while I watch the progress. Perhaps . . ." She stopped speaking, but it sounded as though she had more left to say.

Aden waited for her to finish her thought, hoping she would ask him to join her.

She said nothing further.

"You deserve the rest," he said when the silence grew awkward. "Enjoy it."

"I will."

Was he imagining it, or did she sound disappointed? Aden forced himself to turn his back and walk up the hill. He could ask her to read aloud to him—he could not think of a more delightful way to spend the afternoon—but he knew he had to be smarter than that. Their time was short. The bridge would be completed soon, and she would leave to fulfill her responsibility to the Council.

He went back to his room, the intoxicating scent of the rose hitting his nostrils as soon as he stepped inside. Another petal had fallen that morning. He focused as well as he could on the brown blossom. He had been noting the subtle differences in the few colors he could see, and even though his eye saw the color brown, his mind now registered the rose as red. He could not count the remaining petals, but there were still enough that he could see the bloom, which was a good sign.

Uncomfortable with the tight walls in his room, he made his way to the library. Erich's arrival was upsetting. An abrupt reminder of the outside world. The past few days had seen him fall into a rhythm of normal that he was loath to part with.

Isa had worked diligently on her task, making two of the

scrolls into sturdy bound books ready for travel. She would easily have the final book complete by the time the bridge was done. Aden had spent lazy mornings chatting with her in the library, asking her about different elements of her craft and discussing the stories and writings that had moved them most.

In the afternoons, he often sought Blanca, either interrupting her work with his clumsy attempts to help her or listening to her stories—many of which centered on Isa as a child.

Luca was less inclined to share words with him, but Aden tried to make use of his own brute strength in service of things the older man struggled with.

He paced through the room. The books on the library shelves mocked him, inviting him to escape into their pages when they knew he could not.

The bridge was not done yet, he reminded himself. The rose still valiantly held some of its petals.

He ran the sensitive skin of his soft paw pads along a row of books, feeling the texture, smelling the leather, imagining the contents.

Isa would be back soon, and he would do his best to help her finish her task. He had some time left, and he intended to use it to the best of his ability.

He settled into a comfortable chair in the library. The quiet sound of the rustling leaves from the trees outside seeped through the stone walls of the large room, lulling him to sleep.

He awoke, cozy but disoriented, to the persistent patter of rain on the tall glass windows.

He looked up, surprised. The weather had been warm earlier, but they were in the mountains where things were likely to change. He recalled his first night at the villa when Isa had thrown him out into a light drizzle, which had quickly turned into a raging downpour strong enough to cause a flash flood that carried away the bridge.

The bridge. Isa was at the canyon. Had she returned? How long had it been raining?

Jumping from the chair, he raced out of the library.

He inhaled through his nose as he moved through the eastern wing. He could neither smell Isa's unique scent nor hear her light footfall or confident voice.

He pushed through the double doors of the great hall and stepped out into the rain. It was pouring.

"Isabel!" he called, projecting his voice as loudly as he could. "Isabel!"

The sound of rushing liquid filled his ears. Whether it was the water rising in the canyon down the hill or merely the blood rushing through his eardrums, he could not tell. All he knew was that it fueled his fear.

"Isabel!" He ran down the road, wiping the rain from his eyes as he went.

The falling water deprived him of both scent and sound, barraging his senses with its presence. He focused his eyes on the road ahead, scanning the ground for movement.

"Isabel!" His heart thumped, threatening to overpower even his eyesight. Fear pulsed through him as he struggled to focus through the hazy shadows pressing against his vision. "No, no!" he roared to the emptiness around him. His vision was returning to the state it had been when he'd first woken up to the curse. "Isabel!!"

The canyon was almost in view now. The rushing sound in his ears grew louder.

He saw a movement on the side of the path before he fully recognized the shape of her body. She was on her hands and knees, attempting to lift herself off the ground.

She was covered in blood.

"Isabel!" he howled, a deep, primal roar. All he could see was the deep, bright red of her blood. Its metallic scent, mixed with mud and water, hit his nostrils as he arrived at her side.

In a single smooth motion, he scooped her off the ground, then ran back up the hill as fast as he dared.

He could feel the thick, sticky substance of her blood pulling against his fur as she clung to him.

He could not see her face, but her arms were firm around his neck, holding him tightly.

His lungs begged for air as he pushed himself back up the hill. He growled out a fear-filled sob.

"Aden! Aden."

He was almost to the villa when he realized that she had been repeating his name.

"Listen to me, Aden!"

He kicked open the door, gently lowering his precious burden on the nearest sofa. He gasped for air, his eyes scanning her body in search of the wound.

"What happened?" he growled. "Who did this to you?"

"Nothing, no one." She grabbed his face between her hands, forcing him to still. "I slipped in the mud. I'm fine. What's wrong?"

"You are not fine!" he roared. "Where did all this blood come from?"

"What blood? There is no blood." She removed her hands from his face, her head lifting from the couch to examine her own body.

"Then what are you covered in?" Using the rounded side of one of his claws, Aden gently wiped some of the gooey substance from her arm. Bringing it to his nose, he sniffed it lightly. Dirt. Wet dirt. "It's mud," he breathed, licking it just in case. "Just mud."

Unable to hold himself up, he collapsed to his knees. Dropping his head against the side of the sofa, he gasped for air. He felt her hand on the back of his head.

"Aden, what's going on?" Her voice was quiet, confused.

"It's mud," he repeated, reassuring himself. "It's brown. Not red."

Slowly, his senses returned as his heart rate steadied to a normal pace. The feeling of her hand on the back of his anchored him as he breathed.

"Then why do I still smell blood?" He looked up alarmed, when the distinctly metallic scent once again hit his nostrils. Squinting his eyes, he scanned her body for wounds.

"I think I may have scraped my knee when I slipped, but I'm surprised you can smell that. It barely even scratched the skin."

"That's it? You are sure you are fine?"

"I'm more than fine. I simply slipped in a muddy spot and slid for a moment before catching myself. That's when you found me." She had pushed herself up to a sitting position. "The real thing we should be worried about is you. Are you alright? Why did you think I was covered in blood?"

Aden looked down again, hiding his face. "The curse," he said. "It increased my ability to hear and smell, but distorted my sight."

"In what ways?"

"Some colors are blurred," he muttered.

"Like the color of blood and the color of mud?" she asked.

He nodded. He felt her hand on his chin, raising his face to meet hers.

He cringed, embarrassed that she was touching his wolflike snout.

Her face was a blur in front of his eyes, but he could feel her gaze on him, and he attempted to make eye contact. Even though he was on his knees in front of the couch, his face was level with hers.

"It also makes some things hazy and blurred." He reached toward her face, not fully touching it. "Specifically, things that are closer to me. Things in the far distance are clear, but most objects within a room are too hazy for me to see in detail."

She waved her hand.

His eyes instinctively followed it back and forth, then returned to her face as he realized what she was doing. "I can see movement and basic shapes. But I can't make out details such as words or faces." His mouth was dry. He felt vulnerable and exposed explaining his weakness.

Her hand moved again, and his eyes instantly followed it. She reached up and touched her own face. "Then why do you always seem to be staring at my face?" she asked, sounding skeptical.

"I've been trying to make it out," he said, "because I can't see it clearly."

"You can't see it clearly?" She relaxed into the back of the sofa behind her. "You can't see my face." She sounded delighted.

"At the moment," he replied, "I dearly wish that I could see it, for I get the feeling that it is smiling quite broadly right now, only I can't tell if it is because of some sort of personal joy or if you are laughing at me and my plight."

"I'm not laughing at you," she reassured him. "What do you think I look like?"

"I don't know . . ." Aden said. "I haven't really thought of it."

Of course, he had thought of it. He had thought of it far more than he cared to admit over the last few days.

"Thoughtful," he said quietly, "wise, caring, a touch of fire in your eyes. Soft."

He reached forward and gently touched her cheek with the back of his hand. The sensation on his fur was like a light ripple, barely awakening his sense of touch. The soft pads on the front of his hands were far more sensitive. But as much as he longed to feel her face, he wouldn't dare desecrate her skin by touching it with his curse.

As his hand pulled away, she grasped it in both of her own, gently holding it on her lap between them and lightly stroking his fur.

"Fire in my eyes?" she repeated, making him feel ridiculous.

Why had he said that? He should have said beautiful, exquisite, or bewitching. Something at least remotely flattering.

"I like it," she said, inhaling a deep, satisfied breath. "That's the most wonderful thing anyone has ever said to me."

Aden was afraid to breathe. Afraid to move and shatter the moment.

Her hand stopped moving, and he could sense her eyes looking at him once again. "But you said that you cannot see enough detail to make out words. Does that mean you cannot read any more?"

"I cannot," he replied, feeling as though his last secret had been revealed.

"I cannot imagine being unable to read. That must be miserable. Why did you not tell me?"

Aden sighed, pulling his paw away from her hands. "I already felt so . . . broken. I did not want to shout my weaknesses to the world."

"To me," she corrected.

You are my world, Aden said in his head, wishing he had the courage to say it aloud, but knowing he had nothing to offer except for a few falling rose petals. He stood, breaking the closeness between them.

"I never thought of you as broken," she said, standing as well. "I am angry *for* you that you have been cursed by this awful burden, but I have been continually awed that you spend each day enjoying those around you. I would have crumbled completely under such a weight."

Aden wished he could see her face, but he breathed in the confidence of her words instead, letting them wash over him like a soothing rain.

"Let's go read something together, right now!" she said, her voice light and excited.

"Read something?" he repeated, trying to comprehend the fact that she still wanted to spend time with him even after he had exposed his weaknesses.

"I'll read to you, in the library. Come on." She pulled his arm toward the eastern hallway. "I might even let you choose the book!"

Aden smiled, her joy infecting him. "That sounds wonderful. Oh, wait, actually . . ." He paused, seeing the mud—not blood—on her dress. "Do you want to go get out of your wet clothes?"

She looked down. "I suppose I should, for the sake of the books. I had already forgotten. Meet you there!" She ran off, dancing up the steps and down the hallway.

He still had time—precious little time, but he would make the most of it.

CHAPTER 25

Isa returned to the library, her heart soaring. The Floutast was nearly ready for the Council. The bridge was nearly complete. And their beastly companion had turned out to be very much human after all.

She had been repeatedly repulsed by his constant staring, only to find that he had not been able to see her this entire time.

Maybe that was why her heart felt so light. She could talk to him truly, like a friend.

He was waiting for her at the crackling fireplace. "I asked Luca to light a small fire to fend of the damp," he said.

"Thank you," she responded. She had changed into a dry dress, but her braided hair was still quite damp. She sat down, suddenly feeling self-conscious. She had the sudden desire to continue their conversation, to learn more about his curse. They had argued so many times, yet they had shared very few genuine conversations. "Shall we . . . read?" she asked.

He nodded, seemingly at a loss as much as she was.

"You can choose the book," she said generously, "since it has been so long since you've had the pleasure."

His angular mouth smiled at that. "I choose Floutast," he confidently replied.

"I thought you hated Floutast?" she said, confused.

"I do. And I intend to continue hating him. But I want to see if perhaps I missed something in my earlier assessment. I am very intrigued as to why the Council is so intent on having it." He absently scratched above his pointed ears.

Isa stood and retrieved a newly bound book from her worktable. Settling back into a chair by the fire, she basked in its dry warmth. The crackling flames mixed with the rain pounding on the windows outside to create a cozy atmosphere in the old library.

Aden sat across from her, his massive shoulders hunched over the already-large chair.

"Let's start somewhere in the middle, then," Isa said, opening the book at random. The handwriting was thick and condensed in the typical style from that time, but she was used to parsing the subtle differences in letters and was soon reading freely.

Aden was right. This book was boring. It felt more like a marketplace ledger than a book. She plunged through several pages of supply lists and soldierly formations before closing it in frustration.

"I don't understand," she said. "What in the five kingdoms could the Council be looking for in this text?"

"Your voice is very soothing for reading aloud," Aden responded. "It is energetic but still in a low enough register not to grate on the ears."

"Thank you?" Isa responded. That had sounded like a compliment, unless her voice was grating at other times.

"What do you know of Floutast himself?" Aden asked.

"He was a marshal in the army," Isa replied, "but he paid a peasant to take his place on the battlefield and instead focused his time on writing reports to Queen Delphine. His books are mostly just compilations of that correspondence."

"Queen Delphine?" Aden interjected. "I thought he was later than that."

Isa shook her head. "No, he was in her army."

"So, he himself was a Majis," Aden said.

"Not necessarily," Isa replied. "Many in her troops were coerced into fighting for her."

"But he was a marshal and had enough means to keep himself off the battlefield. It is more likely than not that he was a Majis."

Isa nodded, considering his point. "That would make sense. But how does it change things?"

"I don't know," Aden sighed. "Keep reading a few more pages with that in mind?"

Instead of answering, Isa picked up the book again. She skipped forward a handful of pages and began to read from another place at random.

The content was the same. Boring.

"This is putting me to sleep." She yawned. "The lilting nature of his lists is almost poetical. Ten units of this, and ten barrels of that. They sent troops to accomplish this, and troops to accomplish that. It's like he can't mention one thing without mentioning it's opposite or complement."

"It's harmony," Aden said, sitting up.

"What?"

"It's harmony. If he was part of Queen Delphine's army, they would have been fighting with magic. It's as though he is reporting to the queen that they are keeping everything in balance and harmony."

"I thought you said the magic is based chaos?"

Aden's shoulders slumped back down again. "It is, at least insofar as the examiners have discovered. But there is another part we don't fully understand yet that relies on harmony. My . . . eyesight was worse immediately after the curse, but an old seamstress knew some magic from her ancestors. She went on about harmony canceling out chaos and sang over me, restoring some of my sight. The examiners must have discovered the harmony element of magic, which is why they are requesting the Floutast."

Suddenly, Isa felt too warm. She shifted away from the fire, still thinking about the middle part of what he had said. "You willingly let a Majis perform magic on you?"

Aden's eyes were focused on her, his pupils small and intense. "She restored my eyesight. It was completely different from the attack at the ball. It was calming, and healing."

Isa shook her head. Magic was evil, not to mention absolutely unlawful. "Then why did she not completely break this curse?"

"It cannot be broken," Aden said. "If it could be, I would not be here, hiding in the mountains." His voice was wistful, hopeless. The reminder of his condition instantly dampened his spirits.

Despite their light tension over the use of magic, Isa wanted to comfort him. She had been thinking about his curse, and Blanca's words from that night in the tower came to mind. "Are you sure about that?" she asked. "The curse in *The Queen of Silverreign* was broken when Andrew returned to Amelya, sacrificing his surprise inheritance and promising to take up her responsibility to her oppressed people."

"It's just a myth," Aden said, dismissing her words.

"A myth, a legend, a saga." Isa smirked as she spoke, recalling the same words he had used against her. "A story that is told for the purpose of passing on wisdom from one generation to the next."

His lips twitched as he recognized his own words.

"Say it was a story based on truth," she continued, "and he did use magic to break Amelya's curse. How did he do it?"

"I don't remember the details," he replied. "I wasn't particularly paying attention when I read it."

"Would he have used the magic of harmony or chaos?" Isa mused. "Could he even have been a Majis, though, to wield power? He started as a swineherd. I thought all Majis were nobles."

"If it really was based on truth," Aden said, "and he could wield magic, why did he not use it during the battle? He could have destroyed his enemy sooner and returned to help Amelya before she died. It just doesn't make sense for that part of the story to be true."

"I'm just making theories," Isa said defensively.

"Good theories," Aden replied. "I did not mean to discourage you."

"No, you are right. We do not have enough information and the theory contradicts itself. Though I do wish it would have ended differently so Amelya did not have to die."

Aden raised his dark bushy eyebrows. "I still think you are missing—"

"I know, I know," Isa said, cutting him off. "Then it would not have become a legend."

CHAPTER 26

"Complete." Isa looked with pride at the three leather books stacked on the table below her. They were beautiful both in appearance and function. "Once wrapped in a wax cloth for travel, these books could be tossed from the canyon ledge into the river and still be fine after they had been fished out." She turned to Aden, who was walking toward the table. "Please don't try that, though," she hastily added.

His deep chuckle warmed her heart. How she had ever viewed him as frightening baffled her. His kind eyes expressed more emotion than most humans she knew. He was knowledgeable, yet still humble enough to listen and learn. He carried an immense burden, yet he sought to face it with courage.

She knew he was afraid. Sometimes he asked her to count the remaining petals—they were down to eight. Sometimes she caught him staring into the horizon, his brow furrowed in thought.

He meant to follow his original plan and head deep into the mountains when the rose had only three petals remaining. Isa knew he was afraid of hurting those around him, but she had no intention of letting him leave.

She had meant what she'd said that night, so many nights ago, when they had argued about *The Queen of Silverreign*. She would not leave the one she loved on the eve of battle.

Now, with the Floutast complete and her father's safety secured, she could give Aden her full attention. The bridge would be ready in about two weeks. The petals had been falling faster.

If they fell before the bridge was complete, she would be able to remain with him through the end and still travel back to see her father.

She stopped her own thoughts in horror. That made it sound like she wanted the petals to fall faster, which she did not.

"Isabel?"

She smiled quickly, looking back to Aden.

"You left me. What were you thinking about?"

"Oh, just my father," she said, feeling guilty about the true nature of her exact thoughts. "We accomplished the hardest part. Now it's just a matter of getting them back to Allys, to send to Chendas. My father is safe."

Aden reached for the stack of books. "Or we could just wrap them in waxed linen and toss them into the river. That would likely carry them faster."

She slapped his hand away. "Don't you even dare consider it."

Aden stopped suddenly, twisting his head and lifting his ear. "Someone just knocked on doors at the front entrance."

"They've made it across the canyon?" Isa asked, even though she knew it was the only logical explanation.

Aden nodded.

Isa's feet told her to move toward the door, but her heart

urged her to stay for one more moment in this happy cocoon they had built.

Aden must have been feeling a similar emotion, as he had not yet moved to the door.

She looked up at him, smiling because of their shared time together even if she felt more apprehensive than happy.

His eyes blinked down at her, squinting a little.

Knowing that he could not see her face made the motion endearing rather than invasive.

"Shall we welcome our guest?" she asked, trying to convey with her voice that she wanted the opposite—that she wanted this moment to never end.

"Yes, we should." The tone of his voice also seemed to say the opposite.

Isa turned down the hallway, confused at her own reaction. She had felt isolated from the rest of the world for nearly four weeks. Now that the terrible situation was over, she was nervous to see someone new.

Blanca met them in the hallway. "A gentleman's here, milady! They made it across the canyon!"

"We heard the door," Isa responded, trying to match the servant's excitement.

As she entered the great hall, Isa was met by the sight of the longest feather she had ever seen. It was extending from the top of a hat pointed in her direction. The hat was sitting upon the head of a man bowing deeply before her. The feather swished across the ground as he straightened, then landed daintily across his shoulder.

"Erich Sirilian, Prince of Iseldis, at your service, milady!"

Isa could not hold back her smile of welcome. This young man, dressed in deep purple with gold accents, exuded the most cheerful confidence she had ever encountered. "Lady Isabel Bielsa," she responded. "Welcome to our humble villa."

"The perfect mix of mountain glory and holiday charm," Erich responded, gazing up at the room around him. He pinched his fingertips together, then threw them open for added flair. "It's exquisite." He dipped his head in a much smaller bow, keeping his eyes on her the entire time. "As are you." The ridiculously long feather rippled as he snapped his head back up. "A beauty such as yours should not be relegated to the mountains alone."

Isa's spine stiffened in its old familiar stance.

She was saved from responding to his impudent compliment by a rumbling growl behind her.

"You abominable buffoon!" Erich swept past Isa and threw his arms around Aden.

For a brief moment, Aden seemed to freeze at the abrupt contact. Then his fur-covered arms wrapped around his younger brother. "You're alive," he said, his voice low and gravelly.

Isa watched their reunion, highly intrigued. She had never seen two more different individuals. For the first time, she wondered what Aden had looked like as a human. Would he share Erich's lighter hair? Or would it be dark brown, nearly black, like the fur on his body? If she remembered correctly, their older brother Ian, whom she'd seen at the ball, had dark hair as well. Was Aden the human as tall as Aden the beast? Erich, who was far taller than the average man, stood nearly face to face with the hulking beast. Would Aden's eyes still be insightful and kind? His face expressive?

Her heart filled with sadness that she had never gotten to know the man he really was. What a cruel fate to have found someone so interesting and complex, only to know that she would lose him.

Guilt flooded her heart as she realized his fate was far worse.

To be human but ostracized. To be left alive but given a timeline for death. His would be no happy ending.

"Have you never heard of proper traveling clothes?" Aden said, playfully shoving his brother in the shoulder as he released him from the hug.

"My dear brother, these *are* my traveling clothes," Erich responded, brushing away imaginary dirt from his shoulder where Aden had touched him. "Come, feed me and let me share my news. Ah!" He turned back to Isa, flourishing a folded parchment. "This is for you."

Instantly recognizing her mother's handwriting, Isa tore open the wax seal.

My Dearest Isabel,

I dearly hope that you receive this. Professor Surrell just returned with news of your situation. I cannot sleep for thinking about it. I have found a builder who can oversee the bridge construction, and he is setting out immediately. He assures me that they will have a way over the canyon as soon as possible.

The councilors visit daily, asking for updates. I have explained the situation and begged for more time. I do not know how much longer I can hold them off.

Your father has taken a turn for the worse. And he has no strength left with which to fight.

And now to hear that you are stuck at the villa with a cursed beast! Oh, I pray that you are safe and well and can return to me soon.

The scribbled signature was barely legible. The letter was dated four days prior.

Isa looked up, her eyes instantly seeking Aden's. "The

council has grown more insistent. My mother is fending them off from the very doorstep."

"Your father?" he asked.

She shook her head, her throat closing tightly. "He's worse."

"You must go back and see him," Aden responded. "Immediately."

"The Floutast must go back," she corrected, her heart torn. She did not want to leave Aden, nor was she ready to say goodbye to her father—her hero, the one person who had always been there for her.

Aden turned to Erich. "The rope system you crossed on. Is it safe?"

"For her," Erich waved his hand in an elegant curve toward Isa. "It was quite simple and seemed structurally sound. For you . . ." Erich took in Aden's size. "Probably not. Though you would have to check with the builders."

"Would you accompany her to Allys?" Aden asked.

"Of course, my brother."

"Tomorrow morning. First thing," Aden insisted.

Isa tried to follow what was happening as Aden made the decision without her. "I don't know that I should go. He can take the Floutast. He'd travel faster by himself."

"You are going home to see your father," Aden yelled at her, his voice bellowing.

Erich jumped backward in surprise, but Isa stamped closer to the raging beast.

"I will do what I think is right!" She pointed at her chest.

Aden exhaled. "Yes, of course. This is your decision to make. Please believe me, though, when I say you will regret this. If you do not return now, to see your father a final time and be with your family, you will regret it for the rest of your life. That is a burden you do not want to carry." His voice was much quieter, but the emotion it imparted was far more impactful than his bellows had been.

Isa crossed her arms. "Just as you regret leaving your own family?" she asked.

Aden took a step closer to her, peering down at her with his customary blink. "I loved them too much to stay."

"I will not leave on the eve of battle!"

"You must love them enough to leave me now." His voice rumbled so deeply she could feel it reverberate in the hollow of her own chest.

"They've been falling faster, though," she replied, referring to the rose petals. "How many are left?"

"Stay here." Aden turned, striding quickly down the western hallway.

"Some things never change," Erich said, shaking his head.

Isa looked at him, confused. She had forgotten he was there.

"Don't take it personally. He's always had a testy temper," Erich whispered to her conspiratorially.

"I heard that," Aden growled from the hallway. He reappeared a moment later carrying the rose, which he handed to Isa.

She gingerly examined the blossom, blinking away the tears that had started to seep into her eyes. The leaves looked more wilted than they had the last time she had seen it, and the edges were starting to turn brown. Even the scent had lost its initial clarity. Eight petals stubbornly clung to the base of the pistil. She counted them again to be sure. "There are still eight," she said.

Aden nodded. "You do the math," he said, using the same words she had thrown at him two weeks ago. He reached out for the flower.

She handed it back to him. "Two weeks?"

"Easily," he responded. "Go tomorrow. Take the Floutast. Do

not let your father die in a dungeon cell. Spend time with him. If you wish, come back in ten days' time. The bridge will be done."

"You will wait here for that long?" she asked. "Promise me ten days. I'll return in seven."

"Promise me you will stay with your father as long as he needs you," Aden replied.

Isa nodded. Her heart had never felt so mangled.

He was looking down at her so intently. He clearly wished he had not needed to leave his family, and he did not want her to suffer that pain.

She shook her head. "What if this is the wrong decision? I don't want to be a hero. I don't want them to write legends about us. I don't want to leave you now if it means leaving you forever!"

"I know," Aden responded. "It is a cruel decision to make."

"We never know what tomorrow will bring," Erich said dramatically, "it could be victory; it could be death."

Isa turned to him, confused. She had once again forgotten he was there.

"The last line of *The Queen of Silverreign*," Erich explained, seemingly offended at their questioning glances. "And I thought you were supposed to be the bookish one," he said to Aden, shaking his head in disappointment. The feather danced in response.

"You've read it, too?" she asked. "Do you think Andrew might have been a Majis?"

"What?" Erich stepped back. "No. He was far too honorable to be one of them."

"Then how did he break the curse?" Isa responded.

Erich shrugged.

"Isabel," Aden said, drawing her attention back to him.

"What's important now is what we can control. Go. Prepare the Floutast for travel."

Isa stared back at him, her arms still crossed. "This does not mean I agree to leave in the morning." She stepped away, climbing the stairs to the eastern hallway.

Entering the privacy of the library, her first instinct was to sit down and sob—for her father, for Aden, for herself. But she did not have time for that. If she kept moving, she could avoid the thinking.

Going straight to her work table, she gathered the prepared volumes of Floutast and started wrapping them tightly in some linen she had brought for that purpose.

Not unexpectedly, Blanca quietly entered the library a few moments later. "You poor dear," she said, placing an arm around Isa's shoulder. "This is too much weight for one small person to carry alone. He is right, though."

"Why do you always side with him?" Isa asked, her voice angry and uneven. She hiccupped, her throat taut from trying to keep the tears at bay.

"Will it make you feel better if I stay here with him?" Blanca asked, completely unperturbed by Isa's angry words and seeing straight through to the heart of the issue.

Isa nodded and threw her arms around the older woman's neck. "Would you?" she asked.

"Of course, my dear," Blanca assured her. "And Luca will, too. It was his idea."

"Thank you," Isa whispered. The calm in her mind told her that it was the right decision, even if it was indescribably painful for her heart.

"Now let's get you and Floutast ready to leave first thing in the morning."

CHAPTER 27

"What is this news you bring?" Aden asked his younger brother when Isa was out of sight. He wanted to change the conversation before Erich commented on the discussion that had just taken place.

"Why will her father die in a jail cell if this Floutast is not delivered?" Erich asked, obviously very interested in commenting on the conversation.

"The Council has been using threats to get what they need from even the wealthier families," Aden responded. "Be sure to take this information back to Father. It does not sit well with me."

"That is concerning," Erich responded. "Though news from the shore is not promising. The Majis ships have been raiding along the coast. Even with King Gareth's troops, we've been unable to fend them off. Although they did capture a spy who revealed that the first real attack will be taking place in a few weeks."

"So soon?" Aden replied. "The exile is not complete until this coming silverreign."

"This is war." Erich shrugged. "Honestly, we should be more surprised that they have not attacked sooner."

"What's the plan, then?" Aden asked. Iseldis was his home. His family would be fighting this battle. If they lost, it would cost them their lives. He found himself angry that he would not be there to help them, but he also felt oddly separated from the looming threat. He would not be here to see it. He and his brothers had been preparing for this their entire lives. They had trained in the castle guard and the elite guard, each often bragging about how they would be the hero to defeat the incoming Majis armies. These next years would be the most difficult his kingdom would likely ever know, and he was the first casualty.

"I'm leading three squadrons of the elites to meet with the Chendas troops on the shore," Erich said.

"You're going back?" Aden asked. "When the sea almost just killed you? Brave."

"If we want to talk about brave," Erich retorted, "let's talk about you wooing a woman while you look like that."

Aden growled.

"Alright, alright." Erich held up his hands. "I was only jesting. How have the nightmares been? Did you ever find a way to manage those?"

"Nightmares?" Aden responded, confused. "I've never had a problem with nightmares."

"Oh, you haven't?" Erich shrugged. "Never mind. Anyways, Father won't let Ian out of the capital, as he can't have his heir killed before the war begins, though of course Father himself will be at the shore at the first sign of another attack."

"One of them should remain home, though Ian must be livid."

"He's been spouting on for days about being unable to fulfill his duty and responsibility. It was honestly a relief just to get away from him."

"What were you doing way out here?" Aden asked.

"Tracking a runaway Majis. The one who has the power over the sea seems to have escaped inland. That is, I was tracking this sorceress, until I caught wind of a crazed beast in the mountains and took a detour."

"You should not have stopped for me," Aden said. "The lives of our people are at stake."

"You should not have left," Erich reprimanded.

"I had to. You know it." Aden righteously shut down his brother's attempt to guilt him.

Erich changed the subject. "You won't be here when she gets back, will you?"

"There are only three petals left."

"What?"

"Three petals," Aden explained. "I showed her the wrong rose just now."

"Aden." Erich was speechless, an unusual state for him. "I . . . I knew you had turned into a beast, but that is brutal, Aden, even for you."

"Consider it my last betrayal," Aden responded, his shoulders dropping as he lost the will to hold them up. "We both know how this ends. Take care of her, Erich. See her safely to Allys before you go on to Chendas. See that her family does not need anything, especially if her father dies. Ensure that the Council leaves them alone."

Erich had reached out to place a hand on Aden's shoulder. "I will. You have my word."

"Thank you." Satisfied with his brother's promise, Aden returned to his room to place the decoy rose on the table. He had not wanted to deceive her; he merely wanted to make her decision easier. He could not bear for her to see him when the chaos took control, nor could he bear to hurt her.

Isa and Erich spent the rest of the evening preparing for

their early morning trip. They would not be able to bring the carriage over the canyon, but they could rent a few horses from the villagers on the other side.

When they all said goodnight, Isa had been too preoccupied to give him a proper goodbye. He went to bed with a heavy heart, contenting himself with the thought that he could at least try to find a moment in the morning to thank her for the joy she had brought him over the last few weeks.

He was awoken from a restless sleep by the sound of persistent scratching.

"What is it, Warrior?" he muttered, his eyes flickering open to darkness. "It's still the middle of the night."

A loud snore told him that the small dog was right next to him.

The scratching came again. It was someone at the door.

"Pssst. Aden," a female voice whispered.

Springing out of bed, he threw on a loose white undershirt and breeches.

He opened the door to see Isa, her white robe gleaming in the light of the lantern she carried.

"What's this?" he asked. "Is everything alright?"

"This," she said, with a grin in her voice, "is a secret meeting." She lifted her other arm to show him a basket. "And no one else is invited."

Aden smiled at his visitor. She had not forgotten him. "What about Warrior?" Aden asked, peering back at the pup who was still sleeping soundly on the bed. "Is he invited?"

"Definitely not," Isa confirmed. "He'd eat all the treats I found in the kitchen, and then what would we be left with?"

Aden stepped out of his room, leaving the door open a crack in case Warrior did wake up and panic at being stuck alone in the room without him.

"Which tower shall we choose?" she asked. "The western one or the eastern one?"

"Which wing is Erich's room in?" Aden asked.

"East wing," she replied.

"Then let's go to the eastern tower. It's more dangerous since we'll have to sneak past him."

"That's wicked," Isa reprimanded.

"This whole idea is wicked," Aden pushed back.

Her only response was to start walking away from him down the hallway.

Following her through the dark mansion, Aden could hear her holding in her giggles. Or rather, he could hear her unsuccessfully attempting to hold in her giggles. She seemed in a lighter mood than he would have guessed. If she needed to believe his curse could be broken in order to ease her conscience in leaving him, he would not correct her.

Whatever the cause, her laughter was contagious, and he soon found himself unable to hold in his own chuckles.

"Shhhh," she said, pointing to a door on their left. "That's Erich's room." She made a big deal out of walking on her toes to stifle her footsteps.

Aden saw the lantern sway perilously right before she tripped over her own feet. He reached out to catch her arm, and they both dissolved into a fit of giggles.

Not waiting to hear if they had roused anyone from sleep, they dashed the rest of the way down the hallway and climbed up the tower stairs.

Coming out into the open air of the top room, she turned to face him. "Let the secret meeting commence!" She set down the basket on the center of the floor and opened it to reveal a mini feast. "I stole this from the kitchen after Blanca went to bed."

"Do you think she'll miss it?" Aden asked, sitting on the floor next to her.

"No. I plan on blaming you if she does, though." Isa handed him a piece of meat wrapped in bread.

"What did your older siblings do during these secret meetings they would have without you?" she asked.

"Isn't that kind of the entire point?" he replied. "I wasn't there, so I don't know."

"What do you wish they did? That is what we should do tonight."

Aden looked at her in the lamplight. She was almost ethereal in the way his eyes could only see the glowing shape of her light robe. Her dark hair was loose, puffing out in a voluminous mass of curls that swallowed the light rather than reflected it. He imagined her face once again, daring, slightly reckless as she snuck around her own house with him. Smiling, bold, and confident.

"I'm afraid the things I want to do tonight are very different than the things they did." His voice had deepened, taking on a gravelly texture that was close to a growl. "What did you have planned?"

"I mostly just wanted to build one last memory of you. To speak of the things we have not finished discussing, or to read together again."

"One last perfect memory," he repeated. "If only things had been different and we had forever to look forward to."

"Maybe our forever will live on in the pages of someone else's myth." She looked up at him over the lantern. He wished he could see her expression. "Tonight," she said, "let's give ourselves the luxury of the one thing we were never allowed to do."

"What's that?" he whispered.

"Tonight," she said, "let's dream."

Dream. He swallowed. That would be a luxury they had never allowed themselves. "The proper place for dreaming is under the stars," he replied. The small room had begun to feel smaller, making him uncomfortable.

He stood, leading her through one of the tall open-air windows that surrounded the tower room. They stepped out onto the rampart of the tower. It was a small ledge, wide enough to stand on, with a waist-high solid rock railing.

The tall mountains to the south cut a jagged line against the twinkling stars. He could see the stars clearly, and his breathing became more comfortable as his eyes relaxed.

He sat down, leaning his back against the stone wall of the tower. The railing in front of him was short enough that he could easily see over it.

He looked back up at Isa.

She stepped closer and sat down next to him. "I'm cold," she whispered, nudging his arm.

He lifted it around her shoulders.

She snuggled into his side, hugging her knees with her arms. He liked the feeling of her weight leaning against him.

"What shall we dream about?" he asked.

"Just for a moment," she said, speaking slowly, almost shyly, "let us dream about what might have been."

"What might have been?" His mind seemed to have stopped working. All he could do was repeat her own words.

"Are you asking what it means, or are you asking what really might have been between us?"

"I know what it means," he replied, his voice so deep that it was barely more than a rumble. "Tell me what might have been for you?"

"Invigorating conversations," she responded, her face looking up toward the stars. "Challenging opinions. A shared love of books."

He hugged her tighter. Those were things he would have

appreciated as well. "In a different world, could you . . . would you have loved me as I was?"

"No." Her immediate and confident response cut him to the heart.

He stiffened. Perhaps he had read this evening all wrong.

"I didn't know you as you were then, so how I could I love that person?" Her face had turned to him. "No, I cannot love who you were. I would have wanted to love the person that I know now." She dropped her head to his shoulder. "What might have been for you?"

"I would have gotten lost every day in a pair of fiery eyes," he said. "I would have enjoyed someone who constantly rose to the challenge of an energetic discussion. An opinion that was both lighter and more accepting of the world around her while at the same time demanding more."

"How many petals are on the rose?" she asked, lifting her face once again and twisting to face him. "The real rose?"

"You knew?"

"The stem was too twisted, like our mountain roses. Why did you switch them?"

He looked down at her. "To make the sacrifice for you," he whispered, "so that you did not have to bear it by yourself."

"It was my decision to make," she replied, her voice containing neither anger nor accusation.

"It is your decision, but I still have a strong opinion about it," he replied.

"Is this what could have been?" she asked. "Differing opinions and moonlit nights?"

"I would have loved every second of it," he responded.

"I don't want to leave you tomorrow," she said, a note of grief in her voice. She was speaking as though tomorrow were the past, as though she had already made the decision to leave.

"I don't want you to go tomorrow." He closed his eyes,

inhaling her light scent of rosewater and leather and tree sap. "You smell like books and gum paste."

"I do?" Her voice was concerned.

"It's the most beautiful smell in the world," he reassured her, holding her for a moment longer. "There is nothing left for you here. These dreams that we dreamed will never be. They will be gone with the morning light."

"I know," she whispered. Stretching her neck out, she placed a light kiss on his cheek.

His long whiskers tickled at the unexpected contact and his eyes watered.

He heard the tiniest sniffle catch her breath as she inhaled. And that one small sound was enough to unleash the tears in his own eyes.

They sat there together, holding each other in sorrow, watching their dreams dissipate as the morning light finally broke over the southern mountains.

CHAPTER 28

*I*sa's head spun as she looked at the canyon below her. The builders had created a rope pulley fastened on either side, and they had constructed a kind of saddle-like harness to ferry across humans and supplies.

One of the men had come over from the other side and had just finished securing the ropes around her.

In a few moments, she would be openly swaying above the rushing river far below. Her stomach bubbled uncomfortably.

"Are you nervous?" Aden asked. He stood above her, tugging on the ropes around her to double check that they were secure.

"I'm anxious," she responded, trying to show a brave face. "Anxious to be home, to see my father, to get the Floutast safely out of my care. Anxious to return to you."

"Be safe," he whispered, his deep voice rumbling over her.

"Are *you* nervous?" she asked him.

"Very," he said. "These flimsy threads do not know the treasure they hold."

"I'm glad you care so much for the Floutast," she said, teasing him.

He growled at her, shaking the ropes above her head.

Her feet were still on the ground, so it did not sway her, but she gathered his meaning regardless. "Don't you dare leave before I return," she whispered, speaking quietly so that only he could hear her.

"You will take care of Warrior for me?" he asked, leaning his head closer to hers.

"Of course I will, but we can talk about that when I return and you are still here." She grabbed his hands, burying her fingers in the thick fur around his claws, wishing she would never have to let go.

"We are ready," the worker said, stepping closer to help ease Isa over the edge.

"Goodbye," Aden whispered, squeezing her hands before releasing them.

She felt her feet lift from the ground as they tightened the ropes, slowly inching toward the canyon. "This is not goodbye," she said loudly, not caring who heard her.

She closed her eyes, gripping the ropes that crisscrossed her chest, her mind holding on to the image of his face above hers as his yellow-brown eyes blinked above her.

In a few quick minutes, it was over. Her feet reconnected with the ground on the other side, and several respectful hands removed her from the harness. . As soon as she was free, she shamelessly dropped to the ground, glad to feel it safely below her while they returned the contraption to ferry Erich across.

Isa looked across the canyon, where the figures of Luca, Blanca, and Aden stood barely visible.

He raised his hand in farewell, and she raised hers in return. This was not goodbye. She would not let it be.

Thankfully, Erich left Isa to her own thoughts during their two-day journey back to the Allysian capital. His boundless energy and witty remarks were entertaining, but they felt like a facade. After spending time with Aden's straightforward thoughts and honest emotions, it was exhausting to be around a human man again. Maybe being cut off from the rest of the world had not been so bad after all.

They pushed their tired horses to the limit, arriving on the outskirts of the city in the late afternoon.

"I would give up my right to the throne of Iseldis for a hot bath and a good meal," Erich proclaimed as the houses grew more dense.

"Fortunately, you shall get both in a few moments," Isa responded as the gate to the Bielsa villa came into view. "And I don't think you'll have to give up your birthright for either."

She didn't blame him. She was hot and tired, and her dress felt as though it might be stuck to her skin forever. Erich, on the other hand, for all his complaining, seemed as fresh and spotless as when they had just set out on their journey. He was wearing the orange blue he'd worn that first day on the other side of the canyon. He had even switched out the feather in his hat to match.

As they neared the gate, however, four guards wearing the Allysian uniform approached from the opposite direction. They began pounding on the gate, demanding entry.

"What is the meaning of this?" Isa cried, swinging down from her horse. She landed stiffly but was smart enough to keep her hand on the steed for balance.

"We are here to arrest Carlos Bielsa for crimes against the kingdom of Allys in aiding and abetting the criminal Majis people." The leader of the guard spoke in a practiced monotone, his voice loud and commanding.

"There is no need," Isa replied, fumbling with the pack on her horse to produce the Floutast. "I have returned with the documents my father was supposed to gather for the Council, so he is exonerated from these crimes." She tried not to let her voice display the disdain she had for the so-called crimes.

"I don't know anything about that, miss. I'm just here to carry out my orders, and I don't have the choice not to. If you have a problem with that, you'll have to bring it up to the palace tomorrow where they can review the case. Now, if you will let us in."

"I most certainly will not." Isa went livid. "Carlos Bielsa is deathly ill. To remove him from this house now would be an immediate death sentence. Surely this matter can wait one more day until I can get things sorted. Are the councilors from Chendas still staying at the castle?"

"I don't know. It's not as though I live at the palace. If you cannot grant us entry into this home, then we will make our own way in." He nodded at two of his men, who stepped forward and began to unlatch the gate.

"Good sirs." A new voice joined the conversation.

Erich had dropped from his horse and bowed to the guards as though they were royalty themselves. "Erich Sirilian, fourth prince of Iseldis, at your humble service."

Four heads snapped to attention at both his announcement and the swooping feather that accompanied it.

Isa watched in fascination. She had known Aden was a prince, but she had not had the chance to see him in action as such. Watching Erich instantly demand the attention he wanted was fascinating.

"Your Highness," the head guard started, looking to his fellow guards for confirmation that they were not being fooled by some jester. He bowed.

"My good sirs," Erich continued. "I have only just arrived in your fine kingdom, as you can see." He gestured to his horse with the sweeping hand motion Isa had come to recognize as distinctly his own. "I am quite eager to see my dear friend, August—you might know him, actually. He's the son of your king. Would you be so kind as to escort me to the palace?"

The guards looked at each other, not wanting to be diverted from their orders but not sure how to oppose this new request.

"I am quite weary from my travels and unfamiliar with these outer parts of your fine city, but in the presence of such fine gentlemen as yourselves, I am sure I shall reach my destination safely."

"Of course, Your Highness," the guard stammered. "Two of my men here . . ."

"Two? You would risk my safety with only two of your men?" The feather veritably trembled. "Come now, Captain. Surely you cannot mean that?" Erich pointed at the gate to the Bielsa villa. "If you are worried about your activities here, I shall personally ensure your superiors that I am entirely to blame. Come now, let us make haste. My stomach needs filling and my clothes need cleansing." Not willing to take no for an answer, Erich swung back up on his horse and trotted into the center of the road, waiting for the guards to step in front of him and lead the way.

Seeing no other choice, they did. "We'll be back tomorrow, miss," the lead guard said quietly to Isa as he turned away. He knew he was being played and was obviously miffed about it, but Isa did not care.

Erich shot a quick wink in her direction before he sauntered off.

Isa pushed open the gate and slipped into the courtyard of her childhood home, drawing her horse in behind her. Poor Prince Erich of Iseldis would have to wait a little longer for the bath he had been so loudly looking forward to.

Isa found her family gathered in her father's room. Before any words were spoken, she buried her face in her mother's shoulder. Lady Bielsa looked many seasons older, although they had only been apart a few weeks.

"My dear, sweet girl," she said, her hand on the back of Isa's head, "I am so glad you are here."

"How is Papa?" Isa asked, turning her eyes to the figure on the bed. He looked like a ghost, his skin devoid of any color and sinking into the hollows of his face. He did not even appear to be breathing, the blankets on his chest neither rising nor falling as one would expect them to.

"The physician does not think he will last the night. Come, sit."

Thankful that her mother had not immediately asked for a report, Isa looked around the room. More chairs and benches had been brought in, and she guessed that family and friends had been keeping vigil here for some days.

Her sister Livia had been dozing on a bench in the corner. She opened her eyes, realizing that Isa was home. Jumping up, Livia threw her arms around her sister. "I thought I was never going to see you again!" she cried, slightly more dramatically than their mother had.

Isa stroked her head. "It's alright now, Liv. I'm here and safe."

"Where is the beast?" Livia leaned back to look at Isa's face, eager for news of what had happened in the mountains. "Professor Surrell said there was a terrifying beast that could talk and that he attacked you. The beast, that is, not Professor Surrell—but that he, Professor Surrell, saved you from the beast!"

"Let us focus on Papa tonight," Isa suggested, the exhaustion from her hours of riding seeping back into her bones. She squeezed her sister's arms reassuringly. "Everything is fine and I'm here now, safe."

She sat on a bench and invited her sister to join her. Despite the sadness that hung heavy in the room, Isa knew she had made the right decision to come home to her family.

"I have the Floutast." She moved to stand from the bench, ready to take care of it immediately. "Is there somewhere we can send it tonight?"

"The councilors left for Chendas this morning. We'll have to send it with a messenger first thing tomorrow. There is nothing we can do about it tonight."

Isa sank back onto the bench and leaned against her sister.

She breathed in and out, listening to the silence.

That was, until the door slammed open and Macklin rushed into the room, his head frantically turning back and forth until he found her sitting in the corner.

"Miss Isa!" he cried, far more loudly than a person should speak in a sick room. "You are safe!" He threw himself on his knees at her feet, grasping her hands and looking up into her face. "I thought I would never see you again. I hope you know that every step I took through the wilderness—every agonizing, uncertain, painful step—I took for you."

Completely embarrassed at the raw and inappropriate display of emotion, Isa pulled her hands away.

"Macklin . . ." She threw an exaggerated glance toward her mother sitting by the invalid's bed. "Now is not the place."

Macklin looked over his shoulder, as if realizing they had an audience for the first time. "Of course, come, tell me what happened after I left the villa to save you." He grabbed her hand and pulled her toward the door.

Knowing that the harsh words she wanted to say would also be inappropriate in their current location, she allowed herself to be pulled out of the room. As soon as the door was shut behind them, she wrenched her wrist from his hand.

She reminded herself that Macklin had no idea what had happened after he left the villa. "I appreciate what you did—"

"Isa," Macklin cut her off, "I was so worried for you." He grabbed her hand again.

She pulled her hand away. "Do not touch me."

He placed his hands on her shoulders, stepping forward and hovering over her. "Did he touch you?"

She pushed his hands away. "Who?"

"That monster, if he dared to lay a finger on you!" Macklin's eyes narrowed.

"You mean that monster who grabbed me and dragged me through my own home when you *abandoned* me at its mercy?!"

"Isabel," he said, reaching for her once again.

"Don't call me that, and *do not touch me again.*"

He pulled his hands back. "Silly girl," he said, "that was just a misunderstanding. Do I really need to spell it out for you? That's why I volunteered to brave the wilderness and find help, to redeem myself in your eyes. For you."

"Don't fill my ears with your lies of bravery. That was just another cowardly act. You could not stand to be locked in a remote villa with a beast you did not understand." She pointed to his chest. "You left because you were not brave enough to stay. Don't try to convince me otherwise."

He stepped away from her, his face difficult to read.

"Now, if you'll excuse me, I came to see my father." She turned and slipped back into her parents' room.

Isa spent a long night by her father's bedside. The morning brought no change; he was still breathing but burning with a fever.

Prince Erich returned early the next morning, assuring them he had spoken with the head of the guards and that the arrest warrant had been canceled. He had been called back to Iseldis immediately and could no longer take the Floutast to Chendas personally, but he had already arranged for someone to deliver it directly to the Council with all haste.

Exhausted but happy to have brought some peace to her family, Isa finally made her way to her own room and fell asleep.

She awoke later that afternoon, disoriented and groggy, and went immediately to her father's room.

She opened the door, nearly colliding with a maid.

"Pardon me, milady," the maid said over the pile of cream-colored linen in her arms.

"Let me get the door for you." Isa stepped aside, so the maid could leave the room, then closed the door behind her.

"What was that?" Isa asked her mother, who sat faithfully beside Lord Bielsa's bedside.

"We finished some lighter robes for the monks as you suggested," her mother replied. "Eva just wanted me to check them before she delivers them."

"Is she going there now?" Isa asked, looking back at the closed door.

Her mother nodded.

"How is Papa?" Isa remained standing.

"We managed to feed him some broth this morning, which is more than we could do yesterday."

"How are you?" Isa placed a hand on her mother's shoulder.

"I am well." Lady Bielsa patted her hand. "Don't worry about me."

"Would you mind if I went with Eva to deliver the robes?" Isa asked. "I have a question for Brother Elias."

"Of course, you should go. It was your idea," her mother responded. "Stop by the kitchen before you leave and see if they have anything to send along as well."

"I will stay up with Papa tonight since I slept all day. You need some rest." Isa squeezed her mother's shoulder. "And I'll be right back this time," she called out as she left the room. "Fortunately, there's no canyon between here and the monastery!"

As Eva brought their donation to the brother cook in the kitchen, Isa dashed to the library study where Brother Elias was sitting in his usual place.

"What do you know of curses?" she asked the good monk before she could second-guess her own audacity.

"Why?" His deep-set eyes stared at her shrewdly. "Have you gone and gotten yourself tangled in one?"

"No, not me," she replied, thinking over her words carefully. "It's more about a friend."

"Oh, well." Brother Elias sat back in his chair. "You should rethink the company you keep. Someone who is dabbling in curses probably isn't the best of friends."

"He's not the one doing the dabbling," Isa responded, immediately defending herself and Aden. "He's the one who got dabbled on."

"He?" The old man raised his eyebrows then quickly broke eye contact. "I'm afraid I don't know much about curses, so there's nothing I could do to help your friend."

"I didn't ask you to help him." Isa crossed her arms, staring shrewdly back at him. He knew something and was hiding it.

She turned to the room around her. The haphazard chaos had been sorted into somewhat recognizable piles. "I see the sorting has made some progress. It's almost looking like a proper library in here."

The old man's eyes crinkled into a smile. "That's kind of you to say. It still feels like a small fragment of what we lost."

Isa looked out to the mostly empty shelves in the library outside the study, a brilliant thought taking hold in her mind.

"You know," she said, turning back to the monk, "our library in the mountains is a two-day journey away. Father mostly uses it for the books he doesn't access frequently, but he still complains about not having enough space to house all his 'dear friends' as he calls them. Would you consider housing them here? It would not quite be a donation, more like a loan."

"What a delightful idea," Brother Elias replied, a new light in his eyes. "Only if it would be beneficial to you, though."

"I'll speak to my father as soon as he is well enough to discuss it, though I'm sure he'll be more excited than both you and I combined. They would be cared for properly here, instead of locked away to deteriorate." The more Isa discussed the idea, the more attached to it she became.

"They would be more than treasured here," Brother Elias assured her, his eyes in that far-off place he went to while deep in thought.

"Wonderful," Isa said, turning back to the empty shelves so her face was hidden. "Do you think Andrew could have been a Majis?" she asked, keeping her voice casual.

He paused for a few long moments, as though he hadn't been listening. "Andrew?" he repeated.

"You know," she said, turning back to face him. "Andrew, the swineherd from *The Queen of Silverreign?*"

"Oh, no. Of course not." The monk waved his hand, dismissing her assumption. His eyes still drifted under his half-closed eyelids.

"Then how did he break Amelya's curse at the end of the second volume, if he could not control magic?" Isa hoped he would answer her absentmindedly. She felt mildly guilty about her manipulation.

"Oh, you don't need magic to break a curse—" The old man slapped his hand over his mouth. The far-off look was gone. "Are you trying to get us both killed?" he hissed, looking around her to make sure no one else was within earshot.

"No." Isa stepped closer to the desk and leaned over it, her eyes begging him to trust her. "I'm trying to keep my *friend* alive." She kept her voice a quiet whisper.

Brother Elias exhaled slowly, his eyes scrutinizing every inch of her face. He dropped his hands to the table in front of him.

"Curse," he said softly. His eyes stared at the wall behind her, his gaze softening. "C-U-R-S-E." He nodded to himself as he spelled out the word. "Interestingly, if you switch two letters you get C-U-R-E-S. Cures." His eyes darted back to hers for half an instant.

Isa leaned even closer to him over the table. She nodded, unsure how to decipher his riddle. The only thing she knew about magic was what Aden had shared about the seamstress and the traitorous councilor. "Is it chaos or harmony?" she whispered.

"You've seen one with your own eyes," he whispered back to her, "in Iseldis. Which was that?"

Isa thought back to the ball, remembering the terror of the moment when the room had dimmed, and the orb of light pulsating in the attacker's hands. "Chaos."

"And what is the one thing that can disassemble chaos?" he whispered. His eyes were completely focused on her now.

"Harmony."

He leaned back in his chair. "There you have it. C-U-R-E-S."

Isa had the violent urge to reach across the table and shake the old man. "What are you saying?!" she cried. "I don't have a jar of salve filled with the essence of harmony to go slapping around on people's curse wounds!"

"Quiet, child," he snapped in a sharp whisper. "The walls have ears. I do not know these answers. Even I, as old as I am, have never seen these things firsthand the way that you have. I have studied and read, the same as you, and we seem to have come to similar conclusions. The only way to treat chaos is to soothe it with harmony. I know not how."

Isa slumped over the table. They were so close. "Thank you," she said.

Curse. Cures.

"I need to return home and relieve my mother. I will speak to my father about housing the mountain library here as soon as is possible."

"Child," he called after her as she left the study. "The only thing I do know is you are asking the right questions."

She nodded in response. As she left the villa turned monastery, she heard the monks chanting their prayers. Despite the frustration and uncertainty in her heart, the bass melody soothed her mind.

CHAPTER 29

The next four days passed in a blur. Isa slept while the sun was up so she could remain awake by her father's side at night. Her mother did the opposite so that Lord Bielsa would always have a family member by his side. Even Livia took her turn, though she was too restless to remain in one room for longer than a few hours.

Isa kept a stack of books in the sickroom so she could search for any other remnant of the harmony magic from ancient times. When the occasional feeling of guilt pricked her mind, she told herself that she was not practicing magic, just researching it. Besides, if the Council's examiners had discovered as little as Aden claimed in their two hundred and fifty years of research, then she had little hope of learning something new in the space of a few days.

But she had to try.

Aden had sacrificed himself for his brother. He had left his family and all that he loved. He had accepted his fate. But she was not ready to let *him* go that easily. She wanted so much more than a bittersweet hero's legend. She wanted the love she had dreamed about. She wanted the companionship her parents had found in each other. She wanted to argue with Aden for the rest of their days.

On the fourth night, her mind was too tired to parse the dense passages and ancient spellings of the old texts, so she pulled out her old favorite. She had not read *The Queen of Silverreign* since Aden had spoiled the final volume. It was too hard to read of Andrew and Amelya's love when she knew how the story ended.

But, missing the familiar comfort of her beloved friends, she opened her well-worn book and skimmed through the pages, landing on the scene where Andrew broke Amelya's curse.

The chapter was unbearably sad. Amelya had been cursed with an illness by an evil enchanter and was slowly dying. Andrew rushed back to her side, fighting through spies and enemies who had infiltrated their castle. When he reached her side, she rebuked him for leaving his post. Hurt by her angry words, he yelled back at her, promising her that his love would weather all storms and that, if she became well again, he would sacrifice his own desires in the future for the sake of bearing her responsibilities as Princess alongside her. Eventually, he kissed her. Her sickness did not leave immediately, but she slowly recovered.

Reading the story—especially now that she knew Andrew had fulfilled his promise in the end, fighting on the opposite end of the battlefield to protect their people while Amelya was killed—tore Isa's heart. It didn't feel like harmony. There was far too much chaos involved. The two lovers had spent their reunion at her deathbed yelling at each other!

She closed the book.

Perhaps they had it all wrong. Perhaps the story was merely a myth with no truth behind it.

As the sun rose, her mother entered the room and Isa took

her leave, bringing a few of the books with her to return to the library.

When she entered the library, however, she nearly collided with a strange man carrying a stack of books.

"Could you grab the door for me?" he asked, his arms full.

She held the door for him and watched him leave. Turning back into the library herself, she saw Macklin counting out a handful of coins. She looked back at the closed door, confused. Her eyes saw the change in the room before her mind could fully grasp the situation.

The library was in complete disarray. Stacks had turned into piles, and shelves were mixed.

"What's going on here?" she asked, afraid she already knew the answer.

"Miss Isa." Macklin stood, walking toward her. "Your mother gave me permission to rearrange the library."

"By selling all the books?!"

"Just the less important books, the ones that won't be needed when this is no longer a scholar's house."

"No longer a scholar's house?" she asked, wanting him to spell out exactly what he meant.

"Well, I intend to open a school here, but I won't be needing all the old writers. Only one way to make room for the new, you know."

"What are you talking about?" She had never heard him speak of opening a school, much less in her family's home.

"My dear Isabel," he said, looking at her, "I'm talking about us. Someone will need to step up after your father is dead." His callous words held no regard for the man who was dying a few rooms down the hall.

"Get. Out." Isa's voice was calm with rage. Not the loud, chaotic, screaming kind of rage. The quiet, calculated, terrifying kind of rage.

"What do you mean?" he asked, his eyes narrowing.

"Get out of my house. Get out of my father's house." She walked past him, herding him toward the door. "There is no us. There will never be an us."

"Is nothing good enough for you?" he yelled, his eyes furious at her direct rejection. "Will you never realize that the heroes in your head only exist in books? Just because you are pretty does not mean the whole world will fall at your feet! When will you open your eyes and fall in love with a real man?"

"I am in love with a real man!" she shouted back. "A real man who faces his destiny with true courage, however bleak it may be. You are a coward, Macklin Surrell, and you think only of yourself. Get out!"

"True courage?" He stepped toward her, his face twisted with anger. "I am no coward." He tapped a finger on his chest to punctuate the words. "And I have thought about nothing but you since the moment I laid eyes on you. I'll show you I'm no coward." He exited the library, slamming the door shut behind him.

Filled with rage, Isa set her stack of books on a random shelf and ran back to her father's room.

"Mama!" she said. "Macklin Surrell must be dismissed immediately."

After hearing the full extent of the situation, Lady Bielsa stood. "That is not what I meant when I asked him to see to the library. I shall dismiss him immediately. Would you wait here? Or you can go get some rest if you need. I can call a servant to sit with him. They're constantly offering to."

"I'll wait," Isa responded. "I can't sleep yet." She sank back into the chair beside her father's bed, her body shaking with exhaustion and anger.

Curious about the conversation that was taking place somewhere else in the villa, Isa thought about her mother. Lady

Bielsa was the strongest person she had ever met. It was heart-breakingly beautiful to watch her care for her dying husband day after day, choosing kindness over self-pity.

It reminded her of Aden, devastated by a curse but still taking the time to make Blanca laugh, or ease Luca's burden, or give her a mock exam.

"How do you do it?" Isa asked her mother when she returned a short time later. "How are you so loving when everything around you is turning to chaos?"

Lady Bielsa sat next to her. "I don't know," she sighed. "When you love someone, you just have to keep on giving. It's the only thing you can do. If one person can't pull the weight, then the other one takes over. Like you and I have been doing here, taking turns at his side."

"Was Macklin angry?" Isa asked.

"He seemed hurt. But he said he would leave immediately. He was planning to head back to Chendas to meet with his old tutor anyway." Lady Bielsa reached out for her husband's frail hand. "You should go get some sleep, Isabel," she said. "I'll have you called if anything changes."

Tears tugged at Isa's eyes. Hearing her full name reminded her of the way Aden said it. "I just don't understand why the people who truly love each other have to get hurt," she whispered. "It's not fair."

"Life is complicated, isn't it?" her mother replied. "But that's the risk you take for loving a flawed person. You're bound to have disagreements and illnesses, but those are just part of the rhythm that weaves you together. The chaotic things make the simple happy moments all the sweeter."

Isabel nodded, only half understanding. Her father dying made her *more* sad about the happy moments they had shared.

"You don't need to understand it all at once," her mother continued. "It's fine to feel—"

Isa looked up quickly as her mother gasped.

Lady Bielsa had jumped from her seat, leaning over the sickbed. "Carlo?"

Isa moved closer to the bed to see her father. His eyes were open, staring softly at his wife. They looked tired but clear.

"Lucia?" he whispered.

"I'm here, my dearest," Lady Bielsa whispered. "I'll always be here." She placed a hand on her husband's forehead, then turned to Isa. "His fever is broken."

"I'll summon the physician!" Isa ran from the room.

The physician, pleasantly surprised at this turn of events, assured them that the worst was likely over and that with proper rest and nourishment he had every possibility of recovery.

Isa spent the rest of the day with her mother and sister, attempting to keep her father's room calm and quiet while all they wanted to do was rejoice.

But her own thoughts frequently wandered to Aden. It had been six days since she'd left. She still had no idea whether she could break the curse or not, but she was going to try.

Exhausted from the day's events, she went to her room to sleep through the night. She would leave for the mountains at first light.

"You don't even realize what is right in front of your face," Livia said, bursting into her room.

Isa waved her hand in front of her nose, repeating the jest she had used on Blanca. "Air. Air is in front of my face." She was getting ready for bed, and Livia had come to her room to chat.

"Don't be stupid!" Livia cried. "He loves you and you don't even care!"

Isa dropped her hand, sobering quickly. Macklin had left the morning after she had yelled at him. He'd claimed he had business in Chendas. "He doesn't love me. He loves himself."

"You don't deserve him," Livia said, her eyes filling with tears. "You don't understand him, and you don't even notice or care about the things he does for you. I would do anything for him, but all he does is put himself in harm's way to earn your attention."

"Put himself in harm's way?" Isa repeated. "Don't be ridiculous. If he's fed you stories about the beast, he was most likely lying. Aden is harmless."

"You don't know where he's gone, do you?" Livia's voice held a note of glee, as though she finally had something to hold over her older sister's head.

"Of course I do. He's just going to Chendas to meet with his old tutor." As the words left her mouth, Isa realized something was wrong. The excuse felt hollow.

"Ohh . . ." Livia said, practically bouncing with excitement. "I know something you don't know!"

"What do you know?" Isa narrowed her eyes.

"I'm not going to tell you!"

"That's fine with me." Isa turned away, shrugging her shoulders. "I don't care anyway."

"He's going back to the villa to kill the beast for you!" Livia yelled, unable to handle being ignored. "You don't deserve him at all! Isn't that the most romantic thing you've ever heard?"

Isa stood, throwing open her wardrobe and grabbing a long cloak to cover her nightdress. "That's not romantic at all. That is the most heartless, cruel, obnoxious thing I have ever heard."

"Of course you wouldn't understand." Livia stood. "You don't even have a heart." She dashed from the room.

"Livia!" Isa jumped after her sister and grabbed her by the arm, swinging her around to face her. "You are sure about this? You are absolutely positive Macklin went back to the villa to harm Aden?"

Livia nodded. "He brought other men with him, too. He

talked some men from the tavern into coming with him for the glory and honor of defeating a cursed beast. He said the mountain villagers would be interested in fighting for their safety as well."

Isa let go of her sister's arm and ran toward the courtyard, headed for the stables.

"Where are you going?!" Livia called after her.

"To save my beast!" Isa yelled over her shoulder. She didn't need to pack anything, for she did not plan on stopping until she arrived. The journey would be fastest on horseback again.

"What shall I tell Mama and Papa?" Livia asked, running after her through the courtyard, still in her nightclothes.

"The truth," Isa yelled down from the horse.

"Which is?"

"That I love him!" Isa yelled her declaration in the wind, not sure if it carried back to her younger sister, but not entirely caring. Macklin had left that morning, giving him an entire day's travel ahead of her. If she rode through the night, she might get there in time.

Ride through the night she did, occasionally nodding off as the horse galloped below her. But she never fully let go enough to fall asleep in the saddle. The fear in her heart kept her awake and pressing forward.

$\mathcal{A}$den frequently found himself sleeping in the library. His small room had grown more oppressive since Isa had left. If Luca and Blanca had noticed his new sleeping arrangement, which they surely had, they said nothing.

He could breathe in the library. The tall ceiling and distant walls did not press in on him. The soft scent of leather and Etrarian tree sap comforted him, helping him sleep.

The days passed slowly. He took Warrior on long walks into the woods, scouting out trails. He avoided the canyon, not wanting to interact with the villagers who ferried across the rope pulley each morning to build the other side of the bridge's foundation. By now they surely knew of his existence, but he did not want to test how comfortable they were with that knowledge.

Blanca requested new foods from the village, which were delivered over the pulley. She tried to cheer him up by preparing different meals. He happily ate them with her in the kitchen, dragging Luca into their conversations.

But on the ninth morning after Isabel's departure, another

petal fell, leaving only two remaining. Although it had taken over a week for the petal to fall, he was not willing to risk waiting any longer. The final two might fall simultaneously, or they might cling on for days.

Either way, he could not allow himself to become a danger to those who had selflessly done so much for him.

He also could not afford to wait for the tenth day, as he had promised Isabel—he loved her full name, Isabel.

It was time. They had already shared their goodbyes.

He wished his clumsy claws were dexterous enough to pen a letter, but they were not.

He would secretly prepare a pack of food and sneak out of the castle after dark had fallen. Blanca and Luca would only beg him to stay, and he did not know that he was strong enough to resist their pleas.

"This is delicious, Blanca," Aden said, honestly praising the supper she had made. "I'm always afraid you will try to serve me honey and salted fish, but thus far you've spared me."

"Don't get too comfortable," Blanca responded. "There's always tomorrow."

Aden smiled in response, not wanting to fully agree with her when he knew he would be gone by tomorrow morning. "Thank you for staying," he said.

"You have to stop saying that," Blanca replied. "We were more than happy to remain in these peaceful mountains for an extra time."

"The clean air has been good for my knees," Luca added.

Aden smiled again, but this one felt more genuine. He had no idea how clean air contributed to knee health, but he was not going to contradict the old man. "Wait." He lifted his head, tilting his ear upward. "I hear shouting from the canyon. They're excited. They're closer. I think they've finished the bridge!"

"Oh wonderful." Blanca stood from the table. "I would never have made it across that rope contraption alive."

"Might as well go make sure it's stable," Luca contributed, also standing.

Aden joined them. There was no harm in looking at the bridge. He could hang back and avoid the builders.

Luca grabbed a lantern as they stepped out into the deepening dusk.

Aden found himself tuning out their conversation as they stepped down the road. The shouts of excitement from the bridge were growing louder, and something felt . . . off.

"Stop," he said suddenly. "Those are not shouts of victory— those are battle cries."

They could make out moving torches through the trees. Distant shouts clamored up as the group moved along the road.

"It isn't safe!"

"Kill the beast!"

"Follow me!"

Aden turned to Luca and Blanca, not sure if they could hear it as well. "Back to the villa!"

They ran back as fast as they could.

"Hide yourselves," Aden said, "and do not come out. They're here for me. I'll show myself, then lead them on a chase through the woods."

"No!" Luca replied. "That's the stupidest plan I've ever heard. Bar this door from the inside." He grabbed a table and started dragging it to block the double doors.

Aden grabbed the other end of the table, practically lifting the entire thing from the ground by himself. The old man was right; he and Blanca would be safer if they mob could not get inside at all. He frantically threw furniture in front of the door.

When nothing else could fit, Aden turned to see Blanca

standing behind him with a frying pan in one hand and a wood ax in the other. She handed the ax to Luca.

"Would you like a weapon, Your Highness, or do you prefer to use your claws?" she asked, as calmly as if she were offering him a cup of tea.

Aden brandished his built-in weapons. The long claws slid out, fierce and ready. "Claws, thank you," he responded.

The crowd could be heard clearly now, marching toward the house, shouting and yelling in the kind of rousing ardor that only an angry crowd could conjure.

Aden looked from his claws to the stalwart warriors defending the barricade.

The three of them did not stand a chance. He did not want them to fight for him. His life was at its end; he could not let his curse spread any further. He did not want to fight any of the angry villagers at all. They did not know what they were doing. They likely thought they were heroically defending their families.

"I'm going to lead them off," he said. "Don't let Warrior follow me."

Before they could try to stop him, he raced down the hall to his small bedroom. He grabbed the rose from its jar of water and placed it in his teeth. Throwing open the window, he climbed out and dropped to the front courtyard below. He had planned to run out the front gate, letting them see him and then leading them on a chase deep into the woods where he could outpace them.

But they were already at the front gate, pouring into the courtyard.

"Follow me!" a familiar voice yelled. "I will lead you to the beast!" Macklin the Cowardly ran toward the front entrance of the villa.

Aden could not see his movements, but he assumed the man

had attempted to open the locked door as he started pounding on it moments later.

"We are here for the beast!" Macklin yelled out, as much for his followers as for the inhabitants of the villa. "Turn him over to us and no harm will come to you."

"Get lost!" Blanca called from inside the building.

Macklin and the men around him threw themselves against the door. The old wood groaned in response.

Knowing that the makeshift barricade would not hold for long, Aden looked up at the wall of the villa and leapt into the vines.

"It's him! I see the beast!" a voice yelled out from below.

Another voice screamed in terror at the mere sight of him.

Something clattered against the stone wall next to him. Aden didn't stop to find out what it was. He only increased the speed of his climb. In a few moments, he was standing on the top of the roof. He ran toward the area above the front door, stooping low to the ground as other objects whirred past his head. Removing the rose from his teeth, he slipped it down his shirt.

"Here I am, Macklin the Cowardly!" Aden yelled when he stood above the double doors. "Have you come to hunt or be hunted?"

The mob roared in delight at his challenge. "Kill the beast! Kill the beast!"

Aden stepped back from the ledge. The bright torches below muddled his vision, forcing him to see only shadow and light.

"She will be mine, you cursed monster." Macklin's voice spewed his hatred as he climbed up the vines, following Aden to the roof.

"She is her own," Aden said, his voice not meant to carry to the crowd. "So, I doubt that she will ever be yours." He knew he was playing with fire, but he could not resist poking the cowardly man who had left the woman he supposedly loved to fend off a beast on her own.

"Luckily for you," Macklin responded, climbing over the top of the roof, "you won't live past this night to know what happens to her." He reached behind him, keeping his face turned toward Aden. Hands from below passed up a sturdy spear.

"You don't have to do this," Aden said. "I will disappear into the forest, and you will never hear from me again."

"Who's the coward now?" Macklin sneered.

"I don't think you truly know what that word means," Aden responded. For a fleeting moment, his mind considered letting Macklin have his way. Death by the sword would be quick and controlled. But Aden knew he could not go down without a fight. And no man, cowardly or brave, deserved to be on the receiving end of his fierce claws.

Macklin slowly advanced, the shape of his body silhouetted against the torches in the courtyard below him. He raised his spear, hefting it at shoulder level. He was still several feet away, seemingly afraid to come too much nearer.

Aden swung his paw, claws outstretched, letting out a loud roar that rang throughout the courtyard.

Macklin instantly cowered back.

Using this momentary distraction, Aden turned his back on his enemy and leaped across the roof, dashing toward the eastern wall where he could hopefully escape into the forest below.

A sharp pain tore at his shoulder, and he swung around to find Macklin closer than he'd expected. Swinging his claws toward his attacker, Aden bellowed once again.

Macklin was prepared for it, though, and he didn't cower. Instead, he raised his spear in preparation for an attack.

Aden did not have time to make it to the edge of the building. The side tower was closer.

As Macklin released the spear, Aden used every muscle in the lower half of his body to launch himself upward, away from the rooftop. He flew through the air and landed against the side of the tower several steps away. His claws dug into thick vines as he gasped for air. The spear had missed him, hitting the side of the tower and clattering to the roof below.

Macklin raced to retrieve it.

Aden swung one arm above the other, climbing the tower as fast as he could. He had nowhere else to go. Above him, the thin ledge stuck out like a roof. Fortunately, the vines climbed out over it, and he reached backward and up to precariously swing his body around to the wider circumference of the ledge railing. As he reached over the railing to tumble behind its momentary safety, a numbing force hit his back.

It knocked the breath from his body. He froze, willing his muscles not to let go as he fought to fill his stunned lungs.

The numbness of the impact soon gave way to a wave of intense pain.

He could feel his claws slipping back into his paws as he lost his grip.

With one final effort, he pressed his bottom legs against the wall below him, hurling himself over the final barrier of the railing.

His lungs released the last bit of air they'd still contained, and he landed on the tower ledge with a strangled grunt.

His mind slipped into hazy shadows of its own as pain sank into it.

Somewhere, in the far-off distance, he heard a victorious shout. "The beast is dead!"

CHAPTER 31

Isabel rode into the village just as the sun dipped below the mountains. She had pressed as hard as she could, falling from the horse and sleeping in the bushes for an hour at a time when her eyes absolutely refused to stay open.

She had not overtaken Macklin.

She jumped off the exhausted horse, having brought it to the innkeeper for food and rest. She would go the rest of the way on foot, unable to ask anything further from the poor horse.

"Where is everyone?" she asked the innkeeper, noting the empty tables at the cozy establishment.

"They've gone up to the villa to get rid of the beast. A nasty business for these nasty times." He shook his head.

Isa's heart raced. "Have they finished the bridge over the canyon?"

"Aye, but I would not be heading in that direction if I were you, until they take care of the beast."

She handed him a few coins. "Some bread please, quickly, and see to the horse. I'll be back in the morning." She turned to the door. "Hopefully," she muttered to herself, inhaling the small loaf he had handed her.

The food did not revive her energy as much as she had hoped, but she pressed forward regardless, pretending that it had.

It was fully dark by the time she reached the newly constructed bridge, but she could see it clearly by the light of dozens of bouncing torches on the other side. A raucous group of men swayed down the hill, laughing and yelling and shouting victoriously.

Isa dashed across the bridge as they poured over it. She fought against the flow, keeping her head low to avoid attention.

"We're safe now!" someone cried to the right of her.

"I'd like to see even the Majis themselves take us on!" another said.

"Did you see it? Climbing up that tower with its tail between its legs? Coward!" another spat.

Each passing gibe increased the urgency in Isa's heart. "Out of my way!" she yelled, using her elbows liberally to fight her way across. The bridge was wide, but the wooden planks below her feet responded with a tremor at every footstep.

She was nearly to the end of it when two hands grasped her around the waist.

"My Isabel!" a sickly familiar voice cried. "Have you come to celebrate our victory?" Macklin swayed, whether drunk with the energy of his victory or merely losing his balance on the flexible bridge, she could not tell.

She pressed her hands against his chest, trying to push herself away from him but wary of the flimsy rope netting between her and a fall into the chasm.

"Who's the hero now!" Macklin continued, seemingly

unaware of her struggle, his arms firmly around her waist. "I have freed you and come to claim my prize!"

She threw her head back to separate her body from his.

Misunderstanding her movement, or deliberately taking advantage of it, he leaned forward and pressed his lips against hers.

Shocked and enraged, Isa raised her hand and slapped the side of his head as hard as she could.

He let go of her to grab his face in surprise.

"I told you never to touch me again." Intent on a different goal, she moved out of his range, flinging herself from the swaying bridge onto solid ground.

Wiping her mouth with the back of her hand, she ran up the hill toward the villa.

It was completely lifeless as she approached. No light shone from the inner windows or exterior torches of the courtyard. The stars above cast a dim light over the old stone structure from their twinkling place in the heavens, but even with their help she could only see very little.

"Aden!" she yelled, her eyes frantically searching every shadow.

She was here. She had come back to break his curse or be with him to the end.

She was too late. Macklin had claimed victory.

"Aden!" she yelled again.

She ran to the front entrance. The doors were locked. "Aden!" she screamed.

"Milady?" Luca responded from inside. "Is that you? The door is barricaded. Go through the kitchen."

The familiar voice in the midst of the eerie surroundings flooded Isa with a renewed energy. She ran around the villa, fighting through the shadows to find the kitchen entrance at the back of the building.

Blanca met her at the door with a lantern.

"Where is he!?" Isa cried.

"We don't know yet," Blanca responded. "We couldn't find him in the courtyard. We heard a scuffle on the roof. Luca is trying to find a way to the rooftop."

"The towers," Isa responded, dashing through the kitchen. "Someone on the bridge said he fled to a tower."

But which one? There was a tower in each wing. She paused in the hallway, debating which direction to turn. Remembering their secret meeting in the eastern tower, she wasted no more time making a decision and turned right toward the eastern wing. She realized as she ran that it was the farther tower from the kitchen, but by that point she was already at the end of the eastern hallway.

Isa vaguely realized that Blanca was panting behind her, carrying the lantern, but she pressed forward faster than the older woman could keep up with.

She opened the small door at the end of the hallway and wound her way up the tower stairs. Her own breathing was labored, and her legs begged for relief, but she pushed through, praying that this was the right tower. If it was not, she did know if she could summon the strength to climb the wester tower as well.

Finally, she reached the door of the top tower room, its open-air windows letting in the light of the stars.

"Aden!" she yelled. "Where are you? Don't leave me, not yet!"

Silence greeted her.

Dashing to each window of the circular walls, she leaned through, looking for a shape or shadow on the ramparts around the upper tower.

At the fourth window, she saw it—a dark body sprawled along the thin ledge.

"Aden!" she cried, climbing through the slit-like window.

The mass of fur did not respond as she sank next to it. She reached out, searching for his face. His fur was still warm, but the shaft of a spear lay beneath his motionless body.

She leaned over him, careful not to disturb him, afraid of upsetting any wound she could not see.

A faint hiss greeted her ears as the massive beast exhaled.

"Aden," she cried, tears of relief mixed with tears of sadness falling from her eyes. "Do not leave me," she begged. "I'm here. I came back for you. Don't leave me now!"

"Isabel," he said, the word barely more than a breath. His eyes remained closed.

"Aden, Aden. Aden!" She brought her hands to his face, stroking his fur through her tears. "It's too soon. This is not goodbye. You lied to me—you said it was not the eve of battle. You were wrong. You cannot leave me now, not like this."

"Your father?" he asked.

"He's safe. Safe and well, getting stronger every day."

"Good," Aden said, his voice devolving into a wheezing cough.

"I'm here. I'm here," she sobbed. "The curse can be broken." She spoke the words with a confidence she did not feel.

His breathing was slow and labored. "No. It's too late," he whispered. Lifting his hand from the ground, he brought it to his chest. He was grasping a long stick.

She took the object from his hand, confused until she felt the poke of a thorn against her finger. It was the stem of the rose. The petals were gone. All of them.

"Go," Aden said, his voice no more than a whisper. "I'm not safe. I can already feel my mind slipping."

"I'm not leaving you," she replied. "I won't abandon you to face the chaos alone. If the magic of harmony truly exists, then I will be here, carrying your burden when it is too much to bear alone. I would offer more if I could."

"This is no time to play hero." He attempted to raise his voice, but it was mostly a breathy whisper. He gasped for air, lifting his head from the stone rampart as his eyes frantically searched for her own. "I can feel my consciousness slipping away. You cannot be here when it does. I will not be responsible for hurting you."

"Nonsense," Isa replied. "You would never hurt me. Rest now." She pressed her hand against his forehead, forcing his head back to relax against the stone masonry. She was not afraid. But it was not from bravery or courage; it was from despair. He was weak from his wound, and she could feel blood —not mud—seeping out onto the stones around him. He would not last long enough for the curse to take effect. "Save your energy. We will make it through this. I'm not being a hero. I'm just loving you. Remember what we dreamed? I want all of it. I want it to be real. I want your future, as messy as it might be. I want to live to be happy and old, together. Rest, rest and dream of what could be."

His head thrashed back. "Isabel, you must leave me—I can feel it taking over me. The curse, the chaos. It's too much. I can't fight it."

"Aden," she said, trying to reach through the pain that had taken a hold on his mind. "Aden, stay with me. Don't leave me." Tears streamed down her cheeks.

She leaned over him, using the weight of her body to hold his head still. "Shhhh, rest. Be at peace. You are stronger than any chaos."

She leaned over him, her fingers stroking the fur between his eyes, brushing it upward.

He stilled, his body losing its tension, whether relaxing at her touch or merely having spent its energy, she could not tell.

"I love you, my dearest Aden," she whispered, dropping her head to kiss the spot of fur between his eyes. "I love you now and I always will." She dropped her forehead to his as tears dripped down her nose onto his upturned face. Her mother's words were beginning to make sense. Even if their story ended here, she would always treasure the moments they had shared.

She felt the moment that the last breath left his nostrils. It left his body without a sound, warming her cheek briefly before leaving her alone in the cold of the night. No other warming breath followed.

"Goodbye, my love," she sobbed, not willing to believe that he was gone. "Be at peace."

Grasping the fur at the sides of his head, she let her body sink onto his, sobbing out the fear she had kept at bay while trying to remain strong for him.

A tremor ran through the lifeless body below her.

She tangled her fingers deeper into his hair, refusing to open her eyes. As soon as she did, she would have to face the truth. Her grief needed time, not truth.

But a blinding light pierced her closed eyelids. Blanca and the lantern must have made it up the stairs.

Isa opened her eyes to see a bright light surrounding the body of the beast in front of her.

"Aden?" she cried, unsure what was happening.

The light was not from a lantern, rather it seemed to be pulsing through his body, slowly accumulating in his chest where it formed a sphere.

The sphere thrummed, emitting a power that terrified her, bringing her back to that moment on the balcony in Iseldis when the Majis had cast a ball of light toward Prince Ian on the center dais.

She clutched Aden's head, willing him to remain with her, to not let the curse take him away from her. "Don't take him," she cried. "You've already done enough."

The sphere of light rose out of his body, hovering above it.

"Leave!" she yelled at it. "Go and leave us! Your chaos is not enough to tear us apart!"

The sphere pulsated in the air, hovering just above Aden's chest. Then it split like shards of glass, shattering into the night and disappearing into darkness.

A shudder ran through Aden's body. It had not taken him. It had left him, lifeless and spent.

Momentarily blinded by the brightness of the curse, Isa bent back over him to say her last goodbye. Her tears were spent, but her hands were still tangled in the long fur on his head.

Her body was exhausted. Her relentless ride into the mountains on top of the emotional emptiness of finding Aden wounded had left her completely empty. She could not move. She dropped her head onto his own, realizing moments later that her forehead had landed on the soft satin texture of skin rather than the velvety tendrils of fur.

She pulled away in surprise, gazing around her as her eyes reacclimated to the darkness.

She was not holding on to a beast—she was leaning over a man.

The body in her hands inhaled a long, slow breath.

She was leaning over a living, breathing man.

"Aden?" she cried, disbelief and hope washing over her. "Aden?"

He exhaled, the action turning into a dry cough.

"Aden?" Panic overwhelmed her as the man below her choked on his own cough.

"I'm . . . fine," he hacked. "Let me breathe."

She supported his head through the next fit of coughing until he relaxed back into her hands. She was not holding fur. She was holding hair.

"Aden," she said, "is that . . . is this you?"

The stars seemed to twinkle brighter in the sky above her, illuminating the face of the man in her arms.

He smiled, finally breathing normally. "Isabel?" he asked, looking up at her.

She nodded. She thought her tears had dried up, but she found they were biting at her eyelids once again.

"I can't see your face in these shadows," he said, pushing himself up into a sitting position.

But as he positioned himself to see her better, Isa realized she had seen him before.

"You're him," she said, surprised and confused. "You're Prince Aden."

"Oh, now you finally believe me?" he said, a smile in his voice. "I thought we had already figured that one out."

"I do! We did. I mean, Prince Aden is you, the rude man I spoke to at the Iseldis ball on the balcony."

"You only just figured that out?" He sounded confused.

"Did you already recognize me?"

"Yes, as soon as you started talking about *The Queen of Silver-reign.* I couldn't see your face before then, but I still figured out who you were. How did you not realize it was me?"

"I didn't know I was talking to a prince at the ball! I just thought it was some rude guest avoiding the dance floor until his . . ." She sat back, pulling away from him. "Wait. Don't you already love someone?"

"What?" Aden's mind raced to ascertain what she might mean. He could not think of anyone he was supposed to be in love with.

"At the ball," she explained, "you were staring over the balcony and you saw some woman and said, 'She came!' or something else like that, and you smiled ridiculously and then disappeared down the stairs."

Aden scrunched his eyebrows together. "I said that?"

"Yes. Then you went down and spoke with some lady in light blue that all the men seemed quite intent on speaking with that evening."

Aden's mouth spread into a wide grin as he remembered what she was talking about. "You seem to have been paying close attention to someone you thought was just a rude palace guest," he said. "If I didn't know any better, I'd think you were jealous."

"What, no!" Isa scrambled up, stepping away from him. "I was empathizing with her, since I know how it is to be the center of attention while still feeling like no one can see you at all."

Aden stood as well, stepping toward her. He was enjoying teasing her, but he still had not been able to clearly see her face.

"Well. You're welcome for breaking the curse." She crossed her arms. "Now you can go back to your own kingdom and woo some other woman."

"You have it all wrong," Aden started to explain. "That was Ashlin."

"Oh, so she has a name?" Isa shot back at him.

"So, you are jealous."

"I literally just said 'I love you' over your dying body—of course I'm jealous!" she replied. The bite left her words as she seemed to realize he might not have heard her say it the first time. "Or were you actually dead then?"

Aden took a step closer to her. All thoughts of jesting had left his mind. "No, I heard that part." His voice had dropped to a deeper register, almost as deep as the beast's. Deeper than he had ever remembered it being before the curse.

"Then who's Ashlin?" she asked, her voice barely a whisper. She swallowed as she looked up at him.

"She's a servant girl turned seamstress," Aden replied. He could barely make out her face in the light of the stars, but his eyes sought to register each curve and shape he could see. "My brother Onric is crazy about her, but he thought she wouldn't come to the ball because she had rejected him. When I saw her down below, I went to the main floor to check on my brother."

"You're sure?" Isa asked.

"Sure?" he repeated, confused. "Yes, I'm positive it was Ashlin."

"You're sure that you are not in love with her?" The stars danced in her eyes as she looked up at him.

"How could I be in love with her?" Aden stepped forward, lifting his human hand to gently touch Isa's face. "Isn't it clear that I am in love with someone else?" His heart nearly stopped beating for a second time that night as he felt the soft warmth of her cheek. It felt so right to have control of his human sensations again.

And it felt so right to finally be able to see her face in focus.

"You are beautiful," he whispered.

Isa searched his eyes. He sounded a little awed, but mostly surprised.

"What did you expect?" she replied. "That I would be a burden to look upon?"

"Well, kind of," he replied. "You were so self-conscious about it . . . I thought . . ."

Isa looked down, uncertain how to accept his adoration. Old feelings welled up inside her, fears of being looked at but not truly seen.

"Not that I cared. Seriously." His fingertips brushed her cheek in a way that was almost reverent. "I fell in love with *you* when I could not even see you." His hand slipped down behind her neck and moved closer. "To be completely honest, I can't even fully see you now since it's still dark."

She closed her eyes as his other hand looped behind her neck, his thumbs tracing the bottom line of her jaw. His gentle touch helped to dissipate the tension of her past emotion. She felt treasured by him in a way warmed her from the inside out, bubbling up feelings that she had only ever dreamed of experiencing.

"Do you remember what we dreamed?" he asked.

She smiled at that, opening her eyes to look into his. "Yes, something about fiery eyes and disagreements."

"I want to add an item to that list."

"What item would that be?"

His face was so close to hers that she could feel the warmth of his breath, reminding her that he was very much alive. "It would be easier to show you rather than tell you."

"Show me then," she whispered, placing her hands on his shoulders to stabilize herself as she stood up on tiptoe.

He closed the distance between them, dropping his lips to meet hers.

She wrapped her arms around his neck, pulling herself closer to him, responding to his kiss.

He shifted his head back, breaking their contact. "How do you feel about this addition to the list?" he asked.

She tilted her head to the side. "I'm not sure yet. I'd have to think about it. Maybe we should do it again to help me decide."

He growled, deep in his throat, as his hands left her neck and dropped to her waist. Holding her tightly, he kissed her again.

With a smile at his possessive response, she brought her

hands to his face, holding him in place and willing him never to leave.

The sound of footsteps coming up the stairs startled them, and they quickly jumped apart as the door inside the tower room opened. A breathless Blanca stepped into the room, holding the lantern at waist height.

"Milady," she said, "did you find—" Her words stopped abruptly as she watched the strange young man follow Isa through the tower window.

"Yes," Isa replied. "I did!"

As they explained what had happened to the surprised woman, Isa took advantage of the lantern light to study his face. His hair was quite dark, falling almost to his shoulders. His eyes were brown, flecked with gold instead of yellow. And his eyebrows—thick, dark, and just a touch unruly—reminded her of the beast.

Blanca burst into tears at their explanation, and Isa moved forward instinctively to comfort her. But before she could reach the old woman, Aden had stepped forward and wrapped his arms around her.

"Come, come," she said, standing back and drying her eyes. "We must tell Luca before he falls off the roof in search of you."

"Now that I've seen your face in the lamplight," Aden whispered to Isa as they followed Blanca down the stairs, "I've decided that your eyes are even more fiery than I had imagined."

"Are you sure you weren't just seeing the actual flame of the lantern reflected in them?" Isa teased, even though her heart fluttered at his compliment.

"Oh," he replied. "I guess I hadn't thought of that. I'll just have to stare at them all day tomorrow in the daylight to make an informed opinion, then."

CHAPTER 32

*I*sa found herself staring shyly at the handsome young man sitting next to her during the morning meal.

She knew he was the same, but his transformation had been so dramatic. He felt like a stranger. She wanted time to get to know this new person, same though he was.

"Has anyone seen Warrior?" Aden asked, his eyebrows furrowed.

Isa shook her head. His human eyebrows were as dark and bushy as his beastly eyebrows had been. The sameness of them comforted her, reminding her that he truly was the same person. His dark black hair fell to his shoulders in a tumbled mess.

He had worn his hair tied back at the ball, but Isa found that she preferred it loose, as it was now.

At the ball, he had been condescending, looking down his aquiline nose at the world around him.

Sitting at the table in the kitchen, though, with his hair down and his oversized shirt hanging loosely from his broad shoulders, he was human. Real. Messy. Touchable.

Very touchable.

Her gaze strayed to his lips, which were currently smirking at her.

Embarrassed to be caught staring, she quickly looked back to his eyes. "I'm sorry, what did you ask?"

"I asked if anyone had seen Warrior."

"He slept on my bed last night," Blanca replied, setting a bowl of apples on the table. "He was still fast asleep when I got up. The commotion scared him pretty bad, poor little thing."

"Hmmm." The non-verbal sound came from deep in Aden's throat, almost as though he were still a growling beast.

"What's wrong?" Isa asked.

"I haven't seen him since you broke the curse—"

"Cured the curse," she said, cheekily cutting him off.

"Since you cured the curse," he repeated. "And I don't know if he will remember the old me."

"He'll remember you," she reassured him.

"Do you remember me?" he asked, his brown eyes staring at her unblinkingly.

She smiled. "I do. I remember how rude you were. How you thought your opinion was better than everyone else's. How you walked away from the most beautiful woman in the room."

"I think I've changed a bit," he said, pursing his lips.

"Oh, have you?" She pretended to sound surprised.

"For one, I would never walk away from you now. And additionally, I've since realized that my opinion isn't always perfectly correct." He sniffed, twitching his nose as though he were about to sneeze.

That small movement caused Isa's heart to flutter. It was so human and natural.

"For example," he continued, unaware of the effect his nose was having on her, "I have recently changed my opinion on *The Queen of Silverreign.*"

"Have you?" Isa asked, genuinely surprised.

"I have. I think I far prefer your version of the ending, where Andrew and Amelya get to spend the rest of their days together."

Isa smiled. He wasn't talking about Andrew and Amelya, and they both knew it.

"I think both endings have some merit." She caught his eye, hoping that he understood her concession to his opinion. She might feel a little shy at the newness of their situation, but she also knew she could get used to staring at this new face every day.

"Looks like the bridge is out," Luca said, stomping into the kitchen.

"What?" Isa asked, looking up. "Surely you are jesting."

His face was completely serious. He shrugged. "It's out."

As if in unison, Aden and Isa pushed back their chairs from the table and stood.

"Was there another freak flood?" Blanca asked, joining them as they rushed toward the door.

Isa was confused. There had been no storm or rain during the night.

"It appears to have been cut from the other side," Luca explained as they walked to the canyon.

When they arrived, Isa lay down on her stomach to peer over the edge. Sure enough, the bridge was hanging from their side of the canyon, swinging down toward the river below.

She quickly scrambled back.

A group of villagers were already gathered across the chasm, waving to them.

"What happened?" Luca yelled.

"Someone cut it last night!" a villager yelled back. The wind carried just enough of his voice that they could hear him. "We caught the fellow, though. Sent him back to the capital where he came from. The magistrate can deal with him."

Isa felt a small giggle in her throat.

Aden looked down at her, confused.

"It was Macklin," she said. "He was angry that I rejected him, so he tried to retaliate. Instead, he's given me exactly what I wanted."

"You wanted to be stuck here again?" Aden asked.

"No, I just wanted some time to get to know you," she said. "This new you . . ." Her eyes ran up and down his body.

He was still taller than she was, but he no longer towered over her.

She looked back up at his eyes, her stomach fluttering at the way they looked down at her. "This new you is still different. But now we get to spend a few more days here, just us, getting reacquainted."

His hand reached out and slipped around hers. "I like the way you think," he said.

Her mouth spread into a happy smile. She could get used to hearing that every day.

"AND, I don't think I shall ever tire of seeing your facial expressions," Aden continued, admiring the smiling woman in front him.

Her eyes were bright, despite the deep shadows underneath them from the overexertion of the past few days. Her brown hair was loosely held back, but it seemed to be doing its best to escape its binding as curls twisted free on either side of her face. She was perfect.

"I want to get to know everything about it," he continued,

referring to her face. "Like the way you crinkled your nose just then—were you displeased with something?"

"No, it was just tickling and I was trying to avoid a sneeze."

"It probably would have been a cute sneeze," he responded.

"There's no such thing as a cute sneeze."

"Well, there's only one way to find out. Go wave an old dusty scroll from the library under your nose, and we'll see if the sneeze is cute or not." His kept his face completely serious.

"Well, let's head back to the library and find out," she responded, also looking completely serious.

Luca and Blanca were still shouting at the villagers across the canyon. It sounded as though they already had a plan for re-attaching the bridge.

Still holding her hand, Aden walked back up the hill. He could not tear his eyes away from her. The way she moved, the way she smiled, the way she stole glimpses of him when she thought he wasn't looking.

As they neared the house, a small white ball of fur dashed toward them. Warrior was barking at the top of his puppy lungs.

Aden squeezed Isa's hand. He couldn't tell if the dog was barking in excitement or yelling at this new stranger.

Then the ball of fluff was upon him, jumping in the air, yelping in happiness.

Aden sank to his knees. "Warrior, you remembered me."

The pup jumped into his arms, attempting to lick his face and bounce around in circles at the same time.

"Good boy, Warrior. What a good boy you are."

Aden felt his heart constrict in his chest, stopping his flow of air. His own nose tickled as tears forced their way into his eyes.

He was back. He was really and truly himself, and he was alive. He looked up at Isa.

She leaned down, placing her hand against his cheek and touching his nose with her own. "I love you," she whispered, then tilted her head to press her lips against his.

ACKNOWLEDGMENTS

To Isa, my real-life book-loving friend, thank you for letting me borrow your beautiful name for this book.

Amelia, your positive pep-talks and comments seriously keep me going. You are the very, very best!

Katy and Marta, remember that phone call where you brainstormed up the mud/blood colorblind scene? It's easily my favorite part of this book. Thank you!

And a huge shout out to Allison and Judith for having my back on the grammar side! I appreciate the little inconsistencies you point out and help me to fix. I am so much more confident in my writing because of you.

And last but always first, Ethan, thank you for protecting my writing time and for grabbing us Chipotle when I'm on a deadline.

BUT WHAT HAPPENS TO ERICH?

Life in captivity is horrible.

Pretending to be a prisoner is worse.

Aizel is a Majis and, against her will, a spy. She is supposed to be uncovering secrets for a cruel king, she spends most of her time listening to the haughty, self-absorbed musings of her captor, Prince Erich.

It would be much less frustrating if she could at least complain about it, but the king has silenced her, taking away her voice so that she cannot wield her magic.

If she fails to gather information from Erich, her family will be killed. But if she reports back to the king, her people's only hope for freedom will be exterminated. Can she find a way to communicate with her captor and convince him of the truth about the Majis?